Defying the Curse

Maria O'Rourke

Paperback edition

First published 2024 by Marble City Publishing

ISBN-10 1-908943-70-X

ISBN-13 978-1-908943-70-5

Caveat

In reading this book it is important to point out that, while the life of Arthur MacMurrough Kavanagh inspired this book, the characters, conversations and relationships are imagined. This is a work of historical fiction and should not be interpreted as entirely factual.

Dedication

For David, Jack, Hazel and Rory who encourage me always.
Also my mother, Margaret and my late father, Séamus, who was the
first to tell me the story of the amazing Arthur MacMurrough
Kavanagh.

Contents

Chapter 1

Lady Harriet

On a frosty November day in 1824, the second Earl of Clancarty at Garbally House, Ballinasloe, faced a dilemma. With four daughters in their twenties, none of whom were married or even betrothed, something had to be done. He would have to remedy the situation himself and find suitable suitors for each of them before their tenuous beauty faded.

When his daughter, Lady Harriet Le Poer Trench, first heard that her father had made plans for her to marry the widower, Thomas "The MacMurrough" Kavanagh, she was less than impressed.

'But Papa, he's in his late fifties. How could you expect me to marry one so old?'

'Harriet, dear, he's a gentleman from one of the most noble families in Ireland. The MacMurrough Kavanaghs are directly descended from the great Dermot MacMurrough Kavanagh, one of the ancient high kings, and they own one of the most prestigious houses in the country. Their land stretches over three counties, Carlow, Kilkenny and Wexford. Surely you can overlook the man's age?'

'But he's as old as you are, Papa!'

With raised eyebrows Richard Le Poer Trench replied: 'I honestly didn't know that men of my vintage were so repulsive to young ladies. And, in any case, I dare say that Thomas Kavanagh is a few years younger than I.'

'Don't be flippant, Papa. I won't do it. I don't care if he owns the entire British Empire. I won't be tied to an elderly man with a ridiculous number of children.'

'Harriet, dear, most of his children are fully grown now and his only son died two years ago. You would have a fine house, bear him an heir and live happily ever after. Might I remind you that the fortunes of our family are not what they once were, and this is the best offer you are ever going to get. With four daughters I am not in a position to pick and choose. I insist that you agree to meet with the man. The Hunt Ball is the ideal opportunity and I have already invited him.'

Garbally House in Ballinasloe, the ancestral home of the Le Poer Trenches, was built in 1819 by Richard, replacing the smaller dwelling formerly occupied by his ancestors. Designed by the London architect, Thomas Cundy, the two-storey, square building had minimal ornamentation. The landscaped lawns stretched into the distance, while formal gardens with rosebushes and fountains boasted an obelisk, all of which had cost a lot more than expected. To the outside world, this was an opulent family, headed by an Earl who had been an ambassador and Member of Parliament, but times were changing, and the money was running out.

Turning towards the door, Harriet said: 'I'll meet him, Papa. But don't expect anything and you shan't be disappointed.'

On the evening of the ball, Harriet and her three sisters – Lady Lucy, Lady Louisa and Lady Emily – were putting the finishing touches to their evening wear in Lady Lucy's large bedroom. Dresses and headwear were strewn across the four-poster bed while each of the young ladies in turn stood in front of the long looking glass.

'My corset is not pulled tightly enough,' Lady Lucy complained. 'Emma, will you please do it again? I look like a whale.'

Emma, the girls' maid since childhood, was accustomed to their demands and agreed resignedly. 'I think you look very well, my Lady, but I'll see if I can pull it in another bit.'

'You know Papa is trying to marry us off,' Lady Harriet announced. 'He told me he's invited the ancient Thomas Kavanagh as a suitor for me. You can be sure he has someone lined up for each of you as well.'

'Oh, I hope so.' Lucy held a braid out for Emma to fix in her hair. 'I'm tired of living under this roof. I want a home of my own.'

'I will choose my own husband!' Emily, the youngest of the four, chimed in. 'I'd like a tall, handsome, foreign man with a fortune overseas,' and she looked wistfully out the window as if she could almost see him coming.

'You read too many books!' Harriet answered. 'I'm sure he has some old fossil in mind for you too.' And they all laughed.

'He wants me to marry Cousin William, and I may have to,' Louisa added glumly. 'Nobody else seems interested. I am so unlucky in love.'

Lady Harriet's ball gown was made of floral brocade with a red velvet panel in front. The wide shoulders, puffed sleeves and full skirt emphasised her minute waist, while her fair hair was parted in the centre, scraped back in a chignon bun and kept in place by a narrow braid. By far the best looking of the sisters, although they were all considered plain, they envied her fair skin and elegant posture.

'Do you think this suits me?' she asked, adding a lace pelerine around her shoulders.

'Oh yes,' Lady Lucy said with a wry smile. 'You look like the next Mrs Kavanagh to me!'

'You're perfectly horrid,' Harriet said. 'You don't look like the next Mrs anything! You'll be Miss Le Poer Trench forever!'

With that, the gong sounded for the beginning of the champagne reception and, pulling on their long gloves, the girls demurely made their way down the sweeping stairs to the waiting company.

If the fortune of the Le Poer Trenches was diminishing, one would not guess it from the elaborate function taking place in the ballroom. Liveried servants held silver trays of canapés for guests to sample, while others offered flutes of champagne. In the corner, a quartet of black tie musicians played chamber music as the guests mingled under crystal chandeliers.

To Lady Harriet's surprise, the man presented to her as "The MacMurrough", Mr Thomas Kavanagh, looked younger than his years. Tall and bearded, with an aristocratic air, he quickly moved from conversation about the weather to Harriet's interests and the history of Garbally House.

'I was sorry to hear about the death of the late Mrs Kavanagh and, of course, your poor son.'

'Thank you, Lady Harriet. It's been a difficult time. But this is not the night to dwell on such things. I wonder if I might ask you to dance?'

By this time, the musicians had begun the dance music, and over Thomas' shoulder she saw the approving glances of her mother and father as they took to the floor for the Viennese Waltz. Moving around the great hall in the double-time rhythm, she noticed her older sisters standing together. Her younger sister, Emily, was dancing with a man twice her age who seemed to be stumbling through the steps, while she shuffled to keep up. By contrast, Thomas Kavanagh was nimble on his feet and a confident dancer. He spoke about Borris House and the great functions they used to hold there when his wife was in good health.

'I have agreed that the Hunt Ball can go ahead in Borris this year since the period of mourning is over, and the locals look forward to it so much. I wonder if you might do me the honour of attending?' Thomas asked, adding, 'Of course you could bring one of your sisters along with you.'

'Yes,' Harriet found herself saying, 'I'd like that very much.'

*

After lunch the next day, the Earl and his wife Henrietta asked that Harriet might join them in the parlour, where tea was brought to them.

'Your mother and I wanted to enquire as to how you got along with Mr Kavanagh last evening?'

'Father!' Harriet answered in an exasperated tone, 'I saw you walking in the garden with him this morning. I'll be surprised if you haven't already set the date!'

'There's no need to be facetious, Harriet dear. You know the final decision is up to you.'

Harriet looked to her mother. 'Mamma, I found Mr Kavanagh to be most cordial company, but I'm not sure that married life will suit me. I mean to say, I find the routines so monotonous.'

'Believe me, you will get used to it,' her mother answered unconvincingly.

'But I dream of painting and travelling to interesting places, like the countries Papa speaks about. I want adventure. I know Mr Kavanagh is a good man and rather charming, but something inside tells me there must be more.'

'What more could there possibly be?' Her mother's tone registered surprise.

'A more purposeful existence? Oh, I don't know. I just thought I could be something other than somebody's wife.'

'If there is to be more, my dear Harriet, you will find it in the company of a good man like Thomas Kavanagh. Borris House is as magnificent as Garbally, and Mr Kavanagh is a generous landlord, held in high esteem by his tenants.'

'Yes, indeed,' Richard added. He had remained silent up to now at his wife's request, but this was not going well.

'You can run Bible schools as we do here and encourage the unfortunate people to see the excellence of the true faith. You will be respected and, if you're kind, you will be loved by the peasantry. I'm asking you to go to the Hunt Ball in Carlow and keep an open mind at least.'

Harriet sighed. 'Very well. I'll do as you wish, but I want to bring Emily with me. She understands me best and her opinion means most to me. I'll give you my decision on my return.'

In the intervening three weeks, Harriet received two letters from Thomas Kavanagh. Small white envelopes with several folded sheets inside each one. His cursive handwriting was neat and legible. He told her about his life as an MP in Westminster, places in London he'd like to show her, and charities his former wife was involved with in Borris that she might enjoy. Her replies outlined her love of painting and sketching, as well as her desire to travel to great cities of the world, places very few Irish people had ever seen. He signed off with "Your fond friend, Thomas" while she merely wrote "Yours truly, Harriet".

In mid-November, Harriet and Emily set out for Borris with Emma and their driver. The two-day journey was broken by an overnight stay with the Bernards of Kinnitty Castle, and it was already dusk when their carriage reached the gates of Borris House. Harriet held her breath as they made their way up the cedar-lined driveway and, when the house came into view, she gasped. Her eyes met Emily's as they both took in the square, three-storey Tudor mansion with battlements and an imposing crenelated porch.

While no bigger than Garbally, it had a fairytale quality to it with extensive mouldings over the windows and sculpted heads of kings and queens. Sitting stoutly on the flat Carlow landscape, it seemed as imposing as the majestic mountains in the distance.

'Gosh, I'll look forward to coming to visit you here,' Emily exclaimed, before adding: 'if, of course, you live here.'

'Exactly!' Harriet snapped. 'Remember, you're here to be objective, not to get carried away by appearances.'

'I know. I'm sorry. It's just that…'

But before she could finish, a formally dressed servant opened the carriage door and offered his hand to help them alight.

'You're very welcome to Borris, my Ladies. Allow me to show you to the drawing room. Tea will be brought to you there.'

The entrance hall, although square, was surrounded by marble pillars in a circular shape with magnificent plasterwork on the ceiling. As their bags were being brought in, Thomas Kavanagh emerged from the dining room dressed in tweed hunting clothes with high boots to the knees.

'Welcome to Borris House, Ladies.' He bowed formally. 'I'm so glad you both could come.'

'It's truly magnificent,' Harriet said. 'You remember my sister, Emily.'

'Indeed, I do. Please forgive my attire but I have just returned from a meet in Kilkenny. I look forward to entertaining you both at dinner tonight.'

Walking with them towards the drawing room, he added: 'I'm sure you ladies are tired after your long journey, so dinner will be early, at seven, to allow you to rest before tomorrow's celebrations.'

He seemed nervous and spoke quickly, only glancing momentarily at Harriet before dropping his eyes to the floor again.

'My eldest daughter, Anne, is waiting with tea in the drawing room. I'll show you the way.'

Stepping through the curved mahogany doors, the ladies were warmly greeted by Anne, a striking young lady with long dark hair. She had recently married Henry Bruen of Oak Park House in Carlow and was staying at Borris to help with the arrangements for the ball. Over tea she gushed about Harriet's clothes and her stylish burgundy bonnet, before commenting on Emily's fur-trimmed cape and matching day-dress.

As they made their way to the bedrooms, Emily whispered: 'I like it here.' Harriet said nothing but merely nodded and smiled as if to say 'as do I.'

*

After breakfast in the morning, Thomas invited Harriet and Emily to take a tour of the estate. Clearly proud of his heritage and, less inhibited now that he was walking, rather than face-to-face, he told them story after story of the great MacMurrough Kavanaghs and how they had come to reside in Borris. The current house was built by an ancestor called Morgan MacMurrough Kavanagh in 1731. Clearly aiming to impress, he told them of the bravery of another ancestor, Art

MacMurrough Kavanagh, who received a knighthood from King Richard II but refused to accept it, engaging the crown forces in many battles before his death in the 1400s.

They walked through manicured formal gardens, past the icehouse, taking in magnificent views of the Blackstairs mountains. Kavanagh land stretched in every direction, thirty thousand acres in all, through Counties Carlow, Kilkenny and Wexford, which Thomas showed them with a sweep of his hand. Then, walking toward the gatehouse which opened onto the main street, they passed the sturdy granite cottages where servants and stable hands lived.

'Is that a private chapel I see over there?' Harriet asked.

'Yes, it is. I can show you inside if you wish. There's some beautiful plasterwork by the famous stuccodore, Michael Stapleton. I'll have to send for the key, but we haven't used the chapel for some time.'

'Oh. Why ever not?' Harriet looked surprised. Her family also had their own chapel at Garbally which was used on an almost daily basis. The Le Poer Trenches were devout Protestants who took their duty to proselytize very seriously. 'We love our chapel,' she gushed. 'It's one of my favourite places.'

'This is actually a Catholic chapel,' he said apologetically. 'Our family has roots in both traditions.'

'Oh dear. Well, I'd still like to see the interior, if possible,' Harriet said.

Thomas summoned a boy to run and fetch the keys, while he showed them round the walled garden. When the boy returned, the three made their way up a narrow stairway, strewn with cobwebs, to the cavernous chapel. Vaulted and long, it was a light-filled space. The apse contained a magnificent stained-glass window of The Ascension, with a pipe-organ to the right and an impressively decorated gallery to the rear. A door from the gallery linked it to the main building for access by the family.

'This is truly beautiful,' Harriet said. 'It's a shame not to use it. But those ghastly statues would have to go.'

Thomas turned sharply to look at her as she said this and she blushed, realising she had already begun to make plans for Borris and had spoken them aloud.

Smiling, he said, 'That could be arranged.' And an awkward silence hung in the air.

*

The Hunt Ball was the epitome of style, with gentlemen in tails and ladies resplendent in a myriad of colourful gowns, each with flowing skirts and full sleeves. Harriet wore a pale blue organdie dress with low shoulders and a large bow on the back. Combined with her fair hair and porcelain skin, she exuded an ethereal beauty which didn't go unnoticed by Thomas Kavanagh, and a few others besides. Whispers circulated as he spent more and more time dancing with her, until eventually he sat in the company of herself and Emily, as if to make it official.

When Emily was invited to dance, Thomas leaned over and ventured softly: 'I do hope this is the first of many Hunt Balls you will attend in Borris.'

'If that is a proposal, Mr Kavanagh, it's a very obscure one.' Harriet laughed and Thomas, realising this angelic creature had a feisty personality, coughed and said: 'Well, yes. I suppose it is, if a clumsy one.'

'I have some conditions, Mr Kavanagh.'

'Please, call me Thomas. What would those conditions be?'

'I need some place to do my sketching. An airy room with good light where I can set up my easels, and I need the chapel to be renovated completely.'

A broad smile settled over Thomas' face. 'Consider it done, Harriet. Is there anything else?'

'In fact there is,' Harriet asserted. 'I dream of travelling. To begin with I would like to accompany you on your visits to London and further afield when possible.'

Thomas nodded. 'That can be arranged.' Kissing her gloved hand, he added, 'I hope Borris House will make you very happy.'

Chapter 2

The Curse

In a granite cottage on the main street of Borris, County Carlow, Molly Doyle held court every evening in front of the open hearth. Mary Quigley and Kitty Ryan flanked her on low stools, their stout boots visible under long black skirts. Molly's eyes flashed angrily in the flickering firelight as she took another sip of the tarry black tea she held between her weather-beaten hands. The other women knew that when Molly was like this it was best to stay silent or just nod in agreement. Tiny white beads of froth gathered at the corner of Molly's mouth as she spat out her hatred for Thomas Kavanagh, MP. The gentleman-landlord of Borris House had employed her husband, Johnny, as a farmhand for years, even after Dr Boxwell, the newly qualified doctor in the village, had warned that the next bout of bronchitis might kill him and that he wasn't fit for outdoor work anymore.

'And what do you think the great Mr Kavanagh did for him when he told him that?'

Molly paused to look at her two silent friends. They had heard this story several times and shook their heads as they waited for Molly to continue.

'Nothing! That's what he did! Absolutely nothing!' And she clenched her lips together so that her bottom lip almost touched her nose. 'Just gave him more back-breaking work to do until the poor man fell down.'

'Desperate,' Mary muttered.

'No heart at all,' Kitty added.

From behind the curtain of the settle-bed in the corner, a rasping cough could be heard.

In a low whisper, fruity with venom, Molly said, 'That family will have no luck until it's ruled by a cripple. A cripple! That's what I wish for them, and it'll be good enough for them!'

The other women at the fire nodded and looked at each other with a mixture of admiration and fear.

'Good enough for them is right!' Kitty repeated.

'God bless the mark!' Mary blessed herself slowly with her black beads.

'I never wished ill on anyone before, but God forgive me, I wish it on that man,' Molly said.

*

The gates of Borris House dominated the long main street of the village of Borris with its buttressed, granite walls enclosing the Kavanagh estate. Scores of local people had for generations worked the Kavanagh land, shod their horses and served their table. To most, the family were like benevolent foster-parents, demanding but kindly. Thomas' first wife, Lady Elizabeth Butler of Kilkenny, had borne him ten children, nine daughters and one son, and was liked and respected in the community. His only son, Walter Kavanagh, destined to inherit

14

the fertile acres stretching between the Black River and the Barrow, died aged nine. Now, only three years later and aged sixty-four, Mr Kavanagh remarried with hopes of producing another male heir. "You can never have enough sons" was one of his sayings, and his new wife, twenty-five-year-old Harriet, didn't disappoint.

Lady Harriet – "Lady" being an inherited title – was no sooner settled in the house when workmen began to arrive to do renovations, beginning with the removal of statues from the private chapel.

'That woman will have no luck,' Kitty said. 'Anyone who would take statues from the church and have them buried couldn't have a happy day.'

The chapel, attached to Borris House in the Tudor-Gothic style, had up to Harriet's arrival been Catholic, with locals attending Mass there on special occasions and lighting candles in front of statues of the Virgin Mary and St Joseph. Nobody knew exactly when the family converted to the Established Church, although many suspected it was part of the marriage deal made between Thomas and Harriet's Protestant father. Now, with the removal of the statues, it was official.

'She's turning the church into a Protestant meeting house,' Kitty Ryan said. 'And she got my Joe to take down the statues from their alcoves and throw them into a hole down by the river. The poor man isn't the better of it. He was so upset he went to the priest for absolution.'

'And what did Father Walshe say?'

'He told him the Lord doesn't punish you for following orders. But the poor man hasn't slept all week.'

'Mr Kavanagh and his people before him were God-fearing Catholics until she came along,' Mary Quigley chimed in. 'What was he thinking marrying that one? And she half his age. It doesn't bode well, I tell you. Bad luck is coming.'

At twenty-five, Harriet was often mistaken for one of Thomas' daughters and earned the reputation of being strong-willed as well as a talented artist. Within five years of marriage the couple produced two sons, Thomas and Charles, and a daughter, Harriet, known as Hoddy. Aside from the church incident, the new Mrs Kavanagh slowly managed to endear herself to the tenants of the estate through small acts of kindness. She set up a food and soup kitchen for the less well-off and servants were encouraged to bring home leftovers to feed their growing families, a gesture Molly Doyle disapproved of.

'Are they blind or stupid?' Molly Doyle hissed. 'Can't they see what she's doing?' Her dark eyes squinted around the women at the fire.

'What, Molly? What's she doing?

'She's buying their souls, for God's sake. Gathering the children and telling them stories from the Bible. My cousin in Ballinasloe told me that woman's family, the Le Poer Trenches, converted lots of poor innocent people that way.'

'But where's the harm in stories from the Bible, Molly?' Kitty asked.

Molly laughed, a joyless cackle. 'Oh Kitty, you never had an ounce of sense. It's not our Bible. It's *their* Bible! She's converting them to her pagan practices, and they're too stupid to notice. Why do you think the bishop is coming to Borris next week. It's not to talk about the weather. He'll damn their souls if they keep taking the soup.'

Kitty Ryan's beads were moving quickly through her fingers. 'I'm off home,' she said. 'I don't like that kind of talk. I'll see you at the church on Tuesday night. There'll be a great crowd, I'd say; they're coming in from Ballymurphy and Goresbridge to hear him. It'll be mighty.'

*

On Tuesday evening, against an autumn wind, people processed in twos and threes down Main Street, past the archway of the big house and downhill to the new parish church, which had only been completed a few years earlier. The site was provided by the Kavanaghs before they joined the Established Church. From all directions crowds streamed through the vast doorway, women sitting to the right and men to the left. When every pew was filled with wind-swept parishioners, they began to line the walls under the stained-glass windows, but even still, in the pious silence, the chatter of the crowd trying to gain entry through the open door could be heard.

A hush descended as the surpliced Father Walshe slowly walked across the altar. He raised his voice and held his right hand up for attention. 'His Lordship, Bishop Doyle, would like to address the people of Borris, but since there are too many people gathered to be

17

accommodated inside, he will speak from the front step. Please leave the church and assemble in an orderly fashion outside.'

A murmur of complaint echoed round the vaulted space from those who had come early to get a good seat. 'Remember you're in the house of God,' Father Walshe admonished them. 'Be silent and make your way outdoors.'

Before long the imposing figure of Bishop James Doyle, a man of tall stature, with dark receding hair and strong features, appeared in the doorway. In his late thirties, his powers of oration were legendary. Known to be a friend and ally of the great emancipator, Daniel O'Connell, he stirred excitement in every congregation he addressed. At last, here was a spokesperson for the downtrodden, the equal of any politician.

Bishop Doyle's purple robes billowed in the evening breeze. His mitre almost reached the top of the doorway and, with his crozier in one hand, he gesticulated with the other, first to urge silence and then to drive home his salient points.

'My dear people of Borris, it is with grave regret that I learn of the goings on in Borris House.'

Silence, while he paused and looked up the street to the turreted archway of the Kavanagh demesne.

'You, the faithful Catholic brethren, are rightly and justifiably scandalised by the removal of Catholic artefacts from the church at Borris House. The Kavanagh family, having been staunch leaders in this vibrant community and hailing from the ancient kings of Ireland, have lost their way. It can only be for personal advantage and political gain that they have cast aside the faith of their forefathers. And it is not their first time to do so. But the Established Church will not remain established in this country forever.'

At these words a thunderous applause and cheer rang out loud enough to scare the blackbirds from the trees behind the high wall of the estate so that they swirled and swooped over the heads of the throng.

Bishop Doyle raised his hand again for silence.

'Let us not be triumphant, for pride is one of the deadly sins. Rather, let us examine our consciences in humility. It has come to my attention that the new Mrs Kavanagh entices you and your children to listen to her proselytizing by offering soup and bread for sustenance.' He raised his voice. 'This practice must stop.' And there was a long pause before he continued.

'A good landlord doesn't seek to impose his God on the poor and ignorant. If Kavanagh wants to be generous, let him do so without condition. For those of you who want to learn more about the rich teachings of the Bible, there will be a Sunday school here, in your own church, once a week. This is where you will hear the teachings of the one true church and gain a proper perspective. Be assured of this; educated people will be free.'

Again, the crowd erupted in applause until, once more, the Bishop's right hand was raised.

'My dear people, the day is coming when Catholics will take their place in this country. You have heard of those withholding their tithes. In fact, I'm sure that there are some amongst you who have been brave enough to do so. But let us make haste slowly now, and never, ever resort to violence. There are much more powerful means to achieve the inevitable. I urge you, the noble people of God at the foot of these wondrous mountains, to let your hatred of tithes be as lasting as your love of justice.

'Finally, brethren, I issue a warning. Something will happen at Borris House, at no distant day, that will make the ears of all who hear it tingle.'

There was a gasp from the crowd as they looked from one to the other. Then, as the bishop raised his right hand in an elaborate blessing, they made the sign of the cross and hurried back to their homes to wonder what was about to befall the Kavanaghs. Would it be a rebel attack like the uprising of 1798? Although most believed the bishop would never support a call to arms. Some locals even wondered whether the bishop himself had heard of the peasant's curse.

*

Molly's husband, Johnny Doyle, died in early December 1828 with a cough that made him double over in pain, spitting blood into a tin bowl. He was buried on a bitterly cold day with a throng of villagers stamping their feet to keep warm as they prayed around the graveside. Nobody from the big house attended, although Mrs Kavanagh sent a wreath of fresh flowers which Molly threw into the river, repeating the curse she revealed to the women at the fireside. Two days after Christmas she had a visit from the Kavanagh's agent, Burke, to say that since there was no longer anyone living in this house employed on the estate, the property would have to be vacated by January 15th or the bailiff would be calling. Not one for pleading, Molly stood in front of him squarely and pointed to the three children who still lived at home, the others all being either in England or in service.

'And where, Mr Burke, do you expect these children to live?'

'I'm just delivering the message for Mr Kavanagh, Mrs Doyle. It's nothing personal.'

'Nothing personal! Well may God forgive you for doing the devil's work. You're no better than Judas. But you and your type will get your comeuppance yet! And it won't be long, mark my words.' And she pushed him out the door, striking his head on the low lintel and knocking his hat into the mud outside.

'Bad cess to you,' she shouted after him down the street. 'You can tell Mr Kavanagh, there's a curse on him, and he'll be the sorry man.'

Chapter 3

The Baby

From the moment Doctor Francis Boxwell became the dispensary doctor for Borris and Glynn in County Carlow, he was curious about the occupants of Borris House. Being from the gentrified classes himself, he was aware of the MacMurrough Kavanaghs and their unique place in Irish history. An ancestor of his own, John Boxwell, was private secretary to Queen Mary, but backed the wrong side in the English Civil War, and was removed to Ireland, settling in Butlerstown House, Wexford and building up a vast estate. So Frank, accustomed to the life of a country gentleman, grew up fishing, shooting and riding horses.

His new job as a country doctor, responsible for a large tract of the county of Carlow, suited him perfectly since he was never happier than when riding his horse around the countryside, spotting wildlife and jumping the occasional ditch. The first day he rode up the avenue to Borris House, the hoar frost made the grass shine like silver, and icicles hung from the windowsills and portico. The interior was alive with the chattering of children of all ages and Thomas Kavanagh's second wife looked about the same age as some of the older ones, except she was pregnant with her fourth child.

'The new doctor called today,' Harriet told Thomas over dinner that evening.

'Yes, I've met him before. A nice young fellow.'

'Very nice indeed,' Harriet answered. 'His smile is so very… warm and relaxed. He brought sweets for the children and showed Tom a magic trick, pretending to produce a sixpence from behind his ear. What a breath of fresh air it was to meet him.'

Thomas raised an eyebrow, asking drily: 'And medically, how did you find him?'

'Oh, he was as expected in that regard. Although he said I must stop riding out in the mornings, which I think totally unnecessary, considering this is my fourth pregnancy. He thinks I'm overdoing it.'

'But you will follow his advice, Harriet?'

'Oh, I suppose so. Tiresome though it is, it's only for a few more months.'

*

In late January 1831, Dr Boxwell's carriage was seen sweeping through the archway for the second time in a week.

'Don't tell me she's expecting again!' Nelly Murphy said.

'Sure, why wouldn't she! Hasn't she a nanny and a fleet of maids to look after them?' Molly pitched in. 'All she has to do is push them out and the rest is done for her.'

'Ah I know that, but the last one is barely weaned. I don't understand why she wants to have anything to do with that old goat, Kavanagh. Sure, he's well into his sixties if he's a day and looks more like ninety.'

'God save us, that'll be the man's fourteenth child, and most of them daughters. And it's all our rents that are paying for them dowries.' Molly leaned forward. 'Hope it keeps fine for him. I heard he's not in the best of health.' And she tapped the side of her nose.

On the morning of March 25th, word went out to send for the midwife. To the surprise of the villagers, Dr Boxwell's Tilbury carriage was driven in the gates shortly afterwards. Normally he would leave the work to the midwife and arrive later to check over the new arrival.

'There must be something wrong,' they whispered.

'God save her and the baby,' Kitty Ryan said. 'Isn't it the one suffering all of us women have to go through, rich or poor?'

In fact, Dr Boxwell had told the midwife to send for him as soon as she got word that this baby was on the way. In his previous examinations of Lady Harriet, he detected something not quite right. She was radiant with good health and, it being her fourth child, he didn't anticipate any difficulty with the delivery, but there was something unusual about the way this child sat in the womb and he wanted to be there if needed.

Lady Harriet was lying on her bed when he arrived and Nurse Power had all her shining instruments laid out on a side-table. A maid stood by and occasionally put a cold compress on Lady Harriet's head as she grimaced and sighed with each contraction. The red curtains of the four-poster bed were pulled right back and a white sheet covered her legs. Every now and then she would lean forward in pain, only to lie back again and ask for a sip of water.

She greeted Dr Boxwell, telling him she thought he would not be needed, but it was very good of him to come. Nurse Power nodded as if to say everything was under control.

'Would you mind if I examined you, Lady Harriet, just to be sure?'

'Of course not doctor.'

The curtain on the maid's side of the bed was pulled while Dr Boxwell, watched by the midwife, pressed the abdomen and examined the cervix.

'Can you feel any movement, Lady Harriet?'

'This one doesn't kick like the others, Dr Boxwell, but I can certainly feel movement.'

With that she leaned forward and this time uttered a loud groan.

'I think it's going to be soon, Doctor,' she gasped, as the pain subsided.

Nurse Power's lips were pursed tightly as she held the opium to Lady Harriet's nose.

'I can manage this, Dr Boxwell. I'm sure you have more pressing matters to attend to.'

'Nothing that can't wait, Nurse Power, and I'll be staying until the next Kavanagh is born,' he retorted sharply.

Then, as the tiny head began to emerge, he said: 'Please stand aside, Nurse Power. I'll take charge now.'

Lady Harriet, giving one final thrust, lay back on the pillow as Dr Boxwell drew the tiny creature to himself. 'It's a boy,' he managed to say over the loud crying of the infant, before turning away from the mother with the baby in his arms. Nurse Power shrieked before a heavy hand on her arm silenced her. 'Please cut the cord, Nurse, with expediency, and then ensure the placenta is delivered. And, and… administer some more opium to Lady Harriet.'

As soon as the baby was freed from the umbilical cord, Dr Boxwell carried him, wrapped in a towel, to the other side of the bedroom so he could examine the infant in private. Holding his breath, he dried the blood and vernix so as to have a better look. There was hardly any need to listen to the heartbeat, such was the loud crying coming from the child, but he did so anyway and there was a strong, regular pattern. Perplexed for a few moments, the doctor tried to come to terms with the fact that what was in his arms was the torso of a baby boy, with practically no limbs whatsoever. Never before had he seen an infant with such a deformity. It was as if the limbs had been shorn off by some sharp object in the womb, leaving only the barest of stumps.

Deftly he swaddled the infant in a blanket before presenting him to Lady Harriet.

'Now, my lady, it's not, ahm, what you expected. Ahm. You may not want to hold him, or get too… fond.'

'What do you mean, Doctor? Hand me my baby at once.'

Kissing his perfect head, which was covered in the finest layer of blond hair, she looked puzzled at the young doctor.

'What's the matter, Doctor? He looks perfectly healthy and he gave a good, strong cry.'

Nurse Power was tidying up her instruments and returning them to her bag noisily with shaking hands, glancing every now and then at Lady Harriet and then at the doctor.

'Sit down, will you, Nurse Power!' he said in an exasperated tone. 'And pass me the smelling salts.'

Slowly the doctor pulled back the folds of the blanket, revealing a pink broad chest and shoulders and, finally the stumps where arms should be.

'Oh dear Lord,' Harriet cried. 'Where are his arms?

'And that's not all, I'm afraid,' he said, as he revealed the stumps of two tiny legs.

'Would you like some smelling salts, my Lady?' Nurse Power reached over with the tiny silver pot in her hand.

'I would not.' Lady Harriet breathed deeply as she tried to calm herself.

Doctor Boxwell shook his head silently, not knowing what to say.

'Oh my God, how did this happen?' She looked up wide-eyed at the doctor's face.

'I really don't know, I'm sorry but I really don't. Shall I take him away?'

When Harriet finally spoke again she said: 'Doctor Boxwell, this is my son and my eyes are not offended by the sight of him,' and two large tears trickled down her cheeks, falling on the baby's pink face.

'Thank God he was born to me and not to anyone else. If God spares him, he will have a good life. I will make certain of it.'

*

When Doctor Boxwell went to break the news to Thomas Kavanagh, he found him enjoying a cigar in the library. The afternoon sunlight reflected in the oval panes of glass fronting the walnut cabinets packed with leather-bound books. Holding out the cigar-box to the doctor he said: 'I can hear the child has a fine set of lungs, but you've taken an age to come down. I trust Lady Harriet is quite well.'

'Lady Harriet is very well indeed,' the doctor answered, accepting a cigar. 'But I do have some, ahm, news for you.'

'Well of course you do! Spit it out my good man! Don't tell me it's another girl to bleed my fortune dry? Or is it another spare to the heir, so to speak?' he asked, holding a cigar-box out to offer one to the doctor.

'It's a boy, Mr Kavanagh, but...'

'Yes! Another boy! We'll drink to that,' he said, moving toward the sideboard. 'But, what?' He stopped and looked back at the doctor's serious face.

'He's got some... well... unusual features, ahm, it's difficult to describe.'

'Oh dear. I see.' Thomas resumed his seat in the Queen Anne armchair by the marble fireplace. 'Go on, like a good fellow. Don't beat about the bush.'

As Dr Boxwell described the infant, who was now cradled in his mother's arms, Thomas Kavanagh's face exhibited disgust, although his eyes welled up with tears. Clearing his throat, he said: 'In that case will you find some good woman in the village to take care of him? I assume he won't live long. They'll want for nothing; you can assure them of that.' And he lowered his head to his chest.

'You might like to speak with Lady Harriet before making that decision, Mr Kavanagh.'

Startled, Thomas looked up sharply. 'Well, Boxwell, what else can be done in this type of situation?'

'Talk to Lady Harriet and I'll call again in the morning. And, Mr Kavanagh, as to his general health, it would seem to be excellent.'

When the doctor left, Thomas Kavanagh slowly mounted the stone staircase and crossed the wooden floor to where Lady Harriet lay with the sleeping infant in her arms. Kissing her head, he found it hard to speak. There were tears in her delicate blue eyes as she rocked gently forward and back. Touching her hand, he said: 'My poor dear Harriet. I'm so sorry this happened to you. It's most unfair.'

With tears streaming down her cheeks now, she said: 'Look at him, Thomas. Look at baby Arthur.'

'I'd rather not, Harriet. You know there's no point in getting fond of him. I've asked Doctor Boxwell to find a kindly lady in the village.'

'You what?' Harriet shrieked, making the baby stir and utter a sudden cry. 'How dare you! No son of mine is being reared by anyone but me.'

'Don't be upsetting yourself, Harriet. You've had a hideous fright, and you need to rest. We'll talk about it later.'

'Thomas Kavanagh, you will look at your son right now, or you will spend your old age alone. I mean every word I say. Look at him, now.'

Slowly, Thomas' eyes lowered to the infant who was wriggling and stirring in his mother's arms. Plump cheeks and long eyelashes reminded him of his first-born son, Walter, who had tragically died. Slowly, he peeled back the blanket and gasped, covering his mouth.

'Oh Harriet! How can we keep him? What will he ever do? The Kavanaghs are horsemen and hunters, farmers and politicians. This creature will be… none of those things.'

'Just support me, Thomas, and I will see to the rest.' She wrapped the blanket round him again. 'I've decided something. I'm calling him Arthur after your ancestor, Art Kavanagh, one of the greatest Kavanaghs that ever lived. As a man of faith, you must surely know that God will give us the strength to make a fine man of him. Just agree that we keep him. Please.'

After a moment Thomas lifted her hand and, putting it to his lips said: 'As you wish, Harriet, although I really don't know how you're going to do it. But I will support you, and may God be on your side.'

*

Like dominoes, the village women ran from cottage to cottage, leaning their heads together, only to rush to the next house with the startling news that the Kavanaghs had, after all, produced a cripple. Could it be the curse? Would the Kavanaghs be ruled by a cripple? But the possibility of him being the heir to the family dynasty seemed highly unlikely, as the youngest of three living sons.

'The curse has come to visit them,' Molly said. 'I told you it would. Now young Thomas and Charles better watch out. Their days are surely numbered. The curse will have its way.'

'It's hard to believe it.' Mary Quigley looked frightened. 'I don't like that kind of talk, Molly. It's not right.'

'Bad cess to them all! That's what I say.' Molly was unrepentant.

'Remember what Bishop Doyle said about something happening in Borris House,' Kitty Daly whispered. 'This must be what he meant. It must be because of the statues. God between us and all harm, it's a shocking thing.'

But inside the walls the mood was very different. Lady Harriet forbade anyone to speak of the infant's disability. He was to be treated exactly as her other children, with no exception. In fact, she asked Doctor Boxwell to address the servants on the matter. Sternly he ordered that there was to be no speculation as to why this happened, and no loose talk in the village. 'Nature has its own reasons,' he declared, 'and time will tell what great gifts this child has been given to make up for what he lacks.'

Since their introduction, the doctor found Harriet to be particularly engaging with her love for art and foreign travel. They shared long conversations about the places she had read about and hoped to visit someday, while he recounted tales of his limited time spent in London and Paris. 'I want to go places that nobody has ever been – at least nobody from this part of the world. I plan to go much farther than Europe – perhaps India and Egypt. Who knows?' Harriet declared.

While he had great admiration for her adventurous spirit, the young doctor couldn't help but think that the birth of her newest son might put paid to such ambitions.

After Arthur was born, Boxwell was deeply troubled. Was there some sign he had missed? Could he have done something that would have made a difference? Were the deformities, in fact, caused by the mysterious herbal remedy Harriet took throughout her pregnancy, although she assured him she had taken it for each of her previous pregnancies too. There were no answers, and quickly Doctor Boxwell switched his energies to finding ways to enable this child to live the noble life of his ancestors. In a letter to Harriet, he wrote:

I greatly admire your positivity regarding Arthur. We must make it our joint task to bring him up to be brave and fearless. I firmly believe that his intellect will make up for everything he lacks. Trust me, Harriet, together we can make this happen. I continually mention him at my professional meetings in Dublin and I am assured that some mechanical means can be found which will aid his mobility. We must be patient and instil in him a sense of pride in his noble ancestry. He must feel he has a mission to continue the proud tradition of the MacMurrough Kavanaghs. It will give him a sense of purpose and destiny. Yours Sincerely, F.

In gentrified circles there were rumours of another deformed child who had been born to the Earl of Strathmore in Scotland ten years previously. Referred to as "The Monster of Glamis Castle", he was the rightful heir, but was recorded as having died at birth. Visitors reported that he was confined to a room in the castle and only allowed to exercise at night. While Thomas Kavanagh may have been tempted by such a solution, overcome as he was with embarrassment and shame, both Harriet and the doctor were determined that no such fate would befall Arthur.

After her confinement, Lady Harriet attended to her charities in the village even more assiduously than before, wearing her stylish long skirt and straw hat trimmed with ribbon. Those who were concerned or impertinent enough to enquire after her new baby, were answered in one word: 'thriving.' Baby Arthur's nurse wheeled him about the village in his pram and when nosey people, hoping to catch a glimpse of the unfortunate invalid, engaged her in conversation, all they saw was a sleeping or smiling baby boy covered up to his neck with fine clothes and blankets. The sleeves of his baby gown were tied up like bags, as were the legs, and it was months later before even his own brothers and sisters noticed that there was anything unusual about him.

It was his brother, Tom, who first noticed something was wrong. Being only four years older than Arthur, he was little more than a toddler when he ran from the nursery crying for his mother. 'Mamma, Mamma, the baby's legs are gone! I did nothing! I don't know what happened.'

Lady Harriet hugged him for a moment and then explained: 'God made baby Arthur with very tiny arms, and very tiny legs. But he's already able to move around the floor and he's a big, strong boy just like you. He doesn't need arms and legs. Now go back and play with him as you were. You four children are going to have great adventures together.' And, one by one, she explained it to each of them in this nonchalant way, encouraged by her friend and chief ally, Dr Boxwell.

Anne Fleming was the nurse with responsibility for looking after Arthur as well as Lady Harriet's other three children. A firm but kind lady, at first she was inclined to mollycoddle and spoil the baby, referring to him as "poor Arthur". But when Lady Harriet got word of this, she was furious.

'I will not have you treating Arthur differently to the others,' she admonished.

'But, my Lady, he's such a gentle child and so curious. He's got such intelligent eyes. I just want to help him.'

'The best way you can help Arthur is by not helping him. I want no pandering; do you understand me? If he wants a toy, put it slightly out of his reach. He'll learn to propel himself forward in his own way. Give the others your attention; they need your help more than Arthur ever will.'

'But Lady Harriet…'

'No buts, Anne! That is the way I want him to be treated. It may seem cruel but it is the greatest kindness you can do for him.'

'Very well, my Lady. I'll do my very best.'

'And before you go, Anne. Never let me hear you using the words "poor" and "Arthur" in the same sentence again. Do you understand?'

'Yes, my Lady. I do.'

And so, gradually, Arthur learned to bounce around on his tiny stumps and hold things steady in his mouth, eventually managing to close both stumps across his chest and grip something between them. Anne placed toys just out of his reach, and he learned to wriggle towards them and swipe them up with a quick scissors movement of his tiny limbs. He babbled like any other child and pointed using one of his stumps to indicate what he wanted, speaking full sentences long before his siblings had, with one of his first and favourite sayings being: 'I do it myself!' if anyone tried to help him.

Chapter 4

Fledgling

On his second birthday, Doctor Boxwell brought Arthur for a ride around the estate on his horse. Strapped in front of the doctor, he got his first taste of the speed and excitement of horsemanship, revelling in it like a true Kavanagh. Cheered on by his mother, nurse and siblings, he babbled excitedly on his return, as did the doctor, whose paternal interest in Arthur never waned.

'You will have your own horse one day, Arthur. We will find a way to make it happen, isn't that so, Lady Harriet?'

And flushed with the excitement of seeing her youngest son's exhilaration, she said, 'We will, Doctor. We most certainly will.'

At dinner that evening, Charles and young Thomas recounted the story to their father.

'Father, Doctor Boxwell took Arthur on his horse today.'

'And he didn't take us,' chimed Charles.

'Well it *is* Arthur's birthday, after all,' their father said, patting him on the head.

'But Doctor Boxwell told mother that some day he should have his own horse, and she agreed. Will I have my own horse? I'm much older than him,' asked young Thomas.

'Of course, of course. All Kavanaghs are horsemen. Just be patient. Now could I please have some peace to eat my dinner.'

Once the children were taken away, Thomas Kavanagh asked the servants to leave that he might have a word with his wife in private. Before he spoke, Harriet knew what he was going to say; he had said it in so many different ways before.

'You have to stop this nonsense with Arthur. The child is a cripple. He will never own his own horse. How could he? You and Boxwell have to stop raising the child's hopes and teach him to be realistic.'

'Realistic? And what would you have me tell him? That he should limit his expectations? That he should settle for the life of an invalid? I won't do it, Thomas Kavanagh, and you have no right to do it either. If you showed the slightest interest in that boy, the way Doctor Boxwell does, you would know what I mean.'

'I'm tired of Boxwell keeping this fantasy going. Why is the man turning up here every week? There's nobody ill here. Doesn't he have any sick people to keep him busy?'

'Frank encourages Arthur. He makes time for him, and for me too, which is more than I can say for you!'

Throwing down his napkin, Thomas raised his voice, saying: 'I won't be spoken to like that in my own house. You are quite mad, Harriet. I will speak to Boxwell myself and see if there aren't a few pills he could give you to make you see sense. And since when did you start calling him Frank? Now goodnight!' And he left the dining room, slamming the panelled, mahogany door behind him.

But Harriet revelled in the optimism the doctor inspired in her. On professional visits to Dublin, he discussed Arthur's case in the enduring belief that a mechanical device could, in time, be custom-built to help Arthur move about unaided. He told her that the boy must be made indifferent to fear from the earliest age so that he would not hesitate to take risks when he was older, believing that risk would be necessary for him to live a normal life.

'Give him a sense of mission, of his own destiny. Make him believe that everything is possible for him. Tell him stories of his great ancestry. What he lacks in limbs he will make up for in spirit and determination.' This was exactly what Harriet wanted to hear.

A small chair made of wicker was designed for Arthur by a local craftsman and fitted with straps. This chair was fixed to the back of a large rocking horse in the nursery where Arthur could be strapped into it. Rocking energetically backward and forward, he sometimes leaned precariously to one side, making Anne Fleming or one of the servants rush towards him to help.

'Leave him' Harriet said, whenever she witnessed this. 'He will ask for help if he needs it. He needs to work it out for himself.'

And, more often than not, the toddler shifted his weight so that the seat centred itself again or, if it wouldn't, he laughed loudly, crying out, 'I'm upside down! Look at me, I'm upside down!' And eventually he'd call Anne and ask her to straighten him up again.

The excursions on Doctor Boxwell's horse became a weekly event to which Arthur looked forward greatly. He whooped with excitement when he and the doctor swept under the arch and down onto the Main Street. The villagers would point and gape, but more importantly note that this was a normal, happy child, who happened to have no limbs. Arthur noticed the cats on the granite doorsteps and the children happily spinning tops on the street. He flapped with excitement when they passed another horse or carriage and looked up excitedly at the doctor who stared straight ahead, knowing full well that behind every curtain, all eyes were on them.

*

On his fourth birthday Arthur received a very special surprise. He awoke to his mother, brothers and sister standing round his bed and urging him to get up quickly and look out the window.

'Put me on your shoulder, Thomas,' Arthur demanded and he was hoisted onto his brother's shoulders with a protective arm around his back.

'Look out, Arthur. Look over there towards the bluebell lawn. What do you see?'

'I see Murphy holding the reins of a pony. Is that a new pony? It doesn't look like your one, Tom, or Charles'?'

'It's for you, you silly boy! It's for your birthday!' Lady Harriet kissed him on the head.

'For me?' The boy's face was a vision of shock and delight; his bright blue eyes shining like sapphire. 'My own pony! I don't believe it! Thank you, Mamma,' and he leaned his head over to nestle into the nape of her neck.

'We'll be waiting for you outside,' said Charles. 'You're going to love him.'

'Yes. Hurry, Arthur. I want to hold the reins first,' Hoddy added, running after her brothers down the marble stairs.

By the time Arthur was dressed and ready, the stable-hand, Murphy, had fixed his little wicker seat onto the pony's back. Harriet lifted him into the bucket-like structure and secured him with tight straps.

'Murphy, I want you to walk slowly around the pathway holding the reins until he gets used to it. Then, children, you can all take turns to lead him.'

'Remember what I told you about your famous namesake, Arthur. Go bravely!' Harriet whispered as Murphy led him away.

From the porch, Thomas Kavanagh stood, leaning on a hawthorn stick. His health had been failing for some time and he had grown thin and stooped. He watched the curious scene of his youngest son circling the front lawn sitting bolt upright as royalty would in a sedan chair. After many arguments about Arthur and horse-riding, he had finally given in, since even the doctor seemed to believe it was a good idea. Looking at Arthur now, he wondered: *What if Harriet were right, and there was nothing this child couldn't do?*

'Look at Arthur, Papa. Look at Arthur,' Hoddy called to him, and he raised his arm to wave at the happy family scene; Harriet and Anne Fleming standing under a Lebanon Cyprus and the children excitedly taking their turns to lead the pony around. Over at the yard, some of the stable hands stood outside watching and the gardeners leaned on their rakes taking it all in.

'Wonderful! Wonderful!' Thomas called, 'Well done, Arthur!' before a bout of coughing made him turn to go back inside.

*

While the other children were at school, Arthur often watched Harriet as she painted at her easel, and she used this as an opportunity to educate him. A keen and talented artist, she taught Arthur to hold a paintbrush between his teeth, asking him to imitate simple shapes she made on paper.

'This, Arthur, is a triangle. It has three straight sides, one, two, three. Now I want you to copy it.'

An easel was adjusted to a height at which Arthur could reach, leaning forward while seated on the floor and, with crude strokes, attempt to direct the brush with the movements of his head. While his first attempts were destined to fail, as the brush fell from his teeth or the paint dripped onto the floor before he could complete the task, his mother gently encouraged him.

'Remember the stories I've told you about the great Art McMurrough. He never gave up, no matter what befell him.'

And Arthur would set his face in a determined manner and try again.

Gradually it emerged that he had a flair for drawing and painting with pencil and brush by mouth, which greatly pleased Harriet. As he watched his mother paint expertly, with delicate watercolours and bold oils, gradually his own strokes became more definite and artistic. In this way he developed his motor skills and an enduring patience that would prove necessary to achieve all the things his siblings took for granted.

*

In January 1837, when Arthur was five years old, his father died. A bitter easterly wind made the black coats and shawls of the throng of mourners billow in the wind as they wended their way to the family vault at St Mullins. Tom and Charles wore formal black suits and stood beside their mother at the graveside. Lady Harriet's black bonnet featured lace which partially covered her face, and her high black coat collar protected her from the elements. Anne Fleming was flanked by Hoddy and Arthur in his recently acquired mechanical chair, a wooden, hard-backed seat with two large wheels and two small, which was pushed by Anne. After the prayers, men shook hands with Tom and Charles telling them how proud their father was of them, some calling Tom 'the man of the house now.' 'Big shoes to fill,' another said. Some ruffled Arthur's hair or smiled benevolently at him, but most scurried by and just tipped their hats.

When the crowd dispersed through the open gates and over stiles, Harriet walked over to Arthur and Hoddy.

'You know he was very proud of both of you too. Don't you?'

Looking up with his large blue eyes, Arthur said: 'I don't think he really was proud of me, Mamma. But I plan to make him proud someday.'

Chapter 5

A Time of Change

A pall of sadness and uncertainty hung over Borris House for weeks after Thomas's death. His eldest son, Tom, would someday take his place as head of the family, but at only ten years old, it would be a long time before he could take on that role. He, Charles and Hoddy would soon be going away to boarding school and Harriet, with little or no entitlement to autonomy over the estate, was relieved to know that her father, the Earl of Clancarty, had been appointed as administrator, along with the new agent, Doyne. If Harriet was comforted by this arrangement, the tenants soon found out that Mr Kavanagh had been generosity itself compared to the tight-fisted Earl, who immediately set about cutting costs at the expense of the labourers.

Feeling the need to get away from Borris and on the pretext of finding a school for her stepdaughter, Agnes, Lady Harriet travelled to Torquay, taking Arthur and Anne Fleming with her. It was Arthur's first taste of foreign travel, and he could scarcely believe he was being brought along. He whooped with excitement when he saw the flotilla of boats at the pier in Kingstown where the steamship to Plymouth was docked. Although usually resistant to using his wheelchair, he was happy and excited to have Anne push him all around the ship, and on to the upper deck.

'Gosh, the sea is so huge, Mamma! And look at all the different sailing ships. This is what I want to do when I grow up. I'll sail everywhere.'

'And so you shall, Arthur.' Harriet patted his blond curls, while Anne raised her eyebrows but said nothing.

Suddenly Arthur became aware of a group of children pointing and staring at him.

'Why are they looking at me? Do you know them, Mamma?'

Anne Fleming distracted him by pointing out a huge yacht with billowing sails while Harriet walked towards the children.

'Run along now,' she said. 'Where are your parents?'

'What happened to your boy, Ma'am? Where are his arms?' one of the older boys asked.

'What happened to your manners, young man? I'll report you to the captain. Now, run along!'

'Were they talking about me?' Arthur asked as she walked back.

'Such bad manners!' Harriet said. 'Ignore them, Arthur.'

'They haven't seen a boy like me before, have they?'

'Probably not, Arthur. But that's their misfortune. You are worth ten of them! You're a MacMurrough Kavanagh. Remember that!'

'I know that mother. But perhaps they could have been my friends.'

'You will have lots of friends, Arthur. Don't ever doubt that. Now let's go inside and have lunch. There's nothing like dining on the open sea!'

The promenade in Torquay was milling with people as Arthur's chair was lifted onto the quay. Boats were being loaded and unloaded, stylish ladies with parasols strolled along the strand, carriages waited to bring people to their hotels or for pleasure rides along the seafront. Arthur's eyes were wide with amazement.

'Oh Mamma, this is wonderful. Could we take a carriage ride, please? The horses look so lovely.'

'Our hotel is just over there, Arthur. Look, it's the one with the yellow canopy over the door. We can take a carriage ride tomorrow once we're settled in.'

'Could I just give my apple to that black horse before we go in? He looks just like Tom's pony, doesn't he?'

And, to the astonishment of the carriage owner, the small boy in the wheeled chair held an apple between his two arm stumps and fed it to the waiting horse, speaking quietly to him as only those familiar with horses can.

For the next few days, Harriet looked at some schools in the locality which might be suitable for Agnes, while Anne Fleming spent the mornings reading and painting with Arthur and the afternoons walking the promenade and studying the boats moored in the bay.

'What type of boat would you like to own, Arthur?' she asked.

'Most certainly a yacht,' he answered. 'Like that one over there, with a crow's nest and lots of rigging. I want to be the captain and I'll sail to faraway places that nobody's ever heard of!'

'I don't doubt you will, Master Arthur. You'll make a fine sailor.'

That evening, when Arthur was asleep, Anne Fleming told Lady Harriet about her conversation with Arthur.

'I feel badly, my lady, telling him he can do things when, perhaps, they'll be impossible for him.'

'Nothing will be impossible for Arthur, Anne. If Arthur has the will to do something, he will make it happen. We must make him believe that. Tomorrow I will go to the bookshop on the main street and buy a book about boats and I want you to read it to him and teach him all the right nautical terms. I have entrusted Arthur to the care of our Lord above and I have no doubt he has put him on this earth to achieve great things. Our role is to build his confidence and make him believe that there is nothing he can't do.'

That night, she wrote to Doctor Boxwell to tell him of Arthur's new ambition.

I'm going to buy him a book about sailing tomorrow and I will ask my brother to take him sailing with him as soon as he is old enough. You are absolutely right when you say he must be encouraged to be fearless. There is a spirit in Arthur that is indomitable and who knows where it will take him?

She continued by telling him how Arthur couldn't pass one of the horses in the street without speaking to them and offering them apples, if he had any. She said he was getting used to people looking strangely at him and that she told him to smile and say 'hello' and they would see that *they* were the ones who should be embarrassed for staring, and that he was just a different kind of boy, but a very clever, happy one.

46

I am reluctant to come home, Frank, although I would dearly love to see you and talk with you. I know that when I return, I will be faced with decisions and bills and practicalities which hold no interest for me. My father has written twice to tell me where my duty lies, but, honestly, I have never felt more free and content. Yours truly, H.

Another letter arrived from Harriet's father the very next morning. *My dear Harriet, I must insist that you return forthwith to Borris and reside there permanently. I am doing my utmost to look after the estate as well as my own, but it is your duty to look after your son's inheritance by inhabiting the house and ensuring it is kept aired and maintained. I have catalogued furniture which I believe should be sold which needs your final approval. I will expect you to arrive on Sunday next and will send a carriage to meet you at the port. Your loving father, R le PT.*

Returning with a heavy heart, Harriet was presented with a plan for the future of Borris, valid until Tom reached the age of majority. She would look after the house and gardens while much of the land was to be rented out to avoid paying labourers' wages. Doyne would remain on as agent and her father would oversee the whole enterprise. The sale of items from the house would generate an income which would be for her private use, but the Earl made it clear that she needed to be frugal and that he considered foreign travel an unnecessary expense.

By what means Arthur should be educated was something that troubled Harriet constantly. Clearly, he could not take the path of his siblings, and attending boarding school was out of the question. Convinced that he was at least as bright and intelligent as the others, she was fulfilling the role of educator herself, but this could not go on indefinitely. By reading to him and telling him stories of his brave and fearless ancestors, she had begun to interest him in words and he was becoming an excellent reader. His oral language was superior to his siblings when they were his age and he had an astonishing memory. But his future troubled Harriet greatly and she knew he craved the company of children his own age.

Outside, while riding on horseback together, they counted everything – trees, flowers, animals. Harriet taught Arthur to recognize every tree from its leaves or fruit. He could name every flower in the walled garden and could spell many of them. With his new interest in sailing, Harriet introduced him to maps and he loved to discover the names of faraway countries. By the time he was six years old, he was painting alongside his mother, holding the paintbrush between his teeth, sitting bolt upright in front of his own low easel. But, when Harriet insisted he practice writing in the same manner, Arthur complained loudly.

'Mamma, it's just so hard. Can't I paint for longer and leave the writing? Please?'

'You can paint, once you've written your name neatly between these lines,' she'd say, and with a mixture of his own determination and Harriet's patience, he slowly improved.

The breakthrough came when a set of hooks, supplied by Doctor Boxwell, were attached to Arthur's shoulders. Although they felt awkward at first, they made it possible for him to grip small objects.

By practicing laboriously for hours each day, Arthur first mastered the grasping of large objects, like his teddy bear, books and shoes. Gradually he honed his skills to pick up smaller things, until he could bring a cup to his mouth without spilling a drop. Eventually, he became so adept in the use of his steel hooks that he could hold the reins of his pony, easily keeping pace with his siblings.

'I'm so proud of Arthur,' the doctor said, as he and Harriet walked down the cedar-lined avenue towards the archway, on one of his weekly visits. 'He's such a marvel. His skill and determination are second to none.'

'You know, Frank, there's a quality about him that's almost frightening. It's as if he knows a great destiny awaits him, and he will achieve it come what may.'

'Yes, but he can't do it without you, Harriet, and forgive me for being so bold as to say it, but I'm truly proud of you too.' And he stopped to look into her eyes and touch her arm.

'And I you, Frank.' Her eyes met his unashamedly. 'You have made this happen and I am eternally grateful to you for it.' And there, under the great Lebanon Cedar, they shared a fleeting kiss.

Drawing back swiftly, Harriet's eyes darted all around.

'Oh, I do hope nobody saw us.'

'There's nobody around, Harriet.'

'There's enough gossip about the Kavanaghs already without my adding to it. You know they're up in arms in the village about all the changes my father has made since Thomas died and they were

49

scandalised by the length of time I spent in Torquay. I think they thought I should be confined to my room with a mantilla over my face like a proper bereaved wife.'

Doctor Boxwell smiled at this image. 'I can't quite imagine you in that role,' he said, and they both laughed.

*

On the doctor's next visit to Borris House, Harriet was waiting for him in the drawing room.

'This looks very formal, Harriet. Is anything the matter?'

Waiting until the maid had placed the tray down and closed the door after her, Harriet lowered her voice.

'Frank, what happened between us on the avenue cannot be repeated.'

'It was a fleeting kiss, Harriet. Hardly a cardinal sin.' And he laughed.

'I have been agonising over it, Frank, and I don't find it remotely funny. You know there are strong feelings behind that kiss as well as I do. You are a public figure, engaged to be married to a very respectable young lady. I am recently widowed and officially still in mourning with a very complicated future. There is nothing to be gained from indulging such… ehm… desires.'

The doctor lowered his head for a moment before looking up again.

'You know, I have thought of breaking the engagement.'

'I won't hear of it, Frank,' she said, alarmed by the idea. 'Martha is a fine young woman from a respected family. You simply must marry her. There is no future for us and there will be no future for you around here if you let that young lady down.'

'Martha is a very fine young woman, I agree. But she's not you, Harriet.'

For a moment that felt like an hour, Harriet stared at Boxwell, before finally answering:

'You know, Frank, I have been a wife and mother for so long. I hope to someday discover who the real Harriet is, but I suspect that discovery won't be made in Borris House. It will be in faraway places I have only ever dreamed of, and you cannot accompany me there. It's a journey I must make on my own and, as soon as I have figured out Arthur's future, I plan to indulge that lifelong dream. While I'm away, you will marry and make a life for yourself. You will be a great father if the way you have nurtured Arthur is anything to go by, and I hope you and Martha will be blessed with your own child soon, but my fate is sealed, and it can't involve you.'

'Please don't say I can't be part of Arthur's future, Harriet. That boy is like my own son, you know that.'

'I sincerely hope you will always be part of his life, Frank. He loves you and looks up to you, so please continue to be his mentor. I hope that we, too, can always remain friends. We must sacrifice our own feelings now, for the good of Arthur and Martha and our own destinies.'

*

Over subsequent months Harriet made enquiries as to where Arthur might be educated in a nurturing environment while simultaneously planning a trip to Europe for herself. While she was unwaveringly dedicated to ensuring Arthur would live a full and interesting life, her own independence was equally important. Had she met Frank Boxwell when she was single, perhaps they might have been happy together, although a country doctor would never have been acceptable to her father. But now, having harboured dreams of foreign travel for so long, she was determined to take advantage of her unexpected freedom. Nothing would stand in her way.

But within months all Harriet's plans were shelved when her father suddenly took ill with an unexplained fever and before there was time to visit him in Ballinasloe, he had already died. The shock of his death threw the family into another period of mourning. For a time, Harriet not only felt sad, but also panic-stricken. She knew nothing of estate management and had little interest in learning about it. The only thing to relieve her grief was the realisation that, with the disapproval of her father now gone, there was a genuine chance to realise her ambition to travel. She just needed to figure out the next step in Arthur's education and then, by leaving Doyne in charge of the estate, her fortune was her own and the world beckoned.

Chapter 6

Boyhood

With the help of his steel hooks, Arthur's riding skills continued to improve and before long he was managing completely on his own, with Doctor Boxwell or Harriet riding beside him. The reins were wrapped intricately around his hooks and with slight movements of his shoulders Arthur managed to control his pony, Magpie, beautifully, talking to her all the time. To stay upright he still used the custom-made basket style chair and became increasingly confident about horsemanship and speed, without any sense of fear.

'Look at me, Mamma,' he called out as he sped by her on the driveway, and Harriet bit her lip when she wanted to say: 'Slow down, you'll hurt yourself,' remembering that she and Doctor Boxwell had agreed he must become impervious to danger.

Since proselytizing was something Harriet believed to be her Christian duty, she taught all her children Biblical studies, and Arthur was particularly interested in parables, especially the ones about children and Jesus healing lame or blind men.

'I like Jesus,' he said, 'and I think Jesus would have liked me.'

'He does like you,' Harriet reassured him. 'And all you must do is be a good boy and grow into a fair and just man. Then you will always be in the Lord's favour.'

By now Thomas and Charles were attending the Blue Coat School, a Protestant school located in Blackhall Place, Dublin, while Hoddy would begin boarding the following year. Harriet didn't want Arthur to be a lonely child left to roam around Borris House with no peers for company, and her plans to travel abroad for an extensive period were reaching the final stages. Enquiries into finding a tutor for Arthur led her to an esteemed scholar, a distant relative, the Reverend Greer, who lived in Celbridge in a fine house with his wife and three children. He was a cultured man, educated at Trinity college, and the fact that he was a man of God made him doubly attractive to Harriet who, at all costs, wanted Arthur's faith to be nurtured and expanded. The arrangement was that Arthur and his nurse, Anne, would live with the family while the Reverend tutored Arthur privately with lessons during weekdays. At weekends, Arthur would visit his cousins in nearby Castletown House. This would be Arthur's equivalent to boarding school and he would be close to the consultants in Dublin who were endeavouring to construct prostheses for him.

Samuel Greer and his wife, Maria, ran an efficient, but austere household. There were rules and routines which all the children were obliged to keep, and Harriet's instructions were that Arthur was to be treated no differently. If he misbehaved, he was to be punished exactly as the other children would. At Greer's house, Arthur was introduced to the Classics, he studied Mathematics and Theology, as well as English literature and he showed a great aptitude for learning. Physically, he astonished the Greers with his confident mobility on his short stumps, up and down the stairs and challenging the other children to horseback races across the vast Kildare fields. While, initially,

Arthur was excited about this new development in his life, his letters to Harriet told a different story.

Mother, I am so lonely. I long to be in Borris, riding through the fields on Magpie. How is she? Ask Murphy to give her a special rub from me. When will I see you and Hoddy? I send you a kiss. Your affectionate Arthur.

It was on one of his horseback excursions that the children of Castletown first encountered Arthur. Having just returned from Donegal, where their father was an MP, the four eldest children – Chambré , Thomas, Elizabeth and Louisa – were looking forward to meeting their cousin, whom they understood to be a crippled boy who needed lots of care. Astonished to see him racing on horseback towards a narrow gap, showing no sign of fear, the Connolly children covered their eyes in expectation of disaster as Arthur barely slowed down to get through. Laughing, he expertly manoeuvred his pony, circling back to the group of onlookers.

'I'm Arthur,' he said. 'I hope I didn't scare you. I'm coming to stay with you at the weekend.'

And, like a whirlwind, he brought his mischievous energy into the halls of Castletown House.

On his first visit to the house, Arthur laid down a challenge to the Connolly children:

'If anyone can prise this sixpence from my grip, they can keep it!'

And he clasped his arm stumps together with the sixpence jammed between them. One by one, the Connolly children tried to retrieve it, gently at first since they thought they might hurt him, and then more robustly. But Arthur just threw his head back and laughed as each of them failed.

Anne Fleming accompanied Arthur on these trips and looked after his personal care while in Celbridge. In accordance with his mother's wishes, when he was not under tuition she allowed him to roam the vast estate with the other children. She had been instructed not to restrict him and only to intervene if she thought he was in immediate danger. Arthur loved the company of his lively cousins and the Greer children, turning out to be quite the ringleader, playing tricks on the servants and sneaking downstairs to spy on them.

Reverend and Mrs Greer invited the Connollys to come and play with their children on occasion and this gave Arthur a chance to show off one of his favourite tricks. Clasping a fishing pole between his arm stumps, he held it out the window and tried to entice the ducks below to take the bait. To all the children's surprise, including his own, he caught a duck and hoisted it deftly into the upstairs room. Panic ensued as loud quacks filled the air and they wondered what to do with it now that it was inside and making such a racket. Feathers were flying everywhere, and the laughter and quacks were almost indecipherable from each other. With the help of one of the servants, the unfortunate bird was killed and plucked before Anne Fleming or Mrs Greer, who was very strict, had any knowledge of it. When it was presented on a silver platter for dinner the following evening, Arthur winked at his cousin, Tom, and then ate up heartily.

On another summer's day, when all the children were playing in the gardens of Castletown house, he summoned the children into the greenhouse.

'I dare any of you to let me pierce your ears.'

Laughing, they all backed away, shaking their heads, when the eldest of the Greer family, William, asked:

'What will you give me if I allow it?'

Arthur thought for a moment and, looking at the older boy, asked: 'What would you like?'

'I'd like the hunting knife you have in your room.'

'Done, sir!' Arthur said, 'Now sit here and I'll perform my operation.'

He asked one of the girls to fetch one of Mrs Greer's tapestry needles, and another to get him the coldest stones they could find in the fountain. Then he instructed William to prepare his earlobe by holding the stones on either side for a few minutes.

'Now just hold one stone behind it and sit still.'

The younger children jumped around in anticipation, while the older ones shielded their eyes. Lunging forward with the needle held tightly between his stumps, Arthur pushed the needle through until he felt the firm stone on the other side, laughing loudly as he pulled the needle out again.

'You can call me Surgeon Kavanagh, if you wish,' he announced, as William dabbed the blood with his handkerchief, walking out to the garden so no one would see the tears in his eyes.

'Drop that knife in to my room when you get back,' he called over his shoulder, as the children clapped and patted Arthur on the back.

While Arthur enjoyed his adventures in Castletown and settled in well with the Greer family, at night he lay in bed and thought of Borris. It was all the more difficult knowing that most of the time his mother was not there. In fact none of his family was there. As soon as Hoddy had left for boarding school, Harriet took the opportunity to travel, spending six months visiting friends in London and Paris, before taking in Vienna and Rome. She and Arthur wrote to each other regularly, but the thought of his home without any family present made him really sad.

You cannot think how happy it would make me if we could all live at Borris again instead of merely writing to one another. I dream of having one of our pleasant chats at home.

When might we all be there again, painting and riding our horses together? Please say it will be soon.

But while Harriet was indulging her love of travel, she was also avoiding a big event at home. Dr Boxwell's wedding reception was being held at his family home in Ballyraggett and it was a society affair. All the local gentry would be present and Harriet had received an invitation. She found it easier to reply by saying she sincerely regretted her inability to attend but that she was unavoidably detained abroad, while wishing every blessing on the happy couple. Anne Fleming had written to say that there was some idle talk in the village (which she knew was absolutely without foundation,) that Harriet and the doctor had grown very close. A servant from Borris had written to her in Celbridge with this news.

Of course, my Lady, I don't put any stock on such gossip, but I just thought it best that you know.

It was the second time someone had brought this to her attention. Her own lady's maid told her about a conversation she had overheard in the village.

'There must be a terrible sickness in the big house,' Molly Doyle had said.

'Why do you say that?' Kitty Ryan asked.

'Ah sure, isn't the young doctor up there night and morning!'

'Isn't he only helping the young cripple?' Mary Daly asked.

'Ah, you're an innocent craythur, Mary. There's enough servants up there and a nurse to mind an army of cripples.' Molly gave a dry laugh. 'It's not the child he's there to see at all.'

'Do you think it's herself?'

'Now, I said nothing, but mark my words, there's something going on. A young, engaged man and a widow! Borris House is not finished with scandal yet.'

*

As Harriet travelled throughout Europe, her older sons sometimes came to visit her. She wanted Tom and Charles, who were now becoming young men, to experience the thrill of foreign lands. Arthur longed to be with them, but was never invited. On one such trip, Arthur's letters became even more pleading:

Oh, dear Mamma, you can't think how much I long for your return, which I hope will be very soon. I have written to Tommy and Charlie and begged them not to let you stop at Geneva, but to hurry home to Borris quickly.

By now, Arthur's handwriting was impeccable and, rather than using his hooks, he found it easier to write with the pencil clamped between his arm-stumps. Each letter was perfectly formed in copperplate style that was even and uniform. He spent hours each day lying on his back training his stumps, so that the ends of them had become as sensitive as fingers and could perform a multitude of tasks.

Doctor Boxwell, on his professional visits to Dublin, made constant enquiries as to which consultants might be best equipped to provide Arthur with the most up-to-date prosthetics and finally, he was directed to Sir Philip Crampton, one of the most eminent surgeons in Ireland, who had recently been made a baronet. A surgeon for sixty years in the Meath hospital in Dublin, he had also been Surgeon-in-Ordinary to the queen and three times President of the Royal College of Surgeons. When Arthur was ten, and his mother abroad, Doctor Boxwell called to the Greers' house in Celbridge to break the news to Arthur.

'I have found the expert we've been searching for. If he can't make prosthetics for you, nobody can!' he proclaimed.

'Thank you, Doctor, and I do appreciate it, but I'm quite happy as I am,' Arthur replied. 'Look at what I can do now, come outside in five minutes.'

When the doctor arrived in the stable-yard he saw Arthur, on horseback, strapped into his basket-chair.

'Watch me go!' Arthur shouted, as he took off through the open gate and across the field, leaping over a gate that was at least four feet tall, then turning sharply to jump the same gate on the way back. Doctor Boxwell could hardly look and wondered what force of gravity was protecting the eleven-year-old from certain death.

After a little persuasion, Doctor Boxwell convinced Arthur that a visit to see Sir Philip would be a good idea and, before leaving, made arrangements to pick him up the following week to attend his first consultation. They would travel in the doctor's carriage and Arthur would stay overnight with his cousins, the Steeles, in Dublin. Boxwell had written to Harriet about this appointment and he knew how much she wanted Arthur to have working legs so that he could stand proudly beside his peers. In truth, it was obvious that it meant a lot more to her than to Arthur, but, always eager to please his mother, he agreed to give them a try.

Dr Boxwell pushed Arthur into the imposing Merrion Square residence and immediately Arthur impressed the surgeon greatly with his obvious good humour.

'So, you must be Arthur.' The surgeon extended his hand, before retracting it slowly as he remembered that Arthur couldn't shake hands. 'I'm going to do my best to make your life easier if I possibly can, young man, so tell me the things you like to do.' And he leaned on the front of his desk, taking in the enormity of the challenge before him. Doctor Boxwell stood proudly beside Arthur as if presenting his own progeny.

'Actually, Doctor, I find things pretty easy already, as a matter of fact,' Arthur replied. 'But what I would like to do is to be able to shoot and take part in the hunt. I haven't quite figured out how to manage that yet, but, with your help, I'm sure I will.'

The two men looked at each other.

'Oh, and another thing! I'd like to sail.'

'Good Lord, I wasn't expecting that, young man, but I dare say with that attitude there's nothing you can't do. Now come over here while I measure your limbs and see what can be done.'

Arthur's arm stumps were slightly different lengths, with the longer measuring five and a half inches, while his leg stumps were only a little longer. He had great strength in both sets of limbs as well as strong, wide shoulders. While Doctor Crampton wrote notes in a large ledger, Arthur's attention was drawn to some strange exhibits on surfaces around the room.

'What is this?' Arthur asked, indicating what looked like the skeleton of an animal's head on the windowsill.

'That, my boy, is a giraffe's head.'

'Gosh. A real giraffe?' Arthur's mouth was wide open.

'Yes, indeed. You wouldn't believe all a surgeon like me can learn from studying animals, Arthur.'

'In fact, I would believe it, Sir Philip,' Arthur said confidently. 'I have learned a lot from my pony, Magpie, and I adore dogs and cats.'

'That's wonderful, Arthur. As we become more acquainted, I can introduce you to lots of exotic animals. In fact, I look forward to it.'

However, despite Sir Philip's best efforts, the prosthetics he produced for Arthur caused nothing but chaffing and pain, and rather than making his life easier, they slowed him down. Despite this, the bond that developed between the elderly man and Arthur grew with every visit. Sir Philip loaned him books about wild animals and showed him a selection of skeletons he had collected over the years. He showed him the dissecting room behind his house and explained the extensive research he had done into the workings of the eyelids of birds, while Arthur listened intently. Eventually, Sir Philip brought him to Dublin Zoo, where he was a well-known figure, since he was a founder member of the Royal Zoological Society of Ireland. With its forty-six mammals and seventy-two birds, the zoo was a magically captivating place for Arthur and on the way home he described it as one of the best days of his life.

While Sir Philip, Doctor Boxwell and Harriet were disappointed that no suitable prosthetics could be found, Arthur wasn't in the least. The doctor updated Harriet when she made a brief visit to Borris during the Easter season. The tension between them had receded now that Boxwell was married and time had passed, although eye contact was still difficult.

'I'm afraid that, although the prosthetics are the best and most modern available, Arthur has rejected them,' he reported. 'He says they slow him down.'

'We'll see about that, Frank. I'll speak with him this afternoon.'

Later, Harriet pleaded with Arthur to keep trying to use the limbs Sir Philip had designed for him.

'I'd like you to persist with them, Arthur. They're so realistic and you look so tall and handsome standing on your new legs.'

A flash of anger that Harriet hadn't seen before darkened Arthur's eyes and dropping one of the prosthetics on the floor he raised his voice:

'Mother, am I an embarrassment to you? Is that it? Do you just want me to wear those awful things so you can pretend you have a normal son instead of a cripple?'

Harriet fell back in her floral armchair with shock at this outburst.

'No, Arthur. That's not it at all. Why are you saying such things? I want what's best for you.'

'No, Mother. You want what's best for you! My father was ashamed of me and since he died you want to spend as little time with me as possible. You want me to look normal so your conscience will be clear and you can travel the world and forget about me.'

'Arthur, dear. Please stop. You don't mean those things.'

By now Arthur had begun to cry. Quietly he sobbed:

'I don't mean to hurt you, Mother, and I'm sorry for losing my temper, but I am happy as I am. Of course, I wish I was a normal boy, but I know I never will be. So, I'm going to be better than any boy, like Art MacMurrough Kavanagh. I don't need false legs to do that. I need you to bring me to interesting places the way you bring Tom and

Charles. Let me learn about the world and let the world get used to me as I am.'

Harriet lifted a teacup to her lips to settle herself before answering. She knew there was truth in what her son said, but his outburst was uncharacteristic and worrying.

'Kindly refrain from speaking to me in that tone, Arthur. However, I will give some thought to your request to travel if a suitable opportunity arises.'

For the remainder of his holiday at home, Arthur set his mind to learning new skills, either with the use of the primitive hooks he had become accustomed to or by using his arm stumps on their own. He was learning to fish, which he patiently worked at, crouching over the water with the rod clasped between his stumps. After many attempts and lamenting fish that got away, with one quick flick, he could successfully land a catch and swing it onto the bank, proudly bringing it home for tea.

By now, Arthur was turning into a handsome young man. He continued to be tutored by Reverend Greer and had become like another member of that family. But he was getting restless. His brothers and Hoddy had now accompanied his mother on many of her travels. They spoke of interesting sites and cultures that he wanted to see for himself. So, he made it his mission to convince her that she should plan a trip that included him – an exciting trip, with a hint of danger so he could rise to the challenge and show the family there was nothing he couldn't do.

Chapter 7

Taking Flight

When Arthur returned from Reverend Greer's house for the summer of his twelfth year, there was a surprise awaiting him. As the carriage came to a halt at the doorway, Doctor Boxwell and Harriet stood in the porch with his wheelchair beside them.

'What's this?' Arthur called. 'Am I going somewhere? I've only just arrived.'

Like giddy children, the doctor and his mother said, 'Quickly, Arthur. Get in. We have something to show you in the stable.'

As he was pushed towards the yard, Arthur looked suspiciously from one to the other.

'What is it? A new horse? But I love Magpie! Don't say you've sold her.' And his face fell.

'No, no. Hurry and you'll see,' the doctor answered.

And as they rounded the corner, there standing patiently was his trusted pony with a new, padded chair-saddle on it, specially designed by Doctor Boxwell. Less like a bucket than the previous one, this device was more like a normal saddle with a raised back and slightly higher sides.

'Is that for me?'

'No, it's for the Queen of Sheba! Of course it's for you, Arthur. What do you think? You're much too skilled for that basket-chair now.'

'Help me up, quickly.'

Once settled in the chair-saddle, the doctor showed Arthur how he could strap his leg stumps in so as not to fall off. It also meant that he could control the horse with greater accuracy than before, tightening his muscles and moving sharply sidewards.

'It's magnificent, and so comfortable. Thank you, Doctor. And Mamma. Fix the reins to my shoulders and I'll try it out.' And off he cantered, then trotted, then galloped, until he was a moving speck in the distance.

Day after day, Arthur rode Magpie in this new way and, with the whip under his armpit, his horsemanship became a marvel to all. He disappeared for hours at a time, turning up just in time for meals and nobody, including his mother, worried about him. That is, until the day he didn't come back.

At first, Lady Harriet wasn't at all anxious when Anne Fleming came to tell her that Arthur hadn't arrived home for lunch.

'Oh, you know Arthur, Anne! He's probably talking to one of the villagers. Have you checked the stables?'

'Yes, my Lady. They haven't seen him for three hours and he never misses lunch. The stable-hand was asking if he should go looking for him.'

Standing up, Lady Harriet let her embroidery drop to the floor.

'You don't think something could have happened, do you?'

'I don't know, my Lady.' Anne was wringing her hands, nervously.

'I'll go myself,' Harriet said. 'Ask the stable-hand to saddle up for me. I'll just change my shoes.'

Walking to the stables, Harriet's eyes scanned the estate. Arthur normally went through the woods and into the deer park, spending an hour or more jumping ditches and fences. Sometimes he rode back through the village. But a cold feeling inside told her this was too long. He should be back. Something terrible must have happened.

She met Tom in the stable-yard, already mounted and ready to go. 'I heard about Arthur, Mother. I'll go and find him. You stay here in case he comes back.'

'Very well then, Tom, since you're ready. Go quickly. I'll go to the chapel and pray for his safe return.' And there were tears in her pale blue eyes as she turned away.

Leaning forward, Tom galloped through the woods, trees whizzing by his ears, calling Arthur's name all the way. He could see fresh hoof marks in the mud, but Arthur rode there so often, it was hard to know if they were from today or yesterday. Slowing down to jump the wide ditch into the deer park, he heard a whinny, and drew his horse to a halt. There, in front of him was Magpie, without Arthur. It was only as he drew closer he could see the girth of the chair-saddle had snapped and Arthur was suspended by his leg stumps on the other side of the horse, motionless.

Dismounting, Tom tethered his own horse and approached Magpie, talking gently. Clearly unsettled by what had happened, the horse was traumatised and restless. It took Tom a few minutes to calm her enough that she would let him hold the reins.

'Arthur, are you ok?'

There was no response.

Tom tried to release him from the tangled, leather straps without letting him fall on the ground and finally managed to free him, all the while urging him to, 'Wake up! Please wake up, Arthur.'

But, although his eyes were open, they showed no sign of recognition, and Tom, managing to lay him over his own horse, galloped back to the house with Magpie running after them.

Harriet wailed when she saw the immobile torso and dangling head of her youngest son.

'Is he dead?' she shouted. 'Tell me he's not dead,' and she covered her mouth as if she was about to be sick.

'Be calm, Mother. He's not dead. I can feel his pulse, but send for Doctor Boxwell quickly. I'll carry him into the drawing room.'

Like an infant, Tom cradled Arthur in his arms and walked through the front hall, laying him on the floral chaise longue with his head on a cushion. Anne Fleming knelt beside with a bowl of cold water, holding a compress to his head.

'Fight, Arthur. Come back to us,' she whispered through her tears. There was a large bump on his forehead and a deep gash on his right cheek which she bathed with iodine. His face was deathly white and there was blood on his collar. Suddenly, with a jerk of his head, Arthur's eyes opened.

'Oh my head! What happened? What are you doing, Anne?'

'Oh praised be God,' Harriet called out. 'Arthur, my Arthur.' And she fell to her knees, leaning her head on his chest, crying.

'Are you quite alright, Mother?' he asked. 'What's all this fuss about? I'm fine. How did I get here?' And he tried to sit up. 'Oh my head is really sore. Did I fall?'

'Don't move, Arthur. Doctor Boxwell is on the way to see you. You must stay still.'

'Well, I would have sold tickets if I had known so many people would be here to look at me,' Arthur joked, looking round at his sister and brothers, Anne, his mother and the stable-hand, all staring anxiously at him.

Within an hour, Doctor Boxwell arrived, with sweat dripping down the sides of his face and his black bag in hand.

'I came as quickly as I could. How is he?' His voice was breaking.

'I'm perfectly fine,' the chirpy voice of Arthur came from the chaise longue. 'Such a fuss about nothing.'

Doctor Boxwell smiled but insisted everyone leave the room except Arthur and Harriet.

'Now, young man. I'm going to have to examine you and I need you to tell me everything you remember.'

And, as best he could, Arthur told the story of Magpie bolting when he turned her towards a very high fence.

'The next thing I remember was that the saddle straps seemed to snap and the entire thing turned around. I don't remember anything after that.'

The doctor looked into his eyes and asked questions to check Arthur's memory, before examining his head and torso.

'You seem to be made of steel, my good man, as I knew you were since the day you were born. He's absolutely fine, Harriet. Now, what have we learned from this episode?' He looked expectantly at Arthur.

It was Lady Harriet who answered, in a rare display of nervousness, wondering aloud if Arthur should go back to using the basket-saddle, to which both Arthur and Doctor Boxwell replied in unison, 'Never.'

Sitting up defiantly, Arthur said, 'Mamma, you are the one who taught me to adopt the motto: "Boldness be my friend" from Shakespeare. You can't take it back now.'

'I'll have the new saddle fixed with a stronger girth strap,' the doctor said, 'and Arthur...'

'Yes, Doctor?'

'There is one thing I want you to change.'

'What is it?'

'Don't jump such big fences.'

Arthur's mouth fell open in disappointed disbelief. 'But...'

'That is, until you get a bigger horse.' And they both laughed heartily.

It took a week for the new straps to be fitted to the saddle and Arthur was impatient to get back on horseback, but refused to use the old basket-saddle as a matter of principle.

'No, I've outgrown it. I don't want you to get rid of it, Mother, since I've had such happy times with it, but I won't be using it again.'

As the holidays came to a close, Arthur continually pleaded with his mother not to send him back to Reverend Greer's house.

'This is where I belong, Mother. I don't want to live in exile while life in my beloved Borris goes on without me. Please allow me to stay. Could a tutor not be found who could teach me here?'

'But Hoddy is going back to boarding school shortly and you know I intend to travel, Arthur.'

'I never doubted it, Mamma, but I'd prefer to be writing to you from Borris than Kildare. I'll help with the estate while you're all away. You know how well I get on with people. I'll be an asset, I promise. Please?'

And within weeks, a tutor was found; the humourless young clergyman, Mr David Wood, and although Arthur instantly disliked him, there was nothing he could say since his wish to stay in Borris had been granted. Dark haired and serious, Reverend Wood showed his disapproval for Arthur's mischievous ways by setting his mouth in a straight line and shaking his head. However, Arthur's capacity for learning astonished him. Not only did he show an aptitude for Greek and Latin, but also advanced Mathematics, Science, Divinity, History, Astronomy and a comprehensive knowledge of Zoology which he had learned from Sir Philip Crampton. At Mr Wood's behest, he kept a meticulous log of his fishing expeditions, what he caught and where, and his catches were numerous and varied.

On one of Harriet's brief visits home when Arthur was thirteen, a large banquet was held for the tenantry. Wreaths of evergreen hung from the rafters of the large barn to the rear of the house and candelabras graced the long tables, giving a warm glow to the November evening. Two hundred and fifty tenants feasted on cooked meats and local vegetables – mutton, beef, ham and goose were piled high on platters and served to the ravenous guests. Buttered carrots, turnips and piles of roast potatoes completed the main course, before large trays of trifle and mince pies were held aloft to the 'oohs' and 'ahs' of the assembled crowd. Since Tom and Charles were away at school, Arthur, Hoddy and his mother sat at the top table along with two of his step-sisters Agnes and Anne, Doctor Boxwell and his wife, Martha, Mr Wood and the agent, Mr Doyne.

As the meal was drawing to a close, one of the longest serving tenants raised his tankard of ale and proposed a toast to Lady Harriet and her family. The men followed suit and the ladies raised their sherry glasses. Then, as a hush descended, everyone looked expectantly at the lady of the house to make her traditional speech. But, to their amazement, it was Arthur from his seat at the top of the room, who addressed them. 'Loyal neighbours and friends,' he began, and they all looked from one to the other in amazement. 'In the absence of my brothers, it falls to me to thank you for the warm welcome you have given to my mother and myself tonight and for your loyal service to our family. I would like to wish you and your families good health and happiness.' And raising his glass he exclaimed, 'Good health to you all.' And they raised their glasses with faces as perplexed as if the chair itself had spoken.

At the age of fourteen, Arthur received his Confirmation in the chapel at Borris House, having been meticulously prepared for the sacrament by David Wood. Rather than sitting in the family's seat on the balcony and having to make his way down, he was positioned on a window ledge close to the front where he could be carried to the bishop for the laying on of hands. He looked like a statue with his broad shoulders and straight back, situated as he was in the centre of the ledge with sunlight falling on his pale skin. In silently examining his conscience, Arthur admitted to arrogance, disobedience and wanting things he could not have. However, to the outside world, he presented as cheerful and humble with never-failing determination.

At this time, Arthur reflected many of his mother's stringent religious views, having been repeatedly told that adversity was the will of God which would strengthen, rather than crush a person. She taught him Bible passages where the human spirit conquered life's difficulties, getting him to learn passages off by heart. From the book of Joshua she made him recite: "Be strong and courageous; do not be frightened or dismayed, for the Lord your God is with you wherever you go." And from the Book of Deuteronomy: "Be strong and bold;

have no fear or dread of them, because it is the Lord your God who goes before you."

At fourteen years old, Arthur began his private diary with a quote from a hymn composed by a disabled woman named Charlotte Elliott:

"Though dark my path, and sad my lot,

Let me be still, and murmur not,

Or breathe the prayer divinely taught,

Thy will be done!"

Alone at night, with the pen between his stumps, he wrote in his diary, confessing difficulty in coming to terms with the body he had been given. But no hint of this introspection was visible in his demeanour as he transformed from a boy to a capable, confident young man, a confidante to his sister, Hoddy, and a support to his mother in running the affairs of Borris while his brothers were away at school.

Soon Arthur was old enough and proficient enough at horsemanship to join the Carlow-Kilkenny Hunt and he began using his chair-saddle on one of the bigger horses from the stables. Wearing a kind of kilt which covered his leg stumps and with his hooks barely peeking out from under his jacket, it was only the absence of boots that made him appear different to any other male in the party. But his fearlessness was legendary and the entire field would hold their breath when Arthur launched his horse at the highest fence, only to sigh when he landed safely on the far side.

The hooks, in fact, were used very little by Arthur, preferring the control he had by manipulating things between his arm stumps. But they did prove useful for archery where he managed to steady the bow and release the arrow with precision. Practicing each evening in the stable-yard, he missed so many times in the beginning that the coach house door looked like it had been infested with woodworm. But with steely determination and blistered stumps, he honed his skill, eventually winning a prize in the Leinster archery finals.

Keen that he would be able to dine in a refined manner, his mother insisted that he use the hooks to manipulate cutlery, a skill which took years of practice to perfect. It made eating a slow process and Arthur often loudly complained that his food had gone cold before he could taste it, but gradually he got more proficient, eventually taking only marginally longer than the rest of the family to finish his meals.

When Thomas, Charles and Hoddy brought friends home from boarding school to stay at Borris, they cautiously prepared them for the sight of the limbless Arthur.

'You may find it surprising or even shocking when you first see him,' Hoddy told her friend Mabel, 'but I assure you he is just like us and very mischievous. So, whatever you do, don't feel sorry for him.'

And inevitably these friends were surprised at how quickly they were able to forget that Arthur was physically so different and instead found themselves laughing at his jokes or being beaten at chess by him, as he manoeuvred the pieces deftly using his hooks.

'When is Mabel coming again?' Arthur asked when she left.

'Why, Arthur?' Hoddy teased. 'You were never so interested in my friends before? Do I detect a touch of Cupid's arrow?'

Arthur blushed deeply.

'Actually, Hoddy, I really do like her, but I'm sure she wouldn't feel the same about me. In fact, I doubt any girl will.'

'Arthur. Don't be silly. I've never heard you put yourself down before.'

'I'm not putting myself down. I'm being realistic. Who would want anything to do with a fellow like me when they could have someone tall and able-bodied like Thomas? I can't imagine any family proudly saying "our daughter is marrying the smallest man you ever saw!" ' Arthur laughed at his own joke, but there were tears in his eyes as he turned away from Hoddy.

'Everyone who knows you, loves you, Arthur,' she called after him.

'Yes,' he turned, 'but that's not the kind of love I mean.'

Chapter 8

Wanderlust

The morning of Arthur's fifteenth birthday dawned bright and cold. For what seemed like months there had been hard frost, with wind and persistent sleet showers, meaning Arthur had been largely confined indoors. He and the Reverend Wood were locked in a monotonous routine of lessons, followed by eating and more lessons, and Arthur's diary entries reflected his growing misery.

February 10th: This man is like Cassius in that vile play, Julius Caesar, which he makes me continually read. He seems to enjoy tormenting me. How I wish I could be out and about on my new horse, Bunny.

February 28th: When will this infernal bad weather end? My reason for living lies outside these walls, not inside with that dreadful man. I need to feel the abandonment of speed and fresh air on my face, and adventure.

At breakfast, the birthday gift his mother handed him was a small envelope. They were seated at the large mahogany table in the dining room, with Lady Harriet at the head of the table, David Wood on one side and Arthur at the other.

'Is this my birthday present? It's not very big!'

'Don't be ungrateful, Arthur. Open it. I think you'll like it.'

Wood tutted and shook his head, grimacing.

Sliding one of his hooks through a narrow gap, Arthur managed to slice the envelope as neatly as a letter-opener, and what fell out onto the white tablecloth astonished him!

'What? A ticket to Europe? Oh, Mamma, when? How? Thank you. Thank you. If I had ordered a gift straight from heaven it couldn't be any better! Who's coming with me?'

'Just the two of us, and of course Anne to help you. It will be a short trip, but there's so much I want to show you.'

With a smug smile at David Wood, he said: 'Thank you so much, Mamma. This is the absolute best present in the world. When do we go?'

'Next week.' Looking to David she said, 'Perhaps you could cover some European Art History over the next few days as well as the sights of Paris. It would be good if Arthur knew some background to the delights that await him.'

'I realise it's not my place to say it, my Lady, but I expect you know there will be bad feeling about this trip locally, since the potato blight has rendered many people hungry.'

'You are right, Mr Wood, it is not your place, but since you have so impertinently brought it up, might I remind you that we look after our tenants extraordinarily well and they are in no danger of starvation. I cannot be responsible for the situation elsewhere in the country.'

'Quite so, my Lady. Forgive me. I will see to it that Arthur is well prepared, and I hope he won't fall behind in his studies while he's away.'

'Oh, not at all. Travel is the best education a boy of Arthur's age can get, Mr Wood.'

'I wholeheartedly agree, Mother,' Arthur chipped in and blew a kiss across the table to Harriet.

*

Arriving on the platform of Saint-Germain-en-Laye station the following week, Arthur could barely sit still. His mechanical wicker wheelchair was being pushed alternately by Anne and Harriet to navigate through the crowds, although Arthur was keen to propel it himself with his hooks. He knew that this trip was a trial run for future travels and wanted to show that he could manage independently. He read aloud all the French signage he could see: 'Les horaires', 'Les billets', 'Un quai', and when they couldn't find the exit, he asked in a very convincing French accent, 'Où est la sortie, s'il vous plaît?'

Emerging onto the Rue de Pontoise, he saw his mother's face light up and, for the first time, fully understood her passion for faraway places, and when their blue eyes met, hers seemed to say *welcome to the world, my son.*

One of the first places Harriet took Arthur was the Arc de Triomphe. It was the biggest monument Arthur had ever seen and Anne Fleming, who had never been farther afield than Torquay, was equally impressed. As a veteran traveller, Lady Harriet had a knowledgeable confident air as she brought them from Napoleon's tomb in Les Invalides to the Sacre Coeur Basilica.

From the rooftop garden of Hotel Le Meurice, where they stayed, Arthur gasped at the Parisian vista before him, from the Tuileries Garden to Montmartre and the magnificent, meandering Seine. In his meticulous fashion, he turned a slow full circle in his chair, identifying everything he could recognise and Harriet was happy to point out those he didn't. For breakfast Arthur sampled an array of croissants and pastries, topped with apricot jam. Fruit sculptures adorned the centre of the table, with its white damask linen and fine porcelain ware. The smell of café au lait assaulted the senses, as did the array of fresh fruits, cured meats and cheese at the breakfast buffet.

If people stared at Arthur, and many did, he smiled and said: 'Bonjour Monsieur' or 'Bonjour Madame' and, embarrassed, they looked away. And when an English child, whom he had noticed being obnoxiously rude to the waiter, approached him in the hotel to ask where his legs were, he said: 'I fell under the train, and look at my arms!' When the horrified child saw the hooks, he ran away crying, to Arthur's great amusement.

'Arthur, that was an awful thing to say,' Anne Fleming admonished him, although she seemed to be repressing a laugh.

'Serves him right,' Arthur said. 'He won't ask me again!'

Their next stop was Florence, in northern Italy, having taken an overnight train with a luxurious private sleeping car. As an artist, Florence was paradise for Harriet, and she had visited several times before. Staying at the Bernini Palace Hotel, they were only a stone's throw from the Uffizi Gallery with its classical paintings and sculptures. Harriet showed them Michelangelo's *David* at the Palazzo Vecchio and the Buontalenti Grotto. Arthur loved the loud, gregarious nature of the Italians and quickly picked up some phrases, pronouncing them with gusto.

At night, Arthur asked to be allowed to venture out in his wheelchair alone and Harriet immediately agreed, but Anne Fleming looked dubious.

'But you don't speak the language, Arthur. What if something happens?'

'I speak the language of humanity, Anne. If I fall on the ground, somebody will pick me up. If I can still utter a sentence, I will say "Bernini Palace Hotel." What more would I need?'

And, wearing a cloak to cover his stumps, he ventured into the Italian night, propelling his chair with his hooks and greeting those he met with a 'buona serata,' ignoring their looks of surprise. Making straight for the Via delle Belle Donne, he wanted to see for himself if ladies of the night really existed. Tom had told him that there was a night-time quarter in every European city, but made him swear he wouldn't tell Lady Harriet of anything he had said. Asking the concierge at the hotel, he was given directions with a wink which Arthur returned in the hope that this exchange would be their secret.

And rounding the corner there they were! The ladies in doorways with long, bare legs protruding through slitted skirts and cleavage overflowing from corseted bodices. Arthur wondered would they recoil at the sight of the limbless young man laboriously wheeling himself along the street. But they called to him and beckoned, indicating doorways draped with red velvet curtains, touching the side of his face. And the thrill that went through his body was exhilarating and terrifying at the same time. What would it be like to follow one of them into those dimly lit rooms and surrender to their bewitching charms? He wouldn't do it tonight. He hadn't brought any money, but promised himself that before returning home, this pleasure would be his.

The next day, Arthur was racked with guilt. Looking at his mother over breakfast he thought how horrified she would be if she knew where he'd been and what his plans were. And yet, somehow, he thought that the God who had given him this incomplete body owed him something and had no right to begrudge him the only pleasure he might ever know, since he felt sure no woman at home would ever want to love him. He would follow through with his plan and if eternal damnation awaited him, so be it.

In Rome, the party stayed at the Villa Strozzi and, although Harriet disapproved of all things Catholic, she couldn't but show Arthur the architecture of the Vatican City. Dwarfed by the scale of St Peter's Square, she looked at the mesmerised expression on her youngest son's face and knew that he, like herself, was bitten by the travel bug. In that moment, she decided that she would show him the wonders of the ancient world.

'Isn't Roman architecture amazing?' she asked him.

'More than I could have ever imagined,' he replied.

'Wait until you see what the Greeks and Egyptians built,' she said.

'Do you mean it, Mother?'

'I certainly do!' And she was smiling the happiest smile he had ever seen. 'We'll make our plans when we get home.'

And this was how Arthur found out that the travel experiment had been a success. He had proven himself to his mother, who always believed he could do whatever he wanted, and what he wanted now, more than anything, was to see the world and experience everything it had to offer.

On the journey home Arthur wrote:

I have been awakened in mind, body and senses by this trip so that the future no longer looks so bleak. I am a man, and I will be forever grateful to the dark-eyed lady who showed me that there is beauty in brokenness.

*

Back in Borris, the summer of 1846 was spent planning an ambitious journey to Egypt and beyond.

'Mother, will you let me plan it with you? I'll work out a route with Wood in Geography lessons and put a proposal to you.'

'Very well, Arthur. But bear in mind that I've always wanted to see the sites of the Holy Land, so they must be part of it.'

So Arthur, with Wood's help, planned a route via Marseilles to Alexandria, then Cairo and on to the Holy Land. How, exactly, they were going to navigate the unimaginably tough terrain, Arthur didn't have any idea, but he knew his mother would, and she accepted the plan with enthusiasm. The expedition sounded so exciting that Tom and Hoddy decided to come too, which would be Arthur's first adventure with his siblings. The only drawback was that, despite her children's protestations, Harriet insisted that Wood come to keep their education up to standard. Since there would be hunting involved, the preparations included gathering old shooting jackets, guns, hats, shorter skirts for the ladies, liquorice for medicinal purposes, the Bible and a book of Byron's poems, which Arthur was studying.

'I can't understand why you won't come, Charles,' Arthur said to his brother, Charles. 'It's going to be such gallant fun and you'll be the only one missing out.'

'Someone has to mind the estate,' Charles said, 'and anyway, you know I expect to be called up to the army soon. I can't be half-way across the world when they send for me, can I?'

The truth was, Charles had always been indifferent about travel, and was looking forward to life in Borris without David Wood, whom they all found extremely irritating. Suffering nervous tics since childhood, Charles wanted more than anything to pursue an ordered, predictable life and since he was not heir to the estate, he saw this as his only chance to have a say in its affairs before leaving to serve his country.

As the weeks rolled on, large leather trunks were stacked up in the hallway at Borris House, giving Arthur a rush of excitement every time he passed by. He could scarcely believe this was happening and his only regret was leaving behind his beloved horses: Magpie, whom he was too heavy for now, but still took for short rides, and Bunny, his trusted friend. Their departure was planned for October, and it would be at least three weeks before they reached Egypt.

By now Anne Fleming had been replaced by William Wright as Arthur's personal valet and helper. Harriet deemed it more appropriate, now that her youngest son had reached puberty, that his personal needs should be looked after by a male, although this was never mentioned openly. Anne was given other duties in the house, while the young William, who was only a few years older than Arthur, discreetly accompanied Arthur everywhere.

Doctor Boxwell arrived to see them off on the morning of October 1st, with his six-year-old son, John. Wood and William sat up on top of the carriage with the driver, while Tom, Arthur and Harriet sat on the plush velvet seating behind them. Helping to lift Arthur's wheelchair onto the back of the carriage, the doctor patted Arthur on the shoulder.

'Safe journey, my good fellow. I'm immensely proud of you, you know that. Look after your mother.' And he kissed Hoddy and Harriet on the cheeks, lingering a little too long with Harriet.

'We must go.' She coughed. 'Lead on, driver.'

And, with a crack of the whip, they were off.

'Will you miss him, Mamma?' Arthur smiled, putting his head to one side quizzically.

'Not when I see the wonders of ancient Egypt, I assure you,' she replied as she waved to the villagers who were standing on the street in curious huddles.

'Really?' Arthur said enigmatically, but Harriet didn't respond.

•

'I see she's off again,' Molly Doyle said, 'and half the tenants starving.'

'Ah, it's not that bad here,' Kitty Ryan said.

'Mark my words, the potato blight is going to be everywhere, and that woman couldn't care less. I heard they're starving in Ballymurphy and it's only the soup kitchens are keeping them alive in Carlow.'

'I hope you're wrong, Molly. Surely the potatoes will be better next year.'

'It won't be potatoes the Kavanaghs will be eating on their fancy trip, and they won't be giving the likes of us a second thought.'

'Well, at least she's taking Arthur with her this time. He's turning into a fine young man.'

'For a cripple, you mean! Sure, he'll never be anything only half a man. I don't know what she's thinking bringing him to foreign places. I'd say we'll never see him again.'

Kitty Ryan blessed herself. 'You're an awful woman, Molly. That's unlucky talk. God bless them all.'

'It's not our God they pray to so don't bother blessing yourself. Anyway, I don't know why you're worried about them. Mark my words, bad luck follows the Kavanaghs.'

*

Over the next few days, the travelling party made their way through England and France by boat and stagecoach, finally arriving at the Port of Marseilles, where they rested at the Hotel de Ville. Arthur was mesmerised by the view from the balcony and the bustling sounds that resonated from the quayside. There were sailing boats with billowing sails, small fishing boats with men working on the rigging, rowing boats and yachts. People milled around the dockside, bidding each other farewell, climbing on board vessels, hauling nets and stacking large leather trunks and barrels, ready to be placed onboard. On the other side of the port, large six-storey buildings loomed, their windows glistening in the evening sunshine, some with canopies over the pavement. And behind all of this, an imposing chateau high on the hillside stood like a giant sentinel, overseeing everything.

One group in particular caught Arthur's eye. There were three young ladies in white dresses with colourful shawls and bonnets. With them were two older men with top hats and a woman dressed in long dark skirts and a blue shawl. The excitement of the group was palpable. It was obvious that one of the men wasn't travelling, since they all hugged him or kissed both of his cheeks and finally the two men shook hands amicably. Then, with the help of a man with a waistcoat, soft cap and white shirtsleeves, they boarded a waiting vessel, waving their hats as it sailed out to sea. What a contrast this was to the emaciated travellers they had seen at Kingstown with their plaintive crying and hopeless demeanours, trying to escape the ravages of hunger, dysentery and typhus. Marseilles was the gateway to adventure, and although Arthur felt a pang of guilt, his heart was buoyant with enthusiasm.

Chapter 9

Eastern Promise

Having spent over a week at sea, the party arrived in Alexandria and travelled by camel to Cairo with Arthur's saddle-chair attached. The Bedouin who were leading them were dubious at first that this strange, limbless boy would be able for the journey, but when they saw Arthur's confidence on the animal, they were happy to proceed. William, and the sullen David Wood, were tasked with lifting Arthur on and off as the camels sat patiently with their long, skinny legs folded under them. Arthur whooped with excitement at the thrill of being so high up and even the burning heat didn't deter him. The journey took two days with the party sleeping in square, goatskin tents the Bedouin had erected for them.

Lying on sleeping mats, Arthur and Tom chatted as they stared up at the glimpses of stars peeking through the canopy, which was held up by a strong pole.

'I've waited my whole life for this,' Arthur remarked to Tom.

'You're only fifteen, Arthur. That's not such a long wait.'

'It felt very long to me,' Arthur replied. 'But finally, it feels like my life is really beginning.'

*

In Cairo, having marvelled at the Great Pyramids, Lady Harriet hired two house-boats for their voyage up the Nile, one for herself and Hoddy and the other for Tom, Arthur, David Wood and William.

Showing her vast experience of travel, she ordered that the boats first be submerged to ensure there were no rats. Then she had them both painted sky blue and they began their cruise upriver. Although locals had made it very clear that they thought this journey was perilous, they advised that bandits who preyed on visitors like them were generally respectful of parties which included women. Harriet assured them she was well capable of managing the journey.

On the long, slow voyage, Harriet insisted that Wood resume lessons with Arthur, despite his loud complaints. For these he was sometimes joined by Tom and Hoddy, although they had both been to boarding school. In the afternoons Tom and Arthur fished from the boat, while Hoddy and Harriet read or explored small markets along the way. Everywhere they saw temples, and buildings made from mud which looked exactly like the drawings in their History books. Arthur was enthralled and managed to endear himself to the Arabs who carried him around, treating him like a lucky charm.

What impressed Arthur most was the abundance of wildlife, including rare birds which he longed to hunt. However, he would have spared the delicate hummingbird with its green and purple wings and long thin beak, the smallest bird he had ever seen in his life. He watched them in amazement, flying forwards and backwards in their never-ending search for nectar. So small and yet so perfectly formed. He wondered why his own wings had been clipped so cruelly before he ever had a chance to fly.

They spent Christmas on the Nile. The boats were decorated with streamers and candles and Tom fixed a large cedar branch to the hull of the ship to represent a Christmas tree. At Harriet's request, David Wood led them in a Christmas prayer service and they sang hymns and carols including "O Come All Ye Faithful" and "O Tannenbaum."

For dinner, they ate chicken and mutton with local vegetables and rice. Afterwards, they relished Christmas pudding which had been brought from Borris, and Tom, Wood and William drank whiskey and local beer, called Bouza. Unknown to Lady Harriet, Arthur was also developing a taste for whiskey, which he bribed William to acquire for him. For afternoon entertainment, they played cards and Tom shot pigeons from the roofs of houses on the bank, while Arthur, William and Wood placed wagers on whether he would hit them. Wood was uncharacteristically relaxed, having consumed several tankards of beer, a weakness Tom and Arthur noted for future reference. Arthur longed to be allowed to shoot and begged continually to be allowed to try it, insisting he could handle a gun, but Harriet wouldn't allow it.

'I don't want you incarcerated in Egypt for killing an innocent passerby,' she said, and despite his protestations, she wouldn't give in.

On some of the long evenings Hoddy and Arthur talked by candlelight when they were sure no one else was listening.

'I have a beau,' Hoddy confided in him.

'Is that so? I wondered who you were writing such long letters to.' Arthur smiled. 'So, who is he?'

'He's one of my friend's brothers from school. Remember I went to stay with Annabel in Galway?'

'And what, pray tell, is the young man's name?'

'It's George, but please don't tell Mamma.'

'You know I won't. And is it… em… serious?'

'Well, I'm not going to marry him if that's what you mean. Mamma would never approve. The family are virtually penniless. Annabel wouldn't be at boarding school except for the generosity of her godparents. But I do really love him, if that's what you mean.'

'Lucky you, Hoddy. And does he feel the same?'

'I think he does and I miss him desperately. I know I should forget about him and enjoy this amazing adventure, but I can't stop thinking of him.'

'I envy you, Hoddy. I wish I had someone to miss or someone who might be missing me. But do try to enjoy yourself. We will most probably never be here again and if George is any sort, he'll be there when you get home.'

'I expect you're right. Thank you, Arthur.' She kissed him on the cheek. 'I don't know what I'd do if I didn't have you to talk to.'

*

In mid-January, they moored near Karnak and Lady Harriet, Tom and Hoddy went ashore to visit the historic temple, leaving Arthur studying with David Wood. William had gone to the market in search of fresh fruit and vegetables. Having completed his lessons, Arthur lay back in the sunshine with his head resting against his mother's boat, which was right beside his own. Suddenly a large boat passed by and the wake rocked the two house-boats, making Arthur suddenly drop between them, into the deep water. Like a stone he sank, opening his mouth to call out, but only succeeding in swallowing mouthfuls of water. David Wood, who was also asleep, didn't notice, but luckily a passerby had seen the teenage boy fall. With the aid of a fisherman, he hauled him out of the water, and revived him on the riverbank, astonished and slightly frightened by his unusual physique.

When Lady Harriet returned she found a crowd standing around Arthur who was blue and scarcely breathing. Wood was unable to explain what had happened and she had to rely on the dramatic reenactments of the pair who had rescued him, who clearly had no English. Eventually Arthur was in a position to explain what he remembered, and they pieced together what could have been the final moments of Arthur's short life.

The next part of the journey was the one Arthur had been looking forward to the most. Secured on top of a camel in a caravan of sixty, they set off through Sinai on the trail of the Israelites. This was Lady Harriet's dream, and she listened intently as the guide kept her party abreast of the Biblical references along the way. Through the blistering heat of the desert they trudged, arriving at Elim, where the Israelites were given Manna from heaven, then through the Wilderness of Sin, a vast unrelenting carpet of sand. Rising at 4am each morning, they sheltered from the heat at mid-day in make-shift tents and ate an evening meal at 6pm. In the evenings the boys sat around the fire with the Bedouin who were smoking a mysterious homemade concoction which made them very mellow. Arthur and Tom sampled it after Harriet had retired for the night and found that it made them dizzy in a sort of hazy, pleasant way. David Wood was horrified, but Tom warned him not to reveal their secret to Harriet or there would be repercussions.

With the Sinai Massif looming, they journeyed to the Gulf of Akabar. Arthur again endeared himself to the Bedouin and was greatly amused when one of the Sheikhs offered to build a tent for Harriet if she would stay on as his wife.

'Why not, Mother?' he joked. 'We can look after Borris, and you can visit every couple of years.'

'Don't be ridiculous, Arthur. Now would you mind explaining politely to that man that he is very kind to offer, but the answer is no!'

With his flair for languages, Arthur had mastered the rudiments of the Bedouin's language and they were intrigued by this fearless, limbless boy who could ride a camel like a native.

Finally, they came to Hebron where, like Moses, they could see the Promised Land. Lady Harriet dabbed her eyes as, in the distance, she saw the panorama of Jerusalem to the left, Samaria and Galilee to the north and the snow-capped mountains of Hebron.

'For my entire life,' she sighed, 'this is the sight I've longed to see. Look at the way the road twists and turns to the Holy City, and the walls, and the perfectly blue sky. This is the most special day.' She broke into a rendition of "The Lord's Prayer" in thanksgiving.

Although they thought it odd, all the English speakers in the entire party joined in and somehow it seemed right.

'It really is like a dream, a postcard,' Arthur said. 'I can hardly believe it's real. It's just so beautiful.'

In a letter to his brother, Charles, he attempted to describe some of the amazing sights he was now seeing daily.

The gardens are full of apricots, pomegranates and all sorts of exotic fruits. And there are vineyards and olive groves as far as the eye can see, as well as flowers of every imaginable colour. And that's not all, Charles, the young women with their dark eyes and skin are more charming than any you have ever seen, or at least that I have ever seen! Your loving brother, Arthur.

He doubted Charles would appreciate any of this, except for the girls, but he felt bad that for the rest of their lives he and Hoddy, Tom and his mother would have these memories engraved on their minds which they could recall at will, but Charles would never share them.

*

At Hebron they exchanged camels for horses. These had to be purchased and Arthur chose a white one with a grey mane which he called Dougal McTavish. Although it made him a little homesick for his horses in Borris, it was a delight to be back on horseback and this was how they made their way to Jerusalem for Easter, passing shepherds minding their flocks in the undulating fields. Harriet was in a trance, retracing the footsteps of Jesus and praying at each Biblical milestone, referring to her personal Bible regularly to remind herself of which events happened there. At Calvary Chapel, she was alarmed to see a dispute taking place between Christians of the Latin and Greek rites over who should remove the altar cloth for the Latin liturgy. In the end, it took the threat of prison from a military officer, who removed the altar cloth himself, before the situation calmed.

'Such a lack of respect,' she said. 'Surely they can honour each other's traditions.' And, from nowhere the memory of the statues she had removed from Borris chapel all those years ago came back to her and she felt ashamed.

By now they had been away from Borris for eight months and the news from Ireland was not good. Anne Fleming had written to say that the famine was taking scores of victims daily and fever was rife. The workhouses were overcrowded and people who were strong enough were leaving on ships for America, most probably never to return. Lady Harriet also received a letter at this time saying that her mother, the Dowager Lady Clancarty, was dying in Ballinasloe. Torn between the shackles of duty and promise of adventure, Harriet decided, to everyone's surprise, to spend another winter on the Nile, sending a letter to her mother hoping she would see the "Will of God" in her sufferings and, in time, sense God's endless mercy and love.

'Don't you think the villagers will hold it against us that we continue on our travels while they are enduring such suffering?' Tom asked.

'We can't stop the spread of blight by being in Ireland, Tom. I'm sure it's of little importance to the people of Borris where we are.'

'I'm not sure you're right, Mother. In his letters, Doyne says the people are getting agitated and resentful that grain and butter are still being exported. They're taking it out on many landowners. What would my father expect us to do?'

'Your father does not have a say in this, Tom. Soon you will reach the age of majority and then you can make whichever decisions you wish. This is a journey I have waited a lifetime to experience, and I don't intend to cut it short for anyone.'

'Very well, Mother. I just hope the people don't turn against me before I ever get a chance to be their landlord.'

*

Back on the Nile, after much pleading, and backed up by his brother, Tom, Arthur was given permission to shoot.

'If he can fish successfully for trout, surely he can handle a gun, Mother,' Tom said.

'I don't see any similarity at all between those two pursuits,' she argued.

'Oh, but you know he can do anything he sets his mind to,' Tom insisted, and then, jokingly: 'If he hits three Bedouin, we'll abandon the experiment.'

'That's not remotely amusing, Tom, but I'll allow him to try. Be it on your head if it ends in disaster.'

Delighted with this decision, Arthur practiced by throwing the gun, without trigger-guard, across his left stump, using it to steady the barrel, and flicking the trigger with his right. It was slow, but he was never short of patience when it came to mastering something he really wanted to do. Spending hours each day perfecting this technique, he became an expert shot. So much so that in Tom's next letter home to Charles, he said: *He's a much better shot than Wood, who began shooting at the same time, and he can hit a flying bird with alarming accuracy.*

*

On the return journey, they arrived back in Cairo where Arthur's Bedouin friends recognised him and threw their arms around him, kissing him as if he were a long-lost friend. His 17th birthday was celebrated there with mutton and lamb, wine, whiskey and cake. Now with fine facial hair on his upper lip and chin, Arthur looked very mature compared to when they had left Ireland. With his formal education almost complete, his future was very undecided, something that weighed heavily on his mother's mind. Reluctantly, Harriet had to admit that her Eastern adventure had come to an end and that it was time for her to return with her adult children to face the difficult and uninviting reality.

In a letter to her sister, Harriet wrote:

I don't understand why there is famine at all. I understand that the harvest in Ireland was very good this year. I put the whole thing down to bad government. It really is most tiresome.

Travelling back through France and England, they arrived back in Kingstown in mid-May, having spent eighteen months abroad. Local newspapers announced that "Lady Harriet and Thomas Kavanagh will return from their extensive world tour next week. Mr Kavanagh will attain his majority next August and will reside permanently on the Borris Estate. This will be celebrated widely by his tenantry."

'Not a word about us!' Arthur said to Hoddy drily. 'We are irrelevant! I don't suppose they even missed us.'

Tom sincerely hoped that these predictions of locals celebrating his coming of age would prove true and not the florid imaginings of a newspaper man in need of a story. So it was a relief to him to be met on the road between Bagenalstown and Borris by a brass band which marched in front of them playing "Home Sweet Home," stopping at the gates of Borris to play "God Save the Queen." Yet, while the welcome was warm and genuine, there were rumblings of discontent which wouldn't take long to bubble to the surface.

Chapter 10

Coming of Age

Back in Borris, Arthur reminisced about his time in the Middle East, regaling Doctor Boxwell, his cousins and anyone else who would listen, with stories about the sights and people he had encountered there. At night he read and reread his diary entries from the Nile and the Holy Land, reliving each adventure and experience. Particularly proud of the variety of wildlife he had bagged, he had no idea how or when he would have the opportunity to travel again, confiding in the doctor that he would make it happen somehow.

Tom, on the other hand, was very troubled. The enormity of the task he was taking on as head of the family in turbulent times weighed heavily on him, giving him no time to dwell on his travel experiences. While the family was abroad, the Young Irelanders who were dedicated to political reform and independence had broken away from Daniel O'Connell's Repeal Association, believing it was not radical enough. In May of that year they held an abortive insurrection which ended with most of their leaders being exiled. But the goals of "Fair Rent, Free Sale and Fixity of Tenure" had taken hold in the minds of the peasantry and there were whispers of further rebellion. This was a cause of huge anxiety to many landlords, including Tom.

In July, accompanied on the half-day journey by William and Tom, Arthur went to stay with his great aunt, Lady Ormonde in Garryricken, near Callan in County Kilkenny. Tom returned to Borris the next day.

With minimal help from the stable hands and William to look after his personal needs, Arthur could freely ride around the estate and shoot, as well as fish in the King's River, so named because it was said that a High King had drowned there. With his usual spirit of adventure, Arthur, now aged 17, started riding out at night looking for rebels, who were reportedly active in the area. William was not a horseman and therefore couldn't accompany him.

On one such escapade, Arthur accidentally came across a rebel camp in a clearing in the woods. A group of armed men on horseback were in a semi-circle facing a man standing on the ground with a rifle slung across his back. Arthur brought Bunny to a stop, and whispering to the horse to keep her calm, he watched and listened. Suddenly one of the men shouted: 'Over there!' pointing directly at him. Turning and galloping as fast as he could, Arthur wove his way through the trees with the skill of an expert horseman. Gradually the pounding hooves in pursuit became more distant and he made his way back to Garryricken, shaken but triumphant to have escaped their clutches.

There was another reason for Arthur's nighttime escapades, which took him into the village itself. Unknown to William and his aunt, he was holding secret moonlight meetings with a certain local girl who helped out as a housemaid in Garryricken, named Annie Brooks. She waited for him, sitting on the wall beside the church each night. The priest, who was locking the church one evening, overheard the conversation between the young man on horseback and the young lady, and stayed in the shadows to listen to Arthur's fascinating tales of the Wailing Wall in Jerusalem, the creatures of the Nile and habits of the Bedouin people. Then, Arthur leaned over and kissed young Annie, before galloping off into the night.

Confiding in Hoddy when he got home, he said, 'I met a really nice girl in Callan.'

'What do you mean, you met a girl? Was she a visitor at the house?'

'No, just somebody I met.'

'Arthur! What kind of somebody? You mean a local?'

'Yes! A local! Is that so bad?'

'Don't you know these are dangerous times, Arthur? You can't be going about on your own, talking to locals.'

'Oh Hoddy. A sixteen-year-old girl is hardly dangerous.'

'Potentially more dangerous than a sniper, actually! Whatever did you speak of?'

'Well, that's the interesting bit. She told me about her relatives who have been put off their land and about the workhouse turning people away. I honestly didn't know things were so bad. Did you, Hoddy?'

'There's no point in us concerning ourselves with such things, Arthur. We can't do anything about them.'

'But if people like us can't, then who can?'

'Oh, you ask such difficult questions, Arthur. Was there anything else *interesting* about her?' And she smiled.

'Nothing to concern you,' he answered.

'I knew the girls would love you.' She laughed.

'And what of George from Galway?' Arthur enquired.

'Oh, he seems to have forgotten me. He doesn't write anymore. But I don't mind because I have eyes for somebody else now.'

'Pray tell who?'

'Not yet, Arthur. But you will be the first to know if there is anything to tell.'

*

In August, Tom Kavanagh reached the age of majority and since this meant that he could officially take his place as head of Borris Estate, a huge celebration was held. The banquet on the front lawn was attended by six hundred guests. Canvas awnings stretched over long trestle tables, decorated with flowers and candles, while meats of all descriptions were piled high. Servants scurried in and out of the kitchen, replenishing plates and tankards as casks of ale and cider were placed at the end of each table, from which the tenants could drink freely. Afterwards, a variety of succulent desserts were distributed by the waiting staff. All the Kavanagh tenants were seated on both sides of the long benches and a table for gentry and local dignitaries faced them. When it was time for the speeches, a hush fell over the crowd and Colonel Henry Bruen rose to address the people of Borris and present their new patriarch to them.

'Dear people of Borris, since the late Mr Kavanagh so sadly left us many years ago, we have waited patiently for this day. And now, I present to you this fine young man of noble lineage, Thomas Kavanagh. Like his father and namesake, he is a young man of the utmost integrity, a leader with an extraordinary attachment to his native land, who will stand by you in your trials and be a source of wisdom and solace to you. This evening, at the foothills of these gracious mountains and in front of his ancestral home, he takes his place in history. To mark this auspicious occasion, I present to him the Charter Horn, the most valued heirloom of the Kavanagh family, handed down from O'Donnell, the son of Dermot MacMurrough, in 1175 on submission to the English crown.' To thunderous applause, Tom stood and accepted the gold-rimmed artefact and in his hands it felt like lead.

Tom's address was short and to the point. He thanked Colonel Bruen, whose family had been closely linked to the Kavanagh clan for generations. Proposing a toast to his mother, he included his siblings and remembered his late father. Finally, he expressed the aspiration that the people of Borris would judge him to be a fair landlord who would lead them through the current difficulties to a bright and prosperous future.

This magnificent feast went on for several hours until it was time for the music to begin. Arthur, Lady Harriet, Tom and Hoddy sat together with Charles in full uniform who was now a member of the British Army. Doctor Boxwell and his wife were there, along with other local landowners and dignitaries. But the most fascinating guest of all, and the subject of much pointing and whispering, was a man dressed in Arab attire – a burgundy turban on his head and matching pantaloons, with a silk shirt and cloak. Hadji Mohammad had returned with the family from the Middle East and was now resident in Borris

House, being trained to become Arthur's personal aide, since William had been promoted to Junior Butler. His black eyes scanned the crowd nervously and the only one who spoke to him was Arthur, seated between him and Hoddy.

Tom and Lady Harriet took to the floor for the first dance, opening the proceedings for the tenants, giving Arthur the chance to sample the cider, without Harriet seeing him. Lamps and torches burned all around to light up the dancing area and, in the firelight, the turrets of Borris House seemed to reach to the sky. As far away as Mount Leinster, bonfires could be seen with great plumes of smoke rising into the air. Hundreds came out on the streets and into the estate to celebrate the coming of age of their handsome new landlord. The evening finished with fireworks lighting up the night sky as if the heavens themselves were rejoicing in the new head of Borris House, the new Mr Kavanagh who would bear the title "The MacMurrough".

Having a manservant of his own who didn't speak English gave Arthur a lot more freedom than when he was reliant on Anne Fleming or William, who were regularly quizzed by Harriet. Now Arthur, who had mastered some Arabic, had an ally on whom he could rely, who was also an excellent horseman. So, in the spring of 1849, when Arthur and Hadji began going for night-shoots in the woods a couple of times a week, nobody suspected anything. In fact, Harriet was relieved that he wasn't venturing out alone, and nobody enquired as to where he had been. Sometimes they *did* just go shooting and Arthur delighted in showing the wide-eyed Hadji the extent of the Borris estate and the variety of native wildlife on offer. But, with increasing regularity, he would stop at a large oak tree in the woods and ask Hadji to help him off his horse.

'Lift me down, Hadji. Now, tie up my horse and come back in one hour exactly.' At first, Hadji looked puzzled, but when he saw the young girl stepping out from behind the tree, he nodded in understanding, and left them alone.

Months earlier, when Arthur had returned from Callan, word of his late-night trysts came back to Harriet but she decided not to mention them, since it was unlikely Arthur would be visiting his aunt again in the near future. But lately, at breakfast, she looked at him, now wide-shouldered and manly, and realised that, in all her dreams of a full life for Arthur, she hadn't accounted for love. In fact, the thought of it disgusted her. Nobody in the locality had ever seen the full extent of Arthur's deformity and she imagined gossip and ridicule if they ever did.

His latest sojourns in the woods went unnoticed for a long time, until Hoddy, who had seemed troubled for a few days, asked to speak to Harriet in the drawing room.

'What is it, Hoddy? There's clearly something wrong.'

'Well yes, Mamma, but I'm torn between loyalty to Arthur and loyalty to you.'

'If you think it's something I should know, then say it.'

'You must promise you won't reveal who told it to you. Do you give me your word, Mamma?'

'Does it involve alcohol, because if so, I'm already aware of that weakness and monitoring it closely.'

'No, it's worse than that, Mother.'

'Oh dear, this sounds very ominous. Yes, I promise. Now what is it?'

'Arthur has been seeing Maud in the woods at night.'

'Your friend, Maud Considine from Newtown?' Her voice had risen a notch.

Hoddy nodded. 'When he goes out at night, shooting, he meets her in the woods.'

'But isn't Hadji with him?'

'Not all the time, Mamma. I saw Hadji sitting in the summer house one evening with his horse tied up outside, and when I asked him where Arthur was, he just shrugged. In any case, Mamma, Maud told me herself. She says she loves him.'

'Oh, don't be ridiculous. How could she love him? She's not even in Burke's Peerage! I mean her parents are very respectable landowners, but really, the impertinence of the girl to think she could love Arthur!'

'But Mother, everybody loves Arthur. And I don't think love is confined to those in Burke's Peerage! I'm merely telling you because I think it's serious.'

'What do you mean, serious?'

Hoddy looked down.

'Hoddy! This is no time for embarrassment, what do you mean by serious?'

'Well, Mamma, when I was walking with Maud and she told me about loving Arthur, she said they considered themselves to be married.'

'Married! Has the girl lost her mind? How could they be married?'

'She said they had a kind of ceremony in the woods. They exchanged flowers as tokens of their love – she gave him a Verbena. Haven't you seen it beside his bed? I'm not sure what he gave to her.'

Harriet wrung her hands and held them to her face.

'The boy has clearly taken leave of his senses. Thank you for telling me, Hoddy, and you can rest assured he'll never trace this information back to you.'

*

That night Harriet positioned herself at an upstairs window in darkness and watched as Arthur and Hadji cantered across the lawn to the woods. With guns strapped to their backs they disappeared into the leafy canopy. The clock on the mantelpiece said five to eight. Keeping her eyes peeled on the opening she waited, and at almost five past eight, she saw the white markings on Hadji's horse making their way around the edge of the wood to the summerhouse. So, it was true, and now she must act, but exactly how, she wasn't yet sure.

The following morning, she sent for David Wood.

'Sit down, David, I have a grave matter to discuss with you.'

Fearing his services might no longer be required, Wood sat on the edge of the seat with a worried expression.

'Yes, my Lady?'

'It seems Arthur is philandering again.'

'How could he, my Lady? He's at Borris all the time.'

'There's no need to concern yourself with the details, Wood, what I'm looking for is a solution.'

'What did you have in mind, my Lady? Would you like me to speak to him?'

'With due respect, Wood, I think a lecture from you would be futile.' Wood shifted indignantly on the seat but said nothing. 'I think a prolonged period of travel overseas is what is required to regain perspective.'

'That would be wise, my Lady.'

'I'll need you to travel with him, of course, and I think I'll also ask Tom.'

'Oh, Lady Harriet, I'm not sure I could do that.'

'If you value your position with this family, you *will* do it. With the political situation as it is, I will have to stay here to run affairs while Tom is away. William Wright will travel as manservant, so you'll be a party of four,'

'And what about Hadji, my Lady?'

'I suspect he is, as we speak, waiting at Kingstown for a boat to take him home.'

'Home, my Lady? To Egypt?'

'Indeed! Escorted off the premises at first light.'

Lady Harriet stood up, raising her hand to indicate that she wouldn't be discussing the matter any further.

Getting to his feet, Wood said: 'Do the boys know?'

'Nobody knows, Wood, except you and I, and I'll thank you to remain silent until instructed. Good morning to you.'

And she swept out of the room without another word.

*

When Arthur heard Hadji was gone, he demanded to know why.

'It seems he wanted to return to his own country,' Lady Harriet said.

'But I was with him last night and he didn't mention going anywhere. He seemed very content.'

Something in Lady Harriet's deep blue eyes told him she was hiding something.

'Mother! You brought us up to believe that truth was more important than anything. Now I'm going to ask you a direct question and I want a truthful answer. Did you send him away?'

'Yes, Arthur, I did, but I have absolutely no intention of explaining why.'

In an outburst of rage never displayed by Arthur before, he swiped his hook at a vase on a side-table, smashing it against the fireplace.

'You had no right!' he shouted.

'Arthur Kavanagh, you have only recently turned eighteen, you are not the head of this household and I have every right to employ whomsoever I like, and equally to terminate their employment. Now control your rage, young man, before it controls you.'

'I detest you and your controlling ways. I must live my own life. You had no right to send him away.' Arthur fumed.

'I have every right, and anyway, we won't be needing his services here for the foreseeable future.'

'And why is that? Am I not to have a manservant at all?'

'When you have calmed down, we can discuss my plans for the completion of your education.'

Arthur sat on the low chaise longue and breathed deeply.

'Yes, Mother. What have you planned for me now?'

'I've arranged for you to go on another foreign trip with Tom and Wood. I thought that would be something that would please you.'

'But you never mentioned such a thing.'

'It's a surprise, Arthur, and you should be grateful. William Wright will travel as your aide.'

'And who will manage the Estate?'

'I'll look after that until you and Tom return. Now I must leave as I have an appointment in the village. We will speak about the details later.'

'One more thing, Mother?' he asked as she left the room. 'When is this trip to take place?'

'Next week.'

Chapter 11

Maud Considine

When Arthur didn't turn up in the woods as usual on that June evening in 1849, Maud was puzzled. He was always there at 8pm, sometimes sitting beside the trunk of the large oak, or cantering up on horseback with his Arab friend. She sat beside the tree until 8.30pm, although within a few minutes she sensed he wasn't coming. This had never happened before, so walking home, she reassured herself with thoughts that something must have happened to change his plans and he would get a message to her.

But, for days, no message came and she began to worry that something terrible had befallen him. The only person who knew they had been meeting was Hoddy, so on the pretext of calling to see her, she walked up the long drive to Borris House. She had been visiting the Kavanaghs since she was a small child – her father and mother were occasional guests there, being minor landowners in the area. She and Hoddy had roamed these fields with Arthur, Charles and Tom and her own brother, Philip, playing hide-and-seek in the long grass and climbing the cedar trees with their long, low hanging branches. Arthur was always the ringleader, and she loved his sense of adventure. But, since he came back from his tour of Egypt, something changed between them. At first it frightened her, the quickening pulse and longing to be close to him, but when she realised he felt it too, it was all-consuming.

A servant answered the door and, recognising her, stood back to let her in.

'I'm here to see Hoddy, Edward.'

'Certainly, Miss Considine. Lady Harriet is in the drawing room. I'll bring you there while I fetch her.'

'Good afternoon, Lady Harriet. How are you today?'

Harriet looked up from her book. 'I'm very well, Maud,' she replied, showing only the faintest hint of surprise. 'You're here to see?'

'Hoddy,' Maud answered a little too quickly.

'Of course, and I'm sure you heard Arthur and Tom are away in Europe.'

Maud paled as she plonked onto the chaise longue.

'Away? No, I didn't know that.' Her voice was faltering.

'Well, I'm sure that's no concern of yours. What would you want with them. I'm sure you have a lot more on your mind.'

Maud, stuck for words, felt faint and, afraid she might cry, began to cough a little too dramatically.

'Oh dear. I'll send for a glass of water for you.' But just as she was about to ring the bell, Hoddy came into the room.

'Be a darling, Hoddy, and get Maud a glass of water before you sit down. She seems to have something caught in her throat.'

'No, I'm really quite fine, thank you.' Maud tried to recover herself.

'Well, I'll leave you girls to your chattering, then,' Harriet said as she left the room with a tight smile directed straight at Maud.

As soon as the door closed behind her, Maud let out a whimper and a tear trickled down her cheek. 'What's this about Arthur going to Europe? Why did nobody tell me? Why did *he* not tell me?'

'I have no idea. It's been planned for some time,' Hoddy lied.

'It can't have been. He would have told me. Did he leave a note for me?'

'No, nothing. Were you expecting one?'

'Hoddy, why are you acting like this? I told you Arthur and I were in love and about the ceremony in the woods. He called me his wife.'

'Don't be ridiculous, Maud.' And she gave a dry laugh. 'You're both only eighteen years old. How could you be his wife! I'm sure he'll look you up when he gets back. Now you really need to compose yourself.'

'I can't believe you're being so heartless, Hoddy.' Standing up, she said, 'I'm leaving, but if a letter comes for me, you will give it to me, won't you?'

'That goes without saying, Maud. Do cheer up,' and she showed her to the door.

*

Over dinner, which was taken in the library since there was no one at home but the two of them, Harriet quizzed Hoddy about Maud.

'Mamma, the girl is distraught, and I am caught in the most horrid triangle between my closest brother, my friend and you. But I did what you asked me to do, and that's all I want to say about it.'

'I hope you didn't give her the letter.'

114

'I didn't, Mamma, but I feel awful about it.'

'Sometimes duty makes us feel awful, Hoddy, but we still have to do it. Now I have two more requests of you, and then the matter is closed.'

'And what are they?' Hoddy sighed.

'In your next letter to Arthur you will say that Maud has issued no reply and that she doesn't consider the "ceremony" in Newtown Wood to be in the least binding. Then burn the letter, and any subsequent ones from either party.'

'Oh, Mother, don't ask me to do that. How can you be sure we're doing the right thing?'

'For goodness' sake, Hoddy, the dogs in the street know that a Kavanagh can't marry a Considine, least of all Arthur. Now, as I said, the matter is closed.'

*

When Maud left Borris house she walked towards the woods. Tears were flowing freely down each cheek and she kept pausing to bend over with grief. How could Arthur not have told her? It didn't make sense. He had been so honest and so loving just a few days previously. What could have changed?

Sitting under the tree where they used to meet, she cried until her face was puffed and her eyes red and sore. This was where they had shared their first kiss and where, for the last three months, they had met at least once a week. Sometimes they just sat and talked about places Arthur had travelled to, or the rebellions that were going on all over the country. Other evenings they spent the entire hour until Hadji came back, kissing and whispering in the darkness, his scent filling her senses.

Gradually, their meetings became more intimate. Arthur would ask Hadji to give them a little longer and, with his cloak spread out on the ground, they lay together and his hungry mouth was everywhere.

'Arthur, you do love me, don't you?'

'You know I do, Maud.'

'How do I know, Arthur?'

'Oh, Maud, you ask so many questions. Because I've told you.'

'I need to keep hearing it,' she said.

'Maud, with all my heart, I love you.' And then, 'I have an idea. Tomorrow evening we will hold a ceremony. We'll exchange flowers as tokens of our deepest, heartfelt love, and then you will officially be my woodland wife.'

This had made her laugh, but when it came to it, there was no laughter.

Arthur arrived the following evening with a forget-me-not in his lapel. Maud held a posy of purple Verbana.

'Sit down here and face me,' he said, sitting on the outstretched cloak. 'Now we'll exchange these posies and you must repeat after me: With these flowers, I thee wed.'

And she repeated: 'Arthur, with these flowers, I thee wed.'

'Now, Maud, you are my lawful, woodland wife,' and without any more words they were kissing and lying together, until they heard

Hadji's horse in the distance and she struggled to fix their clothes before he came into view.

How could he not have mentioned going to Europe, when he seemed so sincere? Maud decided that she would write a letter and ask him how this trip had come about, and why he hadn't told her. She'd ask Hoddy to send it to whichever city they were travelling to next. There must be an explanation. She knew Arthur her entire life, and this was just not in his nature.

*

When Hoddy opened the letter intended for Arthur, she blushed with embarrassment. It was clear to her that the intimacies shared between her younger brother and close friend were intense and had been shared for some time. Laying the pale pink pages on the drawing room table, she positioned the one from Arthur to Maud beside it. It was as if she had exposed their raw and beating hearts side by side. The words were so passionate with each of them struggling to understand what had happened. She knew she should follow her mother's wishes and burn them both, but what if love like this never came Arthur's way again? She loved Arthur from the day he was born. He brought everyone around him such happiness. How could she deprive him of such heartfelt love?

Before she could put the letters away, Harriet came into the room with the morning post. 'I recognise David Wood's writing on this one and there's one for you from Arthur.' Then looking at the letters laid out on the table she said:

'Are those what I think they are?'

'Yes, Mamma. And you mustn't read them. They really are private.'

'I have no intention of reading them, Hoddy, but I'll make it easy for you.' Sweeping them off the table, she scrunched them into a ball, and tossed them on the back of the open fire. Hoddy gasped, as Harriet handed her the new letter from Arthur.

'And if there's an enclosure in this envelope for that girl, I expect you to burn it without opening it. There's no point agonising over these things, Hoddy. Love is such a fickle thing at Arthur's age. He'll have forgotten her by the time he reaches Moscow.'

There was a letter addressed to Maud in Hoddy's envelope, with a sketch of a forget-me-not on the back, and another in her next four letters. It was October before these enclosures stopped and Arthur began describing his travels as he used to, exaggerating the scrapes he got into and looking forward to crossing the difficult terrain in Persia, although he always signed off with: "Give my love to all, especially Maud."

When Maud's parents heard of her secret meetings with Arthur they were outraged. It was Lady Harriet who told them, calling on the pretext of inviting them to a harvest banquet. She had spun a version of events where Arthur and his manservant initially came across Maud wandering in the woods alone, and although she normally didn't allude to his disability, she placed the blame firmly at their able-bodied daughter's feet. 'One can't imagine what they would have in common,' she said.

'Well, this is a shock, but I'm sure there's an innocent explanation,' Maud's mother said, fussing over the tea tray with embarrassment.

'Arthur has gone on a world tour, so there won't be any further meetings, I can assure you, but I do wish Maud the very best. Now, tell me, how is Philip getting on in the army?'

And there, as in Borris House, the matter as far as Harriet was concerned was closed.

But not so for Maud.

Her father flew into a rage when she came home. 'A daughter of mine, wandering in the woods, luring that poor crippled boy astray.'

'Don't call Arthur a cripple!' Maud shouted.

'What I call him is nothing to what people will call you!'

'I don't care about people, Father! I care about Arthur.'

'Well, you must stop caring about him. His mother says he'll be away for a year at least, and maybe longer. You will concentrate on your studies and on upholding this family's good name.'

Maud's face was horror-stricken. 'A year? Did she really say that?'

'Go to your room, Maud. You seem to have temporarily lost your mind. Whether it's a year or ten years is no concern of ours. He's a Kavanagh. You're a Considine. There's no more to be said!'

Over the next few months people began to notice that Maud, once an energetic girl who was blossoming into a pretty young woman, was dishevelled and listless. Her long, straight hair was unkempt and she showed no interest in the latest fashions. At the beginning of August, Queen Victoria visited Ireland and young ladies queued to be presented to her at the Vice Regal Lodge in the Phoenix Park in Dublin at which Sir Philip Crampton, Arthur's surgeon, was in the reception party. Although invited, Maud was forbidden by her parents to attend. Still in disgrace, she stayed at home, while Hoddy and other young ladies of a certain class queued with cards bearing their names, to be presented to Her Majesty.

Shortly afterwards, Maud was sent away to an aunt who lived in Switzerland. When friends enquired, they were told she had been diagnosed with a lung condition for which clean cold mountain air would be beneficial. No more specific details of her illness were forthcoming, and when she wrote to Hoddy, she merely enquired about the family in general, without mentioning Arthur at all.

Chapter 12

Wild Oats

Within days of his conversation with Harriet, on the 4th of June, 1849, Arthur found himself at the harbour in Kingstown alongside Tom, David Wood and William Wright. The rough itinerary was to travel from Liverpool to Copenhagen, then Norway, Sweden and on to St Petersburgh before arriving in Persia by crossing the Caspian Sea. Beyond that, the details were hazy, as was the duration of their travels. Tom and Wood maintained that the trip had been planned as a surprise and that Arthur should be pleased instead of looking miserable.

'It doesn't make sense,' Arthur said to Tom. 'Why would no one have told me about it? The trip doesn't seem to be very well thought out and you were just settling into your new role. There's something really strange about this.'

'Will you stop being a wet rag, for goodness' sake. You're going on the trip of a lifetime. I'm happy to be getting away from my responsibilities for another while. Stop moaning and let's enjoy our time abroad.'

'And that's another thing,' Arthur added. 'How long are we staying away? Do you have any idea?'

'No, I don't, but you're not in a hurry, are you? Buck up, Arthur. We're going to need all your charms to get Wood to lighten up and give us a bit of freedom to enjoy the finer things in life, if you know what I mean.' And he raised his eyebrows, giving an exaggerated wink.

Lady Harriet had entrusted David Wood with judging at what point on the journey Arthur had come to his senses, reminding him that he was to keep in regular contact by letter and insist that the boys did likewise. A duration of a year was suggested, but there was no definite return date. Promissory notes were issued to be presented on their arrival in whatever countries they visited or passed through. These were legally binding and would guarantee that whatever expenses were incurred in that country would be paid in full by the Kavanagh Estate. Wood was to ensure that the money was spent wisely and prudently, although Tom, having reached the age of majority, was now officially in charge of the finances.

Arthur's mood was low for the first few days. While he loved to travel and was thrilled with the prospect of hunting in unknown territories, at night he lay awake and thought of Maud Considine. Memories of her scent and soft skin haunted him and he deeply regretted not being able to tell her in person that he was going away. He wanted to, but every time he said he was going on a night-shoot, his mother insisted that David Wood go with him, since Hadji was no longer there. And this foreign trip was sprung on him so fast that all he could do was send a note to her house with Hoddy, but she hadn't sent a reply. The ache in his heart was unbearable at times, making him toss and turn for hours, so that he was tired and out of sorts the next day.

'Cheer up, Brother. You're like a lovesick puppy,' Tom said.

'That's not funny,' Arthur replied. 'Aren't any of you ever going to tell me how this trip came about? I feel like I'm being punished, but nobody is telling me for what, exactly.'

'How could a trip around the world be a punishment? Think of our poor tenants in Borris – any one of them would give anything to change places with you.'

'It's a good answer, Tom, but it's not the point and you know it. I'm tired of all this evasive nonsense. I want you to tell me what's going on.'

'I *have* told you Arthur, and my advice to you is to start enjoying yourself. We arrive in Norway tomorrow. It's time to live a little,' and he clapped him on the back.

Arthur decided to write one more letter to Maud, which he would ask Hoddy to deliver. He wanted her to understand that this trip was not on the cards when they last met and that he hadn't kept it from her. Asking her to reply through Hoddy, he signed off with: *I still have the precious Verbena you gave me. I keep it under my pillow and, when I return, I hope to exchange it for a more lasting token of my affection. Yours, always. Arthur.*

He then wrote a short letter to his mother. It pained him deeply that there was a distance between them. Up to now, no matter how long they were separated or where in the world they both were, he felt there was an invisible connection that kept them close.

I feel that the thread that was so strong between us has been stretched, Mamma, and I fear it will be broken if we cannot be honest with one another. I'm pretty sure this trip is a punishment for me, rather than a pleasant surprise. I will try to enjoy myself, but you need to realise I am a man now and must become the master of my own destiny. I will always uphold the honour of the Kavanaghs, but it may not be exactly as you see fit. I do, however, remain your loving son, Arthur.

With Tom's hasty departure from Borris, Harriet was left to explain to the agent, Doyne and others that the young man who had so recently been presented to them as someone who had an extraordinary commitment to his native land, had left. That the whole thing was organised with such haste set tongues wagging, and Harriet, who would have loved to travel with them, found herself isolated and lonely.

*

'Did you hear that the young Kavanaghs are gone abroad again?' Molly asked the women.

'You must be joking! Sure, they're not long back. Is the cripple gone too?'

'He is. And you're not going to believe why.'

'Spit it out, Molly! Don't keep us waiting.'

'I heard it in the market. One of the maids said she overheard that he had been seeing a young girl and the mother found out.'

'Arthur? Ah, God bless him, he'd hardly be up to much.'

'That's not what she heard.'

'Go away! And who's the girl?'

'She said it's young Considine with the long hair. Bit of a trollop, that one.'

'Well, that's a good one, Molly,' Kitty said. 'And when will Tom, our new landlord who was going to stay with us forever, come back do you think?'

'Who knows? But there's trouble in the big house. They're never far away from it.'

Harriet knew there was talk in the village. She saw the ladies in huddles and knew by the sarcastic way they were asking how Arthur was getting on, that the word was out. It made her furious. She had hidden Arthur's disability for so long and never imagined that he would bring disgrace on the family. The perceived immorality of his activities with Maud Considine was outweighed in her mind by the fact that his disability was laid bare. Although her heart ached to see his empty chair, she wasn't sure if she could ever forgive him.

*

By the time the travellers had journeyed by land through Holland, Germany and Denmark, and by boat to Norway, Arthur was less melancholy. In Oslo, they were invited to dinner with a Mr Crowe and his family who had connections to the Kavanaghs. Although they had heard of Arthur, they found it hard to hide their shock at seeing him carried in on William Wright's back. But, once seated at the table, it was easy to forget that this confident young man was so physically challenged. The meal was a lavish affair with several courses and accompanying wine. Afterwards, David Wood was shocked that even though it was the Sabbath, a large group of people and some musicians arrived for dancing. He indicated that he wanted the boys to leave, but they refused, so he sulked in the library, reading, while Tom and Arthur stayed to enjoy the festivities. Increasingly, they were letting Wood know that, despite the instructions their mother had given him, they would make their own moral decisions on this trip and warned him that his letters to Harriet should confine themselves to what she would like to hear.

The two-day ferry from Stockholm to St Petersburg was calm with cool, bright sunshine and the young men amused themselves by playing shuffleboard on deck and drinking whiskey. In St Petersburg they booked themselves into the Grand Hotel where Arthur found the architecture breathtaking. The mood of his next letter to Hoddy was noticeably more upbeat, telling her that she and Harriet *really must visit Russia. I've never seen anything like it. Borris House is a cottage beside these majestic buildings.* They attended masquerade balls and Arthur attracted a lot of attention by attempting the Cossack dance, for which his short stumps were particularly suited. Hoddy was also relieved to read Arthur describe the Grand Duchess Olga as *quite the most beautiful woman in Russia and one of the handsomest women I have ever seen.*

The journey to Moscow was taken partly by rail, but mostly by stagecoach, which was a lot less comfortable than those to which the Kavanagh brothers were accustomed. They made up for it by staying in the best accommodation available when they arrived. In less than three months of high living, they had managed to spend five hundred pounds, leading Tom to write to his mother saying: *Russia is the most expensive country in the world!* This was not entirely true and mostly the result of their copious consumption of fine food and champagne. When they weren't being hosted by local dignitaries, they dined in expensive restaurants, never looking at the price of anything before settling the bill.

In Moscow, Arthur was troubled by news from home. Famine and death were affecting every part of Ireland, including Borris, and the idea of the tenants he knew and loved suffering such misery was hard to bear. In contrast he found himself looking at some of the most majestic buildings in the world; St Basil's Cathedral, built by Ivan the Terrible, with its candy-striped domes and ornate towers that looked good enough to eat, and the sprawling fortress of the Kremlin.

At night he was also troubled by thoughts of Maud. No letter had arrived from her, even though he had received several from Hoddy and Harriet. In one of them Hoddy said: *Thank you for your recent letter and the one you enclosed for Maud Considine. Unfortunately, she hasn't given me anything to send to you. Incidentally, she also said to tell you that she doesn't consider the 'ceremony' you held in Newtown Park in the least bit binding, whatever that was!* This puzzled and hurt him deeply. How could Maud have changed her mind about him so quickly? She must be angry because he left so abruptly, but hadn't he explained everything in his letters? It was most unlike her to be callous or cruel.

From Moscow, Arthur, Tom, Wood and William Wright travelled to Nijni-Novgorad in Western Russia, where nightly they went to cafes to hear gypsies singing and dancing. It was late August and both Tom and Arthur were keen to return to Borris, but Wood, who had been given the mandate to keep Arthur away for substantially longer, insisted that they travel on. In a letter to Harriet, Tom assured her that Arthur had promised to be sober and steady if they were allowed to return. Certain that his mother would permit them to come back at this stage, Tom tried to convince Wood to turn around and make for Borris, but he disagreed, saying the time was not right. In the end, their fate was to be decided by a game of billiards, at which Wood was particularly talented. If he won, they would travel down the Volga for Astrakhan, if Tom won, they would begin their journey home. Arthur kept the score, cheering every time Tom potted a ball, but much to his disgust, Tom lost.

The journey down the Volga to Astrakhan took three weeks and Wood was increasingly getting on the boys' nerves. There was very little to see except sand and water, with the only entertainment being to shoot whatever birds came their way, mostly cormorants and wild geese. Wood insisted on continuing Arthur's education by having him read Shakespeare, rather than what he considered to be the "sickly sentiment of Byron", which Arthur loved.

'I might actually kill him,' he confided to his brother.

'And what purpose would that serve?'

'We'd be rid of his boring voice and pious sentiments, obviously,' Arthur said.

'And you would languish in a Russian prison for the rest of your days. Is he worth that?'

'I suppose not,' Arthur said ruefully, 'but I'm not sure how long more I can put up with him.'

At Astrakhan the weather was freezing. The night frost glistened on the streets and bushes and the winter was colder than any the young men had ever experienced in Ireland. Eager to escape the bad weather, they quickly boarded a boat across the Caspian Sea which was bound for Persia. The vessel was crowded and there weren't enough cabins. Tom and Wood managed to get one, while Arthur and William Wright had to sleep on the floor. The heaving of the boat meant that everyone, including the crew, was sick. Arthur shared a bottle of brandy, which he had packed in his bag, with the crewmen on duty, rendering them so drunk that they lost their bearings and all awoke to find themselves drifting aimlessly.

Arthur dreamt of Maud. It was almost five months now since he'd seen her and the Verbana she gave him was dried out and pressed between the pages of Byron's poetry. This book used to bring him such joy and he knew almost every poem in it. The one that seemed to speak to him more and more since he left was "When We Two Parted", and he transcribed it in his last letter to her, although by now he expected no reply. With his head heavy from brandy and seasickness, he read the last verse before throwing the book into the sea.

In secret we met,

In silence I grieve,

That thy heart could forget,

Thy spirit deceive.

If I should meet thee

After long years,

How should I greet thee? -

With silence and tears.

Chapter 13

Perilous Journey

Docking in Baku on the Caspian Sea, the travellers were exhausted and dispirited. William Wright carried Arthur on his back as they searched for accommodation, while Tom and David Wood carried the luggage. The party was relieved to find that Baku appeared to be a prosperous place and they quickly found comfortable accommodation in a stylish townhouse. However, their joy was short-lived when they went to find a place to eat and discovered that many places were closed and there were very few people about. They soon discovered the reason for the deserted streets was that Yellow Fever, a fatal disease, was rife there. Resolving to move on the very next day, they convinced their landlady to cook them some food and washed it down with whiskey they had in their luggage.

None of the four weary travellers relished the idea of another sea voyage so soon after their last unpleasant one. Poring over maps of the Caspian Sea, Arthur suggested that travelling to Astrabad in Russia on horseback along the coastline would be exciting.

'And dangerous,' Wood chimed in.

But this only made Tom and Arthur keener to try it. For this journey, they would have to source some horses which were expensive, but the local farrier was happy to help when he realised they were people of means. William set up Arthur's saddle-chair and, glad to be leaving this disease-ridden place, the party set off.

The terrain between Baku and Astrabad was mountainous and difficult to negotiate and soon William Wright complained of feeling unwell. However, the party had little time to focus on his state of health since the terrain was stalked by lions and wild boar, as well as bandits lying in wait to rob from unsuspecting travellers. From a few miles outside the town, they were followed by wild ravenous dogs which they couldn't shake off. The howling and snarling frightened the horses and made them rear up unexpectedly. Shouting and throwing food to the dogs didn't stop them following the party and all four men were relieved when they saw a cluster of buildings in the distance.

On entering the town square, the dogs immediately killed a chicken and tore it to shreds in front of them. The natives, realising that the Kavanagh party was responsible for bringing the dogs into the town, immediately imprisoned them in a cage in the town square. The local men babbled and pointed at Arthur when they realized he had no legs. William lifted him from the horse and both of them were roughly pushed into captivity whereby a large crowd gathered to stare at them. Suddenly, from pockets and bags, the villagers pulled out rotten fruit and raw eggs and pelted the strangers with them. Thinking they were going to die, Tom, Wood and William circled round Arthur with their backs to the crowd and their hands protecting their heads. Eventually the punishment ended, and they were relieved to find themselves released before sunset, when they were shown to a rough loft as sleeping quarters.

'Surely we don't have to lie down in this squalor?' David Wood complained.

'For heaven's sake, Wood, don't you know we're lucky to be alive? Isn't that right, William?' Arthur asked.

It was only then, when all eyes turned to William for a reply, that they realised how weak he was.

'I just need to lie down. This place is fine for me.' William's voice was little more than a whisper and he was shielding his eyes from the light with his arm. His face and eyes were a bright, blotchy red and while Arthur and Tom exchanged looks of alarm, exhaustion meant they decided not to look for a doctor until the morning.

At sunrise, William said he was feeling much better and his colour was closer to normal, so they loaded up their horses, hired a local guide and began the thirty-six-hour journey to Tehran. The route was perilous, the party having to trek along mountain passes and narrow ledges, barely wide enough for a horse to walk. David Wood, in his meticulous manner, measured one of these ledges and announced that it was only fourteen inches wide, advising it was too narrow to cross. But there was no other way. The guide assured them he had crossed it many times before so, with trepidation, they continued. On one occasion Arthur's horse slipped on the muddy surface, kicking stones down into the crevasse below. Teetering on the edge, he struggled to control the terrified beast, only managing to steady him in time to save both of them from a horrible death.

By the time they reached Tehran, where the local guide left them, both Arthur and William were suffering from bouts of fever. Since they were hosts of the British Embassy here, based on their promissory notes, the men were offered comfortable accommodation and a lavish meal. Tom and David Wood were ravenous and ate second helpings of mutton and sausage meat with rice and local vegetables, gorging on pastries with custard filling. However, neither Arthur nor William could face anything more solid than a morsel of local bread dipped in honey, while sipping a sherbet drink said to have medicinal qualities, while servants held cold compresses to their heads.

In November the winter was closing in, and the travelling party wanted to continue their journey to Kurdistan before the weather became more perilous, so after a few days, their horses were saddled up again and they went on their way. As William continually weakened, the temperature plunged below zero and, having spent days trying to keep him alive, they were relieved to arrive in Tabriz, where a Mr Stephens hosted them and summoned a doctor for William. In addition to fever, William was now suffering from frostbite and the doctor deemed that he should be sent home immediately or his life would be in danger. This was a crisis they hadn't anticipated and again Tom and Arthur pleaded with Wood to allow them all to return. But he refused, stating that he had received a letter from Lady Harriet insisting they make their way to India and spend time there before considering the homeward journey.

Arrangements were made for William to travel home alone via Trebizond and Constantinople. He shed tears as he left them, although realizing he was too weak to carry on or to be of any further assistance.

'I'll be alright, old fellow,' Arthur tried to reassure him. 'You look after yourself and travel safely. We'll see you in Borris. Very soon, I hope.' He stared at Wood, who looked at the ground rather than meeting the young men's eyes.

When William had left, Tom and Arthur turned on Wood.

'How am I to manage now, without a manservant,' Arthur shouted, in a rare admission that he couldn't dress or look after his personal hygiene alone. 'What sort of mother would leave me in this predicament?'

'I suppose I'll have to help you myself,' Wood said resignedly.

'You will not touch me,' Arthur hissed.

'It's alright, Arthur, I'll do it, until we reach Tehran. We can hire somebody there to journey with us.' Tom tried to calm the situation.

Arthur shook his head, but said nothing,

'As for you, Wood,' Tom continued, 'you are despicable. I want you to write to my mother at once and tell her whatever she wants to hear that will allow us to come home. Do I make myself clear?'

He stood very close to Wood so that their faces almost touched as he said this, making Wood take a step backwards.

'I'll try,' he said. 'I will try, alright? But your mother is a very determined woman.'

*

The travelling party of three arrived in Tehran in mid-December where, on presentation of their letter from Lord Palmerston, they were introduced to Prince Malichus Mirza. A tall, handsome man in his late thirties, with jet black eyes and beard. He had fifteen wives, spoke French fluently and was an excellent sportsman. Arthur was very impressed with the prince's regal demeanour and arrogance towards David Wood, who immediately seemed to irritate him.

While Tom and David Wood were entertained by the Prince in fine style, Arthur felt wretched and ate very little, even on Christmas Day when there was a lavish feast laid on for the British guests. The prince wore a fine suit which buttoned up to the neck with ornate white collars and cuffs and a tall, conical hat with a white feather at the front. His English was quite good and he told fascinating stories of his hunting exploits. Arthur, who had been assigned a personal servant, was confined to bed all day and missed all the festivities. It was New Year's Day 1850 when he was well enough to get up again. In a letter to Hoddy, he declared it to be his most miserable Christmas ever and declared himself extremely homesick.

Please speak to Mother, dearest Hoddy. I am beginning to wonder if she intends never to see me again. Believe me, there have been times when our lives have been in such danger that I doubted any of us would ever see Borris again. What a tragedy that would be. Tell her I am much more mature than when I left, and I promise to be sober and of good character. Yours as always. Arthur.

Since Arthur was still too weak to travel after another week had passed, Tom and David Wood rode on to Georgia, promising to be back within a week, while the prince offered rest and recuperation for Arthur. What the prince failed to say was that he didn't intend this to take place in his own quarters, but in the confines of his harem. He presented Arthur to the ladies as a 'young, blond god,' and assigned a beautiful lithe black-haired girl to look after his every need. So, while his brother and Wood were experiencing the culture of Georgia, Arthur was having adventures of a different kind.

Although Arthur meticulously kept diaries throughout his travels, he wrote nothing of his days in the harem and wouldn't be drawn on his experiences when Tom and David Wood returned. Wood was horrified to hear where he was being looked after and for another fortnight the prince refused to allow them to communicate with him at all. Even more alarming were the suggestive remarks and rude gestures of the prince each time he was asked how Arthur was getting on.

'As his moral guardian, I must insist that Arthur returns to our company, Prince Mirza.'

'Do not worry yourself about Arthur! I have told the women he is a god and they should treat him as such. He is learning a lot, I can assure you.'

'I want to see him,' David Wood insisted.

At this, the prince stood a little closer to Wood, who was a small man and almost a foot smaller than Prince Mirza. Looking down at him with ebony eyes he said:

'You do know the punishment for infiltrating a seraglio, Mr Wood?'

'Ehm, yes. I believe it's death?' Wood stuttered.

'Exactly. I will let you know when Arthur is ready to leave.'

And that was it. There was no further communication from Arthur. David Wood fretted and complained to Tom, who seemed to find it all quite amusing.

'Arthur will be alright, Wood! I only wish it were me in there.'

'May God forgive you for even thinking such a thing. What will I say to your mother if anything happens to him? How will I explain it? This an absolute nightmare.'

But Tom just laughed. 'If I know Arthur, he'll regale us the whole way to India with stories to make milk curdle. Take it easy, Wood. Nothing will happen to him, at least nothing fatal.' And he laughed again.

When word finally came from the Prince that Arthur was ready to continue his journey, it was in a note brought by a man on horseback. It said: *Mr Kavanagh is ready to leave. Not only is his health greatly improved, but he goes into the world better equipped to understand ladies and has been instructed in the arts of Kama.* Wood, being unfamiliar with the word, had to sit down when he heard it meant "pleasure" and vowed that he would not let Arthur out of his sight for the rest of the journey.

When the three were reunited, Arthur was tight-lipped about his experiences and wouldn't be drawn on what the harem was like. He merely winked at Tom as he told Wood that he was looked after like never before! Wood, deciding to accept what couldn't be altered, contented himself with making the boys promise that nobody would tell their mother.

*

In her next letter, Lady Harriet made it clear to Wood that she was happy to have her sons begin their return journey. Perhaps Hoddy had impressed on her how many times they had been in imminent danger. Although she left it up to Wood's personal judgement, she said she now believed enough time had been spent away from Borris for Arthur to have mended his ways, and she had come up with a plan for him. A farm in Connemara, in which the Kavanaghs had an interest, needed a manager. She would send Arthur there on his return and he could learn the skills of estate management away from the temptations of home, taking his place in suitable social circles.

Not at all sure that Arthur had changed his ways, Wood decided to keep this information to himself and, mounting their horses, the three set off from Tabriz with an English manservant named James, whom the Prince had sourced for Arthur, who would also act as a guide. Venturing through the inhospitable lands of Kurdistan, they faced freezing temperatures and snowdrifts and had to lie down on their horses to protect themselves from the biting winds. After days where very little ground was covered, the horses seemed exhausted and food was running out. By chance they came across an American mission where the occupants allowed them to stay, glad of the English-speaking company. It was weeks before the snowstorm abated and the travelling party set off again.

It was on this journey that David Wood finally enlightened Arthur as to his mother's reasons for banishing him.

'You know why we're on this prolonged journey, don't you?'

'Actually, no, Wood. I don't. Nobody has seen fit to tell me, and I have never understood the haste with which it was organised.'

'Well, you know your mother was displeased with your behaviour.'

'By which you mean because I was in love with Maud Considine?'

'Well yes, that played a major part. But also, there was your reckless imbibing of alcohol and your bursts of temper. She felt you were disrespectful of her and the Kavanagh name and that you would bring disgrace on the family.'

'But that was never my intention. I was just being young – no different to my brothers. Why should I be above enjoying myself a little? Was it not always her intention that I would lead a normal life?'

'Normal, but virtuous I expect, Arthur. But your outbursts were quite explosive and your clandestine meetings with unsuitable young women a cause of great concern to her.'

'Shouldn't I be the judge of who is suitable?' Arthur's face was reddening and he had begun to shout.

'There you go again, Arthur. You need to control that temper.'

Taking a deep breath and lowering his voice again, Arthur said quietly: 'I love Mamma dearly and I never intended to cause her distress, but don't you think sending me to the other side of the world for an indefinite period is a bit extreme? When do you intend to allow me to return, or am I to be banished forever?'

'The time mentioned to me was a year or two, but it seems your mother's attitude is changing. Perhaps you should write to her to apologise and see what comes of it. I believe her heart has softened towards you and she has mentioned that we might all meet in Corfu when she and Hoddy are there in July. Whatever you do, don't mention the harem, or we will all be banished forever.'

Arthur mulled these words over and over in his head as they continued on their journey towards Baghdad. For several weeks they were forced to take refuge in an English camp in the mountains of Loustan since David Wood became quite ill. There was no way to communicate from the camp and to Arthur's dismay, the opportunity to meet with Lady Harriet and Hoddy in Corfu was missed. Tom was also bitterly disappointed, but by the time Wood recovered, it was August 1850, Lady Harriet was back in Borris and the party decided to trek on for India.

Christmas Day 1850 was spent aboard ship crossing the Persian Gulf. The only thing that distinguished it from any other day was that they decided to drink a double ration of rum to mark the occasion. All day, waves tossed the vessel around, with a swell that made their stomachs churn followed by lurching that felt as if they were going to hit the bottom of the ocean, only to rise again seconds later. All four men were miserable and seasick and Arthur wondered if he would ever see Borris again.

Reaching Bombay on January 5th, 1851, Arthur was immediately taken with the opportunities for hunting there, and his homesickness quickly left him. There was no shortage of British settlers to host them and, once they realised that Arthur was skilled and fearless, they introduced him to the exhilarating sport of tiger hunting in the jungle. In his diary, he wrote a vivid account of chasing a tiger through prickly pear bushes and managing to shoot him behind the left ear. Arthur was seated high on the back of an elephant in his saddle-chair, having been hoisted up by two Mahouts, and he proudly described the tiger as being almost nine feet long from toe to tail.

The euphoria Arthur felt at being so high up on this majestic animal and being able to hunt animals he had only ever read about, was intoxicating. During these exciting days, his enthusiasm for life returned and he imagined he could gladly live in India forever. Then word came from Borris that Hoddy had married Captain Middleton, whom she had been courting for almost a year, which set Arthur thinking about home again and prompted him to write to his mother in an apologetic tone.

Dearest Mamma, I have included a letter for Hoddy and I hope she and her new husband will be very happy. How I will miss her at Borris when I return. I have discussed the reason for my banishment with David Wood and now realise the error of my ways. I was horrified to hear that you thought I was being disrespectful, as this would never be my intention. I now know that my hot temper was uncouth, and I am sincerely sorry for this. With God's help I will control it from now on. If you are willing to have me home, we will gladly set out as soon as possible. But whatever your wishes are I am ready to comply with them. Your loving son, Arthur.

Chapter 14

India

All the while he was in India waiting for a reply from his mother, Arthur revelled in hunting, often disappearing into the jungle for days on end with a hunting party. On these excursions an Indian servant was assigned to him, since James had no hunting skills and was anxious to return to Tehran. Each day he meticulously recorded the animals he bagged in his diary – one such entry recalls that he shot "one cheetah, two pigs, four tigers and one boar", although there may have been less, since he was known to exaggerate his hunting prowess. While Arthur was away, Tom and Wood entertained themselves by mixing in fashionable circles, where ballrooms were filled with young ladies looking for suitable husbands.

When the reply to Arthur's letter finally came from Ireland, he could sense a softening in his mother's tone. She made it clear that she would like them to come home at the earliest opportunity and told him of her plans for him to go to Connemara. While Arthur was relieved that Harriet was relenting somewhat, the prospect of exile within his own country didn't please him at all. In fact he felt a new sense of rage. Borris was his home. Was his mother really trying to banish him forever? He would never agree to it. He would make her wait. Tom seemed to be in no hurry to return as he was attending parties every night, and since the hunting was so exciting, he replied with a short note saying that Connemara was something they could discuss, but it would be another few months before they would leave India.

In a letter to Lady Harriet, David Wood defended the fact that they had not yet turned for home, placing the blame firmly on "the boys."

Your sons are such creatures of impulse, particularly Arthur, who has become nothing short of addicted to hunting – talking about it incessantly as well as actually doing it.

He reported that Tom had been quite unwell recently but now seemed to be much better. And finally, he proffered his notice.

I am happy to relinquish my position as soon as you deem it appropriate. Your sons, now aged 23 and 20, seem more than capable of looking after themselves and no longer appear interested in my moral guidance. I await your instruction. Rev D Wood.

It was while Arthur was on a long hunting trip in June 1851 that Tom became seriously ill, coughing incessantly and haemorrhaging from the lungs. When Wood saw blood all over the white sheets of Tom's bed, he almost fainted and immediately ran to get help. The only solution suggested by the doctor, who had no cure or definite diagnosis, was that he immediately embark on a sea voyage where he could rest and breathe fresh air. Oblivious to all of this, Arthur returned and was astonished to find that Wood and Tom had left on a ship for Ceylon without him.

Finding himself alone with his servant in India (although he had made many friends), Arthur was also short of money and angry to be left behind. He had been thinking about returning to Ireland soon and now he wasn't sure how or when that might happen. It was most unlike Tom not to inform him of his plans, and he mentioned nothing of this voyage when they last spoke. Even more distressing was the fact that Tom and Wood had the promissory notes and money with them. Describing their desertion to all his friends as "giving him the slip," he was unaware of how ill Tom really was, and wrote to his mother again in July, asking her for some financial assistance to aid his journey home.

I am not sure how exactly Wood and Tom intend getting home, as I believe they have set off for Java and Ceylon. It looks like they intend to take the long way round, while I am left with nothing but an Indian servant who speaks very poor English. Can you believe Tom left me in this pickle? As soon as possible I will begin my journey home and I look forward to us all being together in Borris again. However, I cannot embark until some finance arrives, as Tom and Wood have the notes with them and I have no means of raising the money.

Leaving as they did in such haste, Tom and Wood hadn't made any provisions for Arthur. Thus, not wanting to depend on the charity of friends, he asked his closest acquaintances to try to secure some employment for him. Wondering what sort of work he could possibly do, they insisted he could stay as long as he wished and were also eager to extend loans to him, but Arthur wouldn't hear of it. He became quite annoyed, suggesting they were questioning his competence and, eventually one friend recommended him to the East India Company, where he was offered a job as a dispatch rider. Nobody believed that he would accept the position or stick with it for very long, since the wages were poor, but Arthur proved them wrong.

The job of a dispatch rider involved riding at great speed, delivering letters and important business documents through dangerous territory where thieves often lay in wait. Some of the parcels contained valuables and were an obvious target. Accompanied by his servant, Arthur had to cover the Aurungabad district in Western India and, far from shying away from the work, he absolutely loved it. He even insisted on learning some of the local dialects so he could converse with the natives along the way. They, in return, loved him and marvelled at the miraculous way he could ride a horse without limbs.

Happy to be able to support himself without relying on friends, Arthur continued to do this work for ten months, until word came from Borris in April that Harriet would be travelling to Corfu again in July to visit Hoddy who was now living there with her husband. She said she would like to meet him there, but still no money arrived. However, by now Arthur had earned enough to make the arduous journey by land and sea. Lying in bed, he wondered what a reunion with his mother would be like. He had such mixed feelings about seeing her and wondered if she had lost all affection for him. She was never one to show her emotions, but he longed for the meeting of minds they once had and he longed to see Hoddy again. With a leaden heart, he decided it was time to go home.

Arthur knew his Indian servant would not want to leave the country, so having broken the news that he was leaving, he asked him to accompany him by land as far as Bombay. A distinguished Englishman living there had agreed to allow one of his manservants, Sai, to travel with Arthur until he got to Corfu and insisted on paying the return fare.

When they reached the port, Arthur and his servant, having spent so long together, fought back tears, knowing they would never see each other again.

'Thank you for all you have done for me. I wish you and your family the very best,' Arthur said, having given him a handsome sum of money.

'Be careful, Master Arthur. This is a dangerous journey.'

'I'll be fine. I'm always fine.' Arthur smiled. And backing away, the servant bowed and made his way down the gangplank.

*

Crossing the Arabian Sea, Arthur befriended an Englishman by the name of Williams. They shared a whiskey together. Arthur explained his hooks by saying he had no arms but omitted to say anything about legs since he was wearing a long cloak and was seated. The poor man almost choked when Arthur hopped down off the seat, to go to his cabin. The ship sailed through the Gulf of Aden and up the Red Sea, by which time Williams and Arthur had become firm friends and Williams agreed to organize a wagon to take him to the port of Alexandria. A ship was sailing for Corfu the next morning and with nowhere else to go, and little money, Arthur and the servant settled themselves among sacks of grain on the quayside and slept till first light. In the morning they boarded the vessel which would take Arthur on the two-day voyage to the reunion with the mother he felt had abandoned him.

Harriet paced up and down the quayside in Corfu, waiting anxiously for Arthur to disembark. His telegram had said he would arrive from Alexandria on this day but didn't say how or with whom. Finally, she saw him making his way along the quay, alone and with only a light bag on his back. It was three years since they had seen each other, and her first impression was that he looked much more manly – quite like his father – and that his hair was receding a little.

Mother and son stood still on the quay for a few moments, not knowing how to bridge the gap of years spent apart. Finally, Harriet spoke:

'It's so good to see you, Arthur.' She bent to kiss his cheek. 'I was beginning to fear that I'd never see you again.'

'As was I, Mother. As was I.' He bit his tongue as what he wanted to say was: *It would be your fault if we hadn't, Mother.* Instead, he commented, 'You look as elegant as ever.'

'Thank you. You look so grown up, so manly.'

'I am a man, Mother. Now, do you have any news of Tom?'

'No, I was hoping you might have heard something. Have you still received no word from them?'

'Nothing. At first I was really annoyed, but now, I must admit to being more than a little worried.'

'I am praying for their safe return, Arthur. I'll put my trust in the Lord. Now come with me. We're staying at the villa with Hoddy and her new husband, William. You'll like him, I'm sure. He's stationed here in Corfu now. There's a carriage waiting over there.'

And Arthur followed her as if no time had passed at all.

'I can't wait to sleep in a comfortable bed,' he said as they mounted the carriage. 'You wouldn't believe some of the places I've stayed, Mother.'

'A mother doesn't need to know everything, Arthur. Just tell me the parts of the story that you think I will enjoy.'

And as the carriage took off, Arthur talked incessantly about snowdrifts and wild dogs, with Harriet shaking her head in disbelief.

*

What Arthur and Harriet didn't know was that Tom had died at sea in the spring of 1852. Wood lacked the courage to pass on the news and when he did write, it was April when the ship was nearing the shores of Australia. It was late July when his letter arrived in Borris and another month before Harriet and Arthur were home to receive it. Wood wrote that it was his painful duty to communicate that tuberculosis had claimed Tom's life. Yet another tragedy had befallen the Kavanagh clan and things were about to get even worse.

Chapter 15

Back at Borris

Arthur and his mother arrived back at Borris House in early August 1852 without the usual fuss and fanfare. Lady Harriet had sent instructions that their arrival was to be low-key, since there was still no word of Tom and, by now, she feared that he might be seriously ill, or even worse. But she tried hard not to allow herself to imagine that. Through the carriage window Arthur could see signs of famine everywhere, deserted streets, people foraging in fields, children begging, and he was quite shocked at how ramshackle the village had become.

'I can't believe how run down everywhere looks, Mother. Is Doyne not doing his job or can things really be this bad?'

'I'm afraid they are, Arthur. He does his best, but you can't expect hungry people to work and they're queuing up for whatever soup and bread we can give them every day.'

'And has Charles been doing anything to alleviate the situation?'

'I told you Charles hasn't been well and you know his heart was never in the estate anyway. Since his illness forced him out of the army, he's shown no interest in it whatsoever.'

'What illness, Mother? The lack of a back bone?'

'You will not speak about your brother like that, Arthur. Charles' health is his own business and I'll thank you not to mention it again.'

'But Mother, if Tom doesn't return…?'

151

'Stop immediately, Arthur. I put my trust in God that Tom will come home safely and take his rightful place as head of the family. I won't have you suggesting otherwise.'

'I'm sorry, but I wasn't suggesting anything. We just need to have a plan.'

'Tom will come home,' she said confidently.

At dinner, when the letters were brought to Harriet on a silver tray, she recognised David Wood's handwriting on a small white envelope with an Australian postmark. Taking a sharp breath she tore it open, believing that it indicated they were both safe. Arthur and Charles stared at her face to read her expression. The words, long-winded as they were, confirmed Harriet's worst fears and she let out a wail, 'No! Oh no!' and covered her face with her hands. There was no need for confirmation, both boys knew that their brother was dead.

For a full week, Harriet could not be convinced to leave her room; it was the first time in her life that she didn't know what to do or how to respond. She would never see her eldest son again. Her first born, of whom she had been so quietly proud, and whose future as head of the household seemed so certain, was buried at sea, where she could never kneel and cry and place a wreath of red roses. And in her heart, she knew that she was the one who had sent him there.

Charles also confined himself to his room. Prone to melancholy, the affairs of the estate had never interested him. Since leaving the army he had met a very nice suitable young lady and was due to get married shortly. He looked forward to a quiet life on her father's estate in

Meath where he could shoot and hunt and raise a family. The sadness of losing his brother was superseded by terror of the responsibility he was now expected to take on. He had always believed that Tom shouldn't have gone abroad and had tried to dissuade his mother from sending him, but she would not listen. It was risky and foolish and now it had ended in disaster for him. When Doctor Boxwell called, he would ask him for medication to calm his nerves. Meanwhile he would stay in bed and refuse to eat anything.

Arthur spent the next few days alone, riding his horse around the estate and noticing the deterioration that had taken place over the previous three years. Some of the tenants' houses were empty and boarded up, fields were overgrown and the lawns, that were usually tended with such care, were full of weeds. Even the house itself had been allowed to fall into disrepair. Paint was peeling from some of the windows and the gate to the farmyard was hanging on one hinge. Tears streamed down his face as he thought of the pride his forefathers had taken in this place and how it had been a jewel in the crown of the locality. Tom would have known what to do, but not Charles, whose birthright and duty it now was. There was nothing anyone could do about that.

Arthur's sadness alternated with a deep anger towards his mother. She had caused all this. It was her controlling pride that had sent Tom to his death. Her extreme reaction to his own youthful behaviour had put all their lives in danger. What loving mother would do such a thing? And now she had jeopardised the future of the very estate she said she was trying to protect. Could such a betrayal ever be forgiven? He couldn't see how.

*

Reading back through all the correspondence she and Tom had exchanged over the previous three years, Harriet's heart ached at the parts where he requested that they might come back home. She cried inconsolably when she read about the game of billiards that decided their destiny. There were so many times when fate could have intervened, when God could have intervened. Where was God? For the first time in her life she doubted His love. Perhaps this was her punishment for the sin of pride. Had she sent Arthur away to protect herself or to protect him? On the other hand, if Arthur hadn't behaved as he did, Tom would still be here. Now the family was falling apart and she knew Charles didn't have the wherewithal to save it. How she wished Hoddy could be here. Her only daughter would be a comfort to her now and might know what to do, but Hoddy was heavily pregnant and unable to travel. She had never felt so utterly alone.

Word went up and down the village that Tom MacMurrough Kavanagh, "The MacMurrough", had died. The big house was struck by tragedy again. Black crepe was hung on the doorways along the main street and prayers were recited for the happy repose of his soul in Protestant and Catholic Churches far and wide.

*

'I know what you're going to say, Molly,' Kitty said.

'Well, aren't I right? There's only one more son to go before the prophecy comes true.'

'God save us, Molly. I didn't want to believe it, but it's frightening to see what's happening.'

'That Charles will be a disaster anyway. Sure, that fella didn't last a wet week in the army. How's he going to run that big estate when he knows nothing about it? And he'd hardly give you the time of day!'

'Anyway, there'll be nothing to look after soon. They're getting in very little rent these days and that big estate won't run on fresh air.'

'True for you, Kitty. The Kavanaghs' days are numbered.'

*

There were no celebrations for the installation of Charles as the head of the family as there had been for Tom. He reluctantly attended meetings with Doyne to try to understand the estate's financial affairs. In January 1853, instead of the assignment Harriet had planned for him in Connemara, Arthur was officially appointed under-agent to the Borris estate, in the belief that together the brothers might be equal to the task, although they rarely saw eye to eye, and Charles' apathy irritated Arthur no end.

Their first challenge was to settle Tom's affairs, which became a lot more complicated with the news that David Wood had also died as a result of an accident in Australia, and that his family was insisting they were owed some money. Shocking as it was that another of their travelling party had died prematurely, Arthur shed no tears for Wood and was adamant that he had already received more than he deserved.

Gathering all the details of payments made to, and drawn down by, Wood on the trip to India, he politely refuted the family's requests for further monies and sympathised with them on their loss.

I am sorry for your family's loss, as I'm sure you are sorry for mine. I don't expect to hear from you again.

But the weight of responsibility was only beginning for Arthur. While he was learning the rudiments of estate management and trying to motivate Charles to act decisively, his brother was distracted with plans of his upcoming wedding which was planned for Saint Patrick's Day, March 17th. Because the family was recently bereaved, it too was to be a quiet affair conducted in Meath at the home of his fiancée, who would now become the new Mrs Kavanagh. The only celebration at Borris House would be a drinks reception for invited guests when the couple returned from their honeymoon. Charles confided in Arthur that his fiancée was greatly distressed by the prospect of being lady of the house in Borris and wanted to remain living in Meath as they had planned.

On February 16th, 1853, with only a month to go to the wedding, a servant brought correspondence to Charles in his bedroom, leaving the letters beside his armchair at the freshly lit open fire. Twenty minutes later, as the servant passed the doorway, he smelled smoke and, on opening the door, found Charles thrashing around on the bed, trying to extinguish the fire which had taken hold of his nightclothes.

'Get water, quickly!' he shouted. 'AAhhhhh! My skin is burning.'

The servant rang the bell by the fireplace and shouted over the banister:

'Fire, fire! Bring water and sand,' and then began beating at the flames himself with a coat.

But by the time help arrived, the drapes of the four-poster bed and blankets were ablaze. Fumes choked the servants as buckets of water and sand were thrown, while Charles screamed in pain and the room turned black with acrid smoke. Eventually the flames were extinguished, but Charles writhed in agony, moaning and intermittently losing consciousness.

When Doctor Boxwell arrived, he was shocked to see the extent of Charles' burns, although he tried to hide his despair.

'I'm afraid, Harriet, this is beyond me,' he whispered in the hallway. 'I'm going to send immediately for Surgeon Cusack. He is an eminent surgeon and specializes in burns. If anyone can do something, he can.'

'I can't lose another son!' Harriet sobbed, in a manner neither Doctor Boxwell nor Arthur had heard since the day she heard the news about Tom.

'I'll make him comfortable, Harriet. He will be virtually unconscious until the surgeon arrives. I'm sorry, but that's all I can do for Charles now.'

Harriet gripped his arm so tightly that her nails left semi-circular marks on his forearm.

'Send for the surgeon straight away, Frank. I can't lose Charles. I simply can't.'

The following morning at 11am, Surgeon Cusack arrived in a black Phaeton carriage and was immediately escorted to where Charles lay in a comatose state. Harriet stood beside the bed, twisting her handkerchief between her fingers, watching the surgeon's face as he pulled back the bedclothes.

'Please wait outside,' he said. 'It's best if you don't see the wounds.'

Arthur, who was sitting on a chair at the other side of the bed, went to leave also.

'No, you can stay,' the surgeon said. 'I believe you're his only surviving brother?'

'That's right, Doctor.'

After a few moments silence while he examined Charles' body, Surgeon Cusack spoke again:

'I'm afraid I have to ask *you*, then, to break the sad news to your mother. These burns are catastrophic. There really is nothing I can do. Your brother would not survive the journey to hospital. I'm very sorry.'

A churning feeling in Arthur's stomach made him feel like he might be about to vomit.

'Are you certain? Won't you even try?'

'I'm certain,' the doctor said, closing his bag. 'It would take a miracle to save him now.'

For the first time in years, Arthur let his head fall to his chest and cried inconsolably.

'Will *you* tell Mamma, please? I don't think *I* can.'

'You are the man of this house now, young man. You need to be a consolation to your mother. Take a moment to compose yourself and we can tell her together.'

Harriet was sitting on an upright chair in the drawing room beside Doctor Boxwell's wife, Martha, with Doctor Boxwell opposite, when Arthur opened the door to lead the surgeon in. Taking a deep breath, Arthur tried to stop his lip from trembling, but his voice broke as he tried to say: 'Surgeon Cusack has something…'

The wail from Lady Harriet brought everyone to their feet. 'Tell me he's going to be alright, Doctor.' She ran and grabbed the surgeon by both arms.

'I'm very sorry, my Lady, there's nothing I can do,' he said, stepping backwards. 'Nature will take its course now and Doctor Boxwell will ensure he doesn't suffer. Boxwell, perhaps you should also give Lady Harriet something to calm her.'

And while everyone in the room cried and tried to console each other, the surgeon left, and by nightfall, Charles was dead.

*

For the second time in her life, Lady Harriet stayed in bed for three days, refusing to speak to anyone. Arthur, stunned by how his life had altered in the space of a few months, wandered from Tom's room to Charles' charred bedroom and cried silently. Servants scurried about doing their daily chores, not knowing whether food should be prepared or served, under strict instructions from Lady Harriet that her bedroom door was not to be opened until Hoddy and her new infant arrived from Corfu, a journey of three days duration. The whispers in the village were of nothing but "the curse."

Arthur sat in his own small chair in the nursery and looked around at the rocking horse, easel, and other toys, recalling the chatter and fun he and his siblings had in this room. Sunlight illuminated the train set Anne Fleming used to put out of his reach so he would push himself forward to get it. He thought of his struggles to write and draw and how his mother had taught him never to give up. He wanted to give her back some of that strength now, but she wasn't ready to receive it. He would wait until all this horrible grief had passed and then he'd make her hold her head high again, proud of the Kavanagh name and especially proud of him.

But there was such a heavy feeling in his chest, heavier than when he had fever in Persia. Tears kept welling up in his eyes when he least expected them to, when he was trying to make plans and stay strong. And when Hoddy stepped through the front door, they both wept and held each other, shaking and crying like never before.

'How can they both be dead, Arthur? I can scarcely believe it. I mean Tom was such a shock, but now Charles too.' And her voice broke as the tears flowed again.

'I know. I know. It's awful. But we'll be alright. I promise.'

'Oh Arthur, you don't have to be strong. You've had such a horrid time. Where's Mamma? I thought she'd be here to meet me.'

'She hasn't been out of her room for three days. I've tried knocking, but she tells me to go away. Do you think I should send for Doctor Boxwell again?'

'Definitely, Arthur. It's most unlike Mamma to stay in her room. Send for him and I'll go and see her. Poor Mamma. She must be heartbroken.'

Knocking on the door, Hoddy called out, 'Mamma, it's me. I'm home.'

There was no reply.

'It's Hoddy, Mamma. May I come in?'

Again, there was no answer, but Hoddy slowly opened the door anyway.

'I said nobody was to come in.'

Hoddy found Harriet sitting, fully dressed, in a wing-backed chair beside the bed. She gasped when she saw Hoddy, but quickly said: 'We have to be strong, Hoddy. This is God's will.'

'Nonsense, Mamma! That's nonsense. What kind of God would want my two brothers to be killed, your two strong sons. I don't believe in your God if that's the case.'

'Hoddy! Never say such a thing in my presence again.'

'Mother, I've travelled night and day to be with you with only a tiny baby for company. My heart is broken and I know yours is even more so. Now stand up and let me embrace you and then come downstairs. Arthur is pining away on his own. This family, or what's left of it, needs to pull together.'

Reluctantly, Harriet stood up and collapsed into Hoddy's arms with loud sobs, echoed by her daughter's, until finally Hoddy said, 'Now, we must eat. Take my hand, Mother, we're going downstairs.'

*

It was a wet and windy day when the body of Charles MacMurrough Kavanagh was lowered into the ground at St Mullins Abbey, with his mother, brother and sister on one side and a semi-circle of house-servants on the other – his fiancée, Emily Butler, was too distressed to attend. Doctor Boxwell and his wife were the only others allowed inside the wall, while the locals huddled in rain-drenched groups around the perimeter. Harriet bowed her head in prayer as the minister said the final prayers, while Arthur and Hoddy looked straight ahead. Arthur sat up squarely in his wheelchair with a black cloak covering his stumps completely. Attached to his pocket was Tom's watch, he wore Charles' necktie and his father's black bowler hat. He was now "The MacMurrough" and nothing would stop him from living up to that title.

'Will you look at the pitiful sight of him,' Kitty Ryan whispered into Molly Doyle's ear. 'Sure how could the likes of him rule a big estate like Borris? It'll go to rack and ruin for sure.'

'Ah, I don't know, Kitty. He's made of steely stuff. Didn't he make it back from India and his fine strong brother didn't.'

'Sure, that was just because of the curse! His brothers were never going to live. But what's going to happen now? That's what I'd like to know.'

'God save us all, Kitty. Sure, what's going to happen to any of us? These are terrible times.'

'That's for sure.'

And as the clods of clay fell on top of the wooden coffin, those inside and outside the wall were all wondering the same thing.

Chapter 16
Arthur "The MacMurrough"

At breakfast the following morning, Arthur, Hoddy and Lady Harriet sat at the large oval table in the dining room in silence. Arthur and Hoddy ate plates of eggs and bacon with freshly baked soda bread while Lady Harriet picked fussily at a piece of boiled fish. Servants cleared dishes and served tea wordlessly with heads bowed.

Eventually, Harriet broke the silence. 'I want to speak to you both in the drawing room after breakfast. I think it's time we discussed the future of Borris.'

Arthur raised an eyebrow.

'What do you mean, Mother?'

'We'll talk after breakfast,' she said, indicating the presence of a servant with a nod of her head. 'When we're alone.'

In the drawing room Arthur moved around nervously on his stumps, while his mother waited for the scullery maid to finish lighting the fire.

'Arthur, for goodness' sake, sit down. You're making me dizzy.'

Perching on the side of the chaise longue, Arthur announced, 'I'm puzzled.'

'What do you mean, Arthur? I haven't said anything yet,' Harriet replied with irritation in her voice.

'I mean to cause you no offence, Hoddy, but I fail to see why you are part of the discussions on the future of Borris. You have your new life with your husband in Corfu. Borris is my responsibility now.'

'No offence taken, Brother. I am as surprised as you are to be summoned here. Why are you doing this, Mamma? Can't we just be allowed to grieve for now and leave decisions until later?'

'Exactly!' Arthur agreed. 'And when the time is right, you and I will discuss the future. There's no need to trouble Hoddy with it.'

'It's just that… ehm, Arthur… I never really thought it would come to this… and… well… I mean, how are you going to manage?' Harriet's voice had a plaintive tone.

'The estate? Do you mean how am I going to manage the estate? Or how am I going to manage without arms and legs?'

'Don't be facetious, Arthur. Of course I mean the estate.'

'Ah but you don't, Mamma. What you really mean is how am I going to manage the estate without arms and legs. And I'll tell you how! I'm going to manage it the same as I have managed everything since the day I was born, with the courage and confidence you instilled in me. It disappoints me greatly that at the biggest moment of my life you seem to have lost faith in me, but I'll forgive you since I know you are grieving. But let me promise you this, I solemnly vow this day to try to attain the same distinction in public life as my father and to manage this estate as he would want it to be managed. All I ask is that you continue to believe in me as you used to.'

'Well said, Arthur,' Hoddy gushed, her eyes filling up.

And for a moment, Lady Harriet seemed stuck for words, before saying quietly:

'Forgive me, Arthur. It's just that I've lost so much. Believe me when I say I really do have faith in you. I'm just so worried, and everything has gone so badly wrong. I *do* believe in you. In fact, I've always had a feeling you might be the greatest Kavanagh of them all.'

'May I say something, Mamma, although I know I really don't have a place in this discussion?'

'Of course, Hoddy.'

'All my life I have been proud to call Arthur my brother. I wish with all my heart that I still had three brothers, but I know that Thomas and Charles would trust Arthur implicitly, and I do too. I believe our family's future is in safe hands.'

Arthur felt his eyes beginning to water and, afraid he would cry at this pivotal moment, he hopped up and asked to be excused.

'Excuse me, I have business to attend to,' he attempted to joke, while making his way towards the oak-panelled door and out into the open air.

*

The deprivation of famine was evident in the streets of the village of Borris and all over the Kavanagh estate. Houses were falling into disrepair, very few tenants were in a position to pay their rent and there was no end in sight. Political agitation was on the increase as people began to question the system of land ownership which had been accepted for years. The Tenant Rights League was formed to advance the rights of tenant farmers throughout Ireland and was gaining traction. Their goal was to achieve the three F's – Fair rent, Fixity of tenure for those who paid their rent and Free sale of their interest in their holding to a new tenant. This new movement was a huge challenge for Arthur, a twenty-two-year-old young man of the privileged class with little or no experience.

But Arthur responded quickly and decisively. The dilapidation in the village disturbed him and he was determined to help his tenants out of the dire poverty they were experiencing. He believed his tenants would remain loyal to the Kavanaghs if their living conditions improved. So, in conjunction with the executors of the estate, it was agreed to hold an auction of antiques and items of value from the big house which were surplus to requirement. Many valuable pieces of furniture, jewellery and paintings were sold in order to put the estate back in good financial straits. Money needed to be raised quickly, and if Kavanagh family heirlooms had to be sold, so be it. There was some opposition from Lady Harriet, but Arthur held firm.

'We have more than we need,' Arthur insisted. 'And I'm not selling anything that can't be replaced when times improve. We have to put people before possessions, Mother.'

'I agree, but you must ensure that none of the artefacts from our travels go under the hammer. They are my prized possessions.'

'Trust me, Mother. Nothing personal or sentimental will be sold.'

By now Hoddy was back in Corfu and Lady Harriet was still deeply troubled. Confiding in her friend, Dr Boxwell, she said:

'You know I believe in Arthur, and he seems much more mature and steady since he came home, but I'm unable to sleep at night thinking of the future of the estate. I mean, what about the Kavanagh legacy? For the first time ever, there won't be an heir. Does the Kavanagh line end here and what does that mean for all of us?'

'But Harriet, dear, why do you assume there will be no heir?'

'Oh, you know I've never dwelled on Arthur's, ehm, difficulties, throughout his entire life, but I never really envisaged that he would marry, much less have a child.'

'Didn't you? I always assumed that he would.'

'But surely that won't be… you know… possible?'

'Why not? We have no reason to assume that Arthur can't father children. In fact, if you were to listen to gossip in the village, which of course you don't, there may be one or two already. And, if our suspicions about the sudden departure of Maud Considine all those years ago are correct, he may have already done so there too.'

'We agreed never to speak of that again, Frank, and we don't know it to be a fact.'

'Yes, but it does seem very relevant now, doesn't it? In my opinion what you need to do is look around for a suitable wife for Arthur before he finds an unsuitable one all by himself!'

'Do you think so? Yes, I suppose I probably should. Oh dear, I'm not sure he'll be guided by anyone though, least of all me.'

'Perhaps you could enlist the help of one of your brothers? Some young lady within the extended family might be approached. Remember, Arthur is now a very eligible bachelor and his personality more than makes up for anything he lacks.'

'Yes. Perhaps you're right. Thank you. That's very sound advice. I'll write to my brother Richard this evening.'

*

Doyne, a rotund man with a sharp nose and a pronounced limp, had managed the Kavanagh estate since the death of Thomas Kavanagh senior. Although a good manager, the locals viewed him as a middle-man – a status for which they had no respect. He had taken his fair share of abuse on behalf of the Kavanaghs over the years, particularly when the ravages of famine were everywhere and the family was perceived to be living the high life abroad. Arthur needed to use every ounce of his charm to win back the favour of the tenants, and he needed to learn the rudiments of estate management very quickly if his tenure as Master of Borris was to be successful.

Having auctioned valuables from the big house to fund repairs to his tenants' homes, Arthur was convinced that the best way to secure a future for the workers, and ultimately for Borris House, was to develop local industries where people could earn a living without depending on the land. While he had lots of ideas, he realised that investment was needed and money was in short supply.

'Money must be spent,' he told Harriet, 'if money is to be earned. Heaven knows where it is to come from. And it may be many years before all rents are paid again unless some drastic steps are taken to provide more income for all.'

While figuring out how to raise money, he busied himself with repairing the decaying buildings on his estate and in the village. With advice from other landowners, he brought farming methods up to date to be more efficient and cost-effective. Using the skills he had learned in India, he drew up plans for a row of cottages which were built along the main street in the village. The design was of such a high standard that he won a medal from the Royal Dublin Society for the best cottage at the lowest cost.

While he was busy learning about the estate, Arthur was completely unaware that plans were being made to find a suitable match for him until his mother announced that a distant cousin, Frances Leathley, would be coming to visit with her aunt. It was March 1854 and the foliage around Borris House was just coming back to life after a hard winter.

'I do hope you'll show her around the estate. It's a very long time since she was here. You remember she came to spend some time here when her mother died? I think she was seven or eight?'

'Yes, I remember Frances. A small, serious girl? In fact, I met her again when I was in Castletown with the Greer family. I look forward to showing her around. If I remember correctly, she's very fond of horses.'

'That's right. I'm sure you'll have a lot in common.'

A week later, when the carriage arrived from County Louth, Arthur waited to greet it on horseback. With his straight back and cloak covering his stumps, he looked regal, with broad shoulders and handsome features. As Frances stepped from the carriage, a gust of wind blew her hat across the courtyard and her long, chestnut-coloured hair blew in front of her face. They all laughed as Arthur cantered over to retrieve the hat from the top of a bush with one of his hooks and, as he handed it back to her, he noticed her dark eyes and tiny waist.

'You're welcome to windy Borris,' he exclaimed, and as his mother emerged from the porch to bring the older lady inside, Arthur spoke quietly to Frances.

'I've asked the stable-hand to saddle up a horse for you. Do you still like to ride?'

'Oh, I'd love that.' She blushed. 'Just give me a few moments to change into suitable clothes and I'll join you.'

And so, the courtship began. Arthur found Frances both attractive and engaging, with an interest not just in horses, but art and architecture. She constantly asked him to tell her stories of his travels across the continent to the East and marvelled at the artefacts he had managed to bring home. He was equally impressed by her quiet confidence. Her knowledge of the political situation was unusual for a woman of her age and standing, and her compassion for the plight of struggling tenants made her all the more intriguing to Arthur.

'May I come and see you when you leave?' he asked on the evening before she departed.

'I fully expect it,' she said with a smile.

A distant cousin, and two years younger than Arthur, Frances was the granddaughter of Lady Harriet Osborne, a great-aunt on his mother's side. She had known and liked Arthur as a child, so wasn't shocked by his appearance, although she needed convincing to consider him as a husband. Unlike other marriages that had been arranged in the family, Frances brought no wealth or status, but the fact that she was willing to consider marrying Arthur, and possibly producing future MacMurrough Kavanaghs to carry the family name, was enough for Harriet.

At night Arthur thought about Frances, and although he knew he shouldn't, he compared her to Maud. While he didn't long for her anymore, he had never forgotten the thrill of anticipation as he set out each evening to meet her, a feeling he couldn't recapture with Frances. The fact of his mother's whole-hearted approval almost stole the excitement from the relationship and banished desire. Yet she really was lovely, and he felt a curious mixture of contentment and admiration in her company. He would marry her, and with God's help, their union would bring happiness back to this blighted family.

Having first gained her father, the Reverend Leathley's permission to marry, Arthur wrote a letter of proposal:

My dear Frances, I am writing this letter to you in the hope that you will give my proposal due consideration. While I would like to fall on bended knee and put this question to you in the traditional way, obviously that is not possible! On a serious note, though, while I sincerely hope you will agree to marry me, and I assure you that my love for you is unfailing, I want to be sure that you will not do so out of pity or any sense of duty. You are a beautiful young lady and I'm certain you could have many suitors. What I can guarantee is my loyal, faithful love and protection for the rest of your life in a beautiful place where, in time, we might be blessed with a family to make our joy complete. I will await your reply anxiously. Please don't delay. Your loving Arthur x

Within two days a reply came. In beautiful handwritten script, the letter was short and to the point.

Dearest Arthur, it will bring me the utmost happiness to be your wife and to make Borris my home. With all my love, Frances x

The wedding, held in March 1855, was a discreet affair, held away from the grandeur of Borris House. Lady Harriet insisted it would be indelicate to have a large celebration and banquet given the political situation, but equally she was keen to have the matter settled, away from prying eyes and gossip. So, at the home of her sister, Lady Louisa le Poer Trench, at No. 1 Mountjoy Square in Dublin, a handful of relatives gathered. Lady Harriet, now fifty-four years old and rather more plump than in her youth, wore a dark green brocade dress to her ankles with a velvet bonnet. The bride, wearing white taffeta with a pearl necklace left to her by her mother, was given away by her father Reverend Joseph Leathley. Arthur wore a tweed jacket and waistcoat over a kilt which covered his stumps.

The entire ceremony lasted less than twenty minutes, with Arthur and Frances sitting throughout. When it was time for the rings to be exchanged, Arthur held the ring on one of his hooks, and Frances removed it, placing it on her own finger. Then she put a gold chain with a ring hanging from it around Arthur's neck, and vowed to be his lawful wedded wife, for better or worse, until death would them part.

From Mountjoy Square, the wedding party was ferried by two coaches to the Shelbourne Hotel on St Stephen's Green. As the horses clip-clopped along the cobbled streets, people stopped to look at the stylish occupants of the carriage and Frances waved regally. Drawing to a halt outside the hotel, they were greeted formally by a doorman in top hat and tails. His smile turned to a look of shock as he saw the groom being carried in on a servant's shoulders, before he regained his composure and held the door open wide for them.

The party was shown to a large, light-filled room overlooking St Stephen's Green. Here they were joined by Dr Boxwell and his wife, Reverend Samuel Greer who performed the ceremony, Mrs Greer, and Sir Philip Crampton who maintained a lifelong friendship with Arthur. Since Frances was an only child, and her mother deceased, her family group was small and consisted of her father, two aunts and a cousin. In all, the party numbered twenty. Unfortunately, Hoddy was unable to make the journey from Corfu as she was, once again, about to give birth.

Arthur and Frances sat at the centre of a long table, replete with a garland down the middle and three candelabras decorated with carnations. Removing his white, starched napkin from its silver holder with his hook, Arthur shook it dramatically like a magician, before tucking it under his chin. Then he tapped the side of a wine glass, making a tinkling noise.

'Before I ask the Reverend Leathley to say grace, I'd like to say a few words.'

All eyes were on Arthur.

'Very few words, in fact, as I hate long speeches. Firstly, I would like to thank my mother for the strength and confidence she has given me throughout my life. I especially want to thank her for giving me the chance to see the world. I will treasure those memories forever. Therefore, I would like to propose a toast to my mother.'

Harriet nodded gracefully as the assembled company clinked their glistening wine glasses in honour of her.

'Secondly, I would like to thank my new beautiful wife. I can't imagine what she sees in me, but I know what I see in her. I see beauty, intelligence and strength of character. But most of all, I see kindness. I want to thank her for agreeing to marry me, and I pledge that I will endeavour to be the best husband I can be. To my beautiful wife!' And they all raised their glasses again.

'Finally, I would like to propose a toast to absent friends. I'm thinking especially of my father and two brothers and, of course, Hoddy, who would have loved to be here.'

Harriet lowered her head as he said: 'To absent friends!'

'Now, Reverend Leathley, could I ask you to lead us in the grace before meals?'

'Not so quick, Arthur,' the Reverend said, rising to his feet. 'Don't worry, this won't take long, but I must pay tribute to my wonderful daughter, Frances. My only daughter, my only child. Since her mother died, Frances has been my companion, my helper and my advisor. While it pains me to lose her, I want nothing but happiness for her. I know that in Arthur she has found a good man who will look after her and I would like to propose a toast to the happy couple. Long life and happiness to Arthur and Frances!'

Once grace was recited, a banquet of fine meats, fish and vegetables was served on large silver platters, reflecting the light from the crystal chandelier. Arthur deftly used his hooks to eat with a knife and fork and, once seated, looked exactly like any bridegroom with his broad shoulders and clean-shaven countenance. Gilt-edged, fine china bowls of treacle tart and trifle laden with custard were served as dessert, followed by a selection of cheeses with sweet wine. Finally, the party went their separate ways, with Arthur, Frances and Harriet returning to Borris House. There was no time for a honeymoon, since urgent business on the rebuilding of the estate couldn't be postponed. But Arthur pledged that he would make it up to Frances by taking many journeys together in the future, and she contented herself with her new role as lady of the house.

Chapter 17

Rebuilding Borris

The two ladies of Borris House, Harriet and Frances, spent the following few weeks getting to know each other. Frances was introduced to other ladies of the region – the Butlers of Kilkenny, the Bruens of Oak Park, the Stopfords of Wexford and many others. Harriet entertained in the drawing room of Borris and the other ladies duly invited Frances and Harriet in return. Frances, who was often more content to listen than speak, looked to her new mother-in-law for advice, and Harriet mentored her in the art of opening conversations, which family members to enquire about and which to gloss over, and how to excuse herself when a suitable amount of time had passed.

When they were alone one morning, Harriet hinted that she hoped everything was going well between herself and Arthur and, by the way she indicated upstairs with a flick of her head, Frances knew she meant the bedroom. Blushing profusely, Frances said: 'Oh yes, absolutely, absolutely,' taking solace by gulping another mouthful of tea.

'I'm so very glad to hear that.' Harriet smiled. 'Of course you are free to do as you wish, but I never, I mean I have never, discussed Arthur's… ehm… situation with anyone and I suggest that perhaps you might do likewise. I find if one doesn't discuss something, it doesn't exist. Don't you agree?' And, raising her eyebrows, Harriet smiled again.

Frances merely nodded nervously in agreement.

By early June, the two ladies had developed an ease between them, and Harriet looked forward to their morning conversations.

'I have something I would like to mention to you today, Lady Harriet,' Frances said as the maid left the room one sunny morning.

'I would very much like if you called me Mother, Frances. Sadly, I have too few people left to call me that.'

'Thank you. I'd be honoured to do that,' Frances replied.

'And what is it that you would like to mention?'

'Well, Mother. It's very good news. Another Kavanagh is on the way.'

'Oh, praise the Lord. That is the best news I have heard in a very long time. I couldn't be happier.' Harriet gave her hands a gentle clap before placing them back on her lap. 'This is wonderful. Now we must look after you. You must not over exert yourself.'

'I'm feeling very well indeed,' Frances answered. 'Very well.'

'I know what I'll do,' Harriet enthused. 'I will show you some lace-making skills I learned when I was in Corfu. I have some lovely patterns you can work from. It will be ideal for the rest of your confinement.'

'Thank you, Mother. I'd like that very much. But I really feel quite well able to be active.'

'Of course, of course. I'm fussing. But I'll teach you anyway. I'd love to show it to you.'

Ten and a half months after their wedding, Frances gave birth to a son whom they named Walter. Although nobody mentioned it, the midwife and Doctor Boxwell immediately checked the baby's limbs, before presenting him to his exhausted mother.

'Ten fingers and ten toes!' he declared proudly. 'Well done.'

The doctor suddenly felt quite emotional, as if this baby could somehow make up for all that had gone before.

'Thank God, and thank *you*, Doctor,' she said. 'Call Arthur to come and see him straight away.'

Arthur, who had been hopping up and down the landing waiting for news, beamed as he made his way over to the bed. He climbed up beside Frances and, kissing her cheek, looked down on the fine blond hair of his first son.

'I'm so proud of you, Frances. Well done. Imagine, we have a son of our own.' And tears trickled down his face.

'His arms and legs are perfect, Arthur. Look.'

Arthur lifted a tiny hand with his stump, bringing it to his mouth and kissing it gently, then, examining the minuscule toenails, he repeated the action with each perfectly formed foot.

'I've never prayed for anything so hard in my entire life,' he whispered, kissing the baby's head again.

'You are a Kavanagh, baby Walter, and some day this estate will be yours,' he said. 'There's nothing you can't achieve with those fine arms and legs.' And he and Frances cried again.

*

Word went up and down the street in Borris. 'Mr Kavanagh has a son and heir. A perfectly formed baby boy!' Burning tar barrels lined the street that evening, and bonfires could be seen in the mountains. The parish church bell rang out and people gathered along the main street singing and dancing in celebration. There was an heir to the Kavanagh estate. Something seemingly miraculous had happened and the future of their little village was secure.

'Looks like the curse is over,' Molly Doyle said to her cronies that evening.

'Do you think the family will get some peace now, Molly?'

'Well, none of you believed me when I told you that one by one the Kavanagh sons would die until we were left with the cripple, so you'll hardly believe me now!' And she sipped her black, tarry tea conspiratorially.

'Come on, Molly, tell us what you think. We *do* believe you now!' Kitty said.

'The curse was that the family would have no luck until it was ruled by a cripple. That's happened now, so there'll be peace. But only for a while, mind you.' She sat forward. 'And I'm not talking superstition this time.'

'What do you mean, Molly?'

'The wind is changing for families like theirs. Hungry people won't stay down forever. It won't be just the Kavanaghs who'll suffer, and it won't be today or tomorrow. But mark my words, a different day is coming.'

*

Although not privy to these conversations, Arthur instinctively knew that a new approach was needed to bring Borris back from the brink of despair. People needed work and the means to earn enough to keep their families. Agriculture, and particularly the potato crop, could not be depended on. As his father before him had done, he began holding listening and counselling sessions under the Oak Tree in the Courtyard at Borris House. There, sitting on an old stone mounting-block, he heard tales of disputes over property, family arguments and trauma. He heard about relatives starving and being evicted in other parts of the country and others leaving for America just to stay alive. By listening, he learned the mood of his tenants and they accepted his good-natured advice or admonishment.

One tenant, Johnny Moran, came to Arthur one day. For a while the conversation was general: 'Mr Kavanagh, the crops in the low field are coming on well. Do you think it'll be ready to harvest soon?'

'Oh, I'd give it another few weeks, Johnny. But you didn't come here to talk to me about farming, did you?'

'No, Mr Kavanagh. It's a bit… awkward.'

'Well, Johnny, if this tree could talk it would tell of murder, deception and infidelity, to mention but a few. Have you anything stranger than that to discuss?' And the two men laughed.

'Indeed, I haven't, Mr Kavanagh. It's just that, well, I haven't long to live.'

'Oh dear, Johnny. I'm very sorry to hear that. Are you sure?'

'The doctor is very sure, Mr Kavanagh, but I don't expect you to do anything about that. What I want is not for myself, but for my daughter, Mary.'

'Mary? What age is Mary now?'

'She's twenty now, Mr Kavanagh, and she's the only one we have left at home. The others all went to America.'

'All of them?'

'Yes, Mr Kavanagh. One after the other. And the thing is, I don't want my poor wife to be left with no one when I'm gone.'

'How can I help?'

'I know you might think it forward of me, but I've heard that you've arranged matches before and if you could find someone suitable for Mary, maybe she'd stay and my wife would have family around her. I hope you don't think I'm being forward asking you.'

Arthur had, by then, been responsible for many matches in the area. He discreetly introduced many lonely men to young women and gave character references for people living in isolated places without the means of socialising. He had gained a reputation as someone who could arrange a good marriage, and some came back to thank him with a baby in their arms a year or two later.

'You're not being forward at all, Johnny,' Arthur said. 'I think you're doing a great deed trying to look after your family when you're gone, and I'll do my utmost to help. Send Mary up to me on Saturday and I'll take it from there.'

As Johnny left, out of the corner of his eye Arthur could see the two Brennan brothers waiting to speak to him. One was leaning against the stable wall, while the other was on his hunkers under a tree. He summoned them forward and the hostility between them was like a thundercloud ready to burst. They both started talking together:

'Mr Kavanagh, he…'

'It was him.'

Raising his voice, Arthur said: 'My good men, I'll speak first, and you will listen. The dogs in the street can see there's a dispute going on between you two. If you came here for a solution, sit down, facing each other. If you came to argue and blame, there's the gate.' And he indicated the open gates leading to the main street.

Chastened, the two men sat down and the older one spoke. 'It's about a fence, Mr Kavanagh. My father said the hilly field was to be divided between us when he died, but this fella has fenced off the biggest, driest bit for himself.'

'And what's your side of this story?' Arthur asked the other brother who was sitting with his head bowed.

'Tom was always my father's favourite and I've had enough of it. I have six children to feed. He has only three and his wife gets money for the scrubbing that she does. I need the land more than he does.'

'If Jimmy doesn't move that fence, Mr Kavanagh, I'm going to move it for him, and he'd better not stand in my way.'

Hopping down off the stone, Arthur stared hard at Tom. 'If you threaten violence in my presence, you'll find yourself in front of a magistrate. Is that clear?'

'Yes, Mr Kavanagh.'

'I'll ride over to the field this afternoon. Be there at 2 o'clock. The fence will be in the correct position within an hour. Then, Jimmy, I'd like you to come and see me tomorrow and we'll see if there's anything else we can do for your family. Good day, gentlemen.'

Some mornings, as many as ten people were waiting to share their difficulties with him, and with the patience of an Indian guru, he offered spiritual as well as practical advice to them all. Meanwhile, Arthur was seeking advice from others about how Borris could be developed to make it a self-sufficient entity in the future. He believed that the land would not be able to sustain everyone and that a local industry offering regular employment needed to be developed as soon as possible.

When riding out one morning along the banks of the Mountain River, an idea came to him. The current flowing from the Blackstairs mountains through the estate was powerful. On his travels he had seen many successful working mills and understood enough about engineering to know that this small river would be sufficient to run one. Given the plentiful supply of timber on the estate with trees being felled all the time, a sawmill would be ideal. All he needed to do was to identify the best location along the riverbank.

Like many of Arthur's ideas, there was initial opposition, especially from Harriet. It wouldn't work, it would be too expensive, there would be no market for the wood. But once the seed of an idea became embedded in Arthur's head, he pursued it relentlessly. Through consultation with engineers from Dublin he identified an ideal location for the new mill and plans were drawn up. Local limestone was used and labourers were delighted with the opportunity to work on this new building project, which took six months to complete. Then, once it was fitted out with turning-lathes, saws and machinery, Arthur brought in experts to teach some of his tenants the skills needed to fell local wood and use it to make wooden items for use in other industries. Before long, he had secured contracts for the supply of bobbins to the cotton industry in England, the Kavanagh name helping to open many doors and ensuring that the mill prospered.

A constant supply of wood was needed to provide the sawmill with raw material and there was nothing Arthur liked more than to personally fell trees on his own land. Like everything he did, he had practiced it until he was an expert. Using an axe which had his initials engraved on it clasped between his stumps, he moved around the tree, studying the trunk until he found the perfect angle. Then, urging all present to stand back, he expertly hacked so that the tree fell exactly where he expected, swinging his whole body energetically. While this was nerve-wracking for the party of workers with him, he found it exhilarating and all agreed that the "plate" left behind on the tree stump was as clean as any professional could wish for. Axing became part of his daily routine and he even organised competitions which, nine out of ten times, he won.

The sawmill gradually expanded and more and more men from the locality gained regular work there. Others sold their timber for a good price to the mill and there was employment for those with the means of transporting the cut timber to Dublin and the port of Wexford. A manager was appointed, but Arthur remained the overseer of every stage of production. What worried him most was the slow, horse-drawn means of transport for the wood produced in the mill. Other parts of the country were beginning to benefit from the railway system which, since first opening with the Dublin to Kingstown line in 1834, was spreading competitively throughout the country. Looking at the horses and flat carts leaving his timber yard, and knowing how long it would take them to reach Wexford, Arthur wondered could there be a railway in Borris? But that would take a huge investment of money that he simply didn't have.

At 25 years old, the burden of responsibility weighed heavily on Arthur's shoulders. Along with managing the estate he was also Chairman of the local bench of Magistrates and was called upon to officiate at many public meetings as a member of the aristocracy. The only time he could truly relax was when at sea in his yacht, *The Corsair*, which was berthed in New Ross. His childhood dream had become a reality and he had assembled a small crew to help him. It was on the open sea that he felt at one with nature where his skills as a sailor were all that mattered, and the financial and political situation of his homeland could be temporarily left behind.

As Christmas approached it seemed timely, now that things were improving, to celebrate with typical Borris House lavishness. Arthur and Frances made meticulous lists of their employees, tenants and people in need in the area. Together with the staff of Borris House they prepared hampers of meat, preserves, blankets and clothes with small toys for the children in each house. These were tied into parcels, many of which Arthur delivered in person on horseback to families living on the mountainsides. The happiness these packages brought meant more to him than any gift he had ever received himself. When the families heard the horses' hooves approaching, their children would crowd in the doorway while the mother or father stepped forward to receive the wrapped bundle. The men would tip their caps in deference to the generous landlord with promises of prayers and blessings on his family, and as he rode down the road he could often hear the cheers of the children as the contents spilled out on the flagged floor.

Back at Borris House, a huge Christmas tree was set up in the great hall, filling it with a rich scent of pine, and the children from the village school were invited to sing around it, with their teacher accompanying them on the piano. The servants brought refreshments for everybody afterwards and Frances was charmed by the excitement of the chattering children. In the evening, a banquet was held for the villagers where the doors of the house were thrown open. Fine food, desserts and wine were served and those present were encouraged to take a look around the kitchens and other downstairs reception rooms – something they had never had the opportunity to do before. They pointed and whispered about the huge cookers and serving tables and the smell of roast duck and pheasant. Marvelling at the array of silver and glass in everyday use, one woman commented:

'There's one silver spoon in my house. My grandmother gave it to me. She might even have stolen it from here, but no one is allowed to use it, we treasure it that much.'

And Arthur, acting as the congenial host, was keen to show that he was as loyal to the villagers as they were to him and that he valued their service.

After the party, when the last of the locals left with armfuls of leftover food, Arthur summoned the staff to the Christmas tree for a nightcap. When everyone was ready to sing "O Come All Ye Faithful," the butler announced that Burns, the footman, wasn't present and neither was Mrs Foley, the cook.

'Let's begin and they will probably arrive,' Arthur said, bellowing out the first line as everyone joined in.

As the second drink was poured, Arthur made his way to the kitchen himself to find that Burns and Mrs Foley had passed out at the long trestle table with a large bottle of whiskey between them. Putting the whiskey back in the drinks cupboard, he discreetly made his way back to the party, and as the night came to a close, whispered to the butler:

'You might make sure Mrs Foley and Burns are helped to bed. They seem very tired.' And he winked to show there would be no repercussions.

Meanwhile, throughout Ireland, there was turbulence and violence. Hungry tenants were refusing to pay their landlords and some big houses had been set on fire or vandalized. However, despite the turmoil elsewhere, for now peace reigned in and around Borris House. Arthur was sure that if he kept his tenants comfortable and in employment they would continue to serve his family as they always had. He believed his fairness and generosity would be enough and that demands for land ownership would pass him by. But the movement was growing, and it would take more than goodwill to stop it.

*

In August 1857, Frances gave birth to a second son, whom she named Arthur Thomas after both her husband and his father. A dark-haired boy this time, he resembled Frances' family more than the Kavanaghs, and again his limbs were perfect. No one was prouder than Arthur himself as he travelled by carriage through the village of Borris with his wife and two sons. People stood at the side of the street to greet them, and there were few in the village who were not happy to see that the fortunes of the big house had turned and their little village had a leader who was second to none.

Chapter 18

The Iron Road

While Arthur concerned himself with building and expanding local industry, Lady Harriet, true to her word, began daily lessons in lace-making with Frances. The two ladies worked through the intricate lace patterns which Harriet had brought home from Corfu years before, each of them sitting at the large window of the drawing room at Borris House. Harriet patiently explained where she had acquired each piece of lace and how to master the tiny stitching. Being a keen artist herself, she was intrigued by the delicate needlework and communicated this enthusiasm to Frances who proved to be an excellent student.

Harriet explained the difference between Italian lace and other laces produced in Ireland. The Italian ones were "tape laces" created by using lace tape, with designs held together by piloted bars or a net. Decorative filling stitches enhanced and embellished the lace making designs which were very popular for handkerchiefs, lace collars and ruffles, tablecloths and centrepieces. Each piece took lengthy periods of concentration and needed excellent eyesight and Harriet, who was now in her late fifties, wore reading glasses on the end of her nose as she worked. During these sessions the two ladies bonded in a way that might never have happened without the lace-making and Frances, although remaining shy, became more and more confident.

One day, when Harriet and Frances were walking in the village distributing food and clothing parcels to tenants, Frances had an idea.

'I wonder if we could teach local women to do lacework as a means of making money for their families? The lace is so popular and fashionable and we could probably find a market for their work. What do you think, Mother?'

'I think…' Lady Harriet paused. 'I think that's a wonderful idea. I wonder how would we teach them? And would many women take to it? Let's discuss it with Arthur when he gets home and we'll figure out how best to approach it.'

Soon classes began at the big house, attended by women who had scrubbed their hands and faces to attend Lady Harriet's lace lessons. Starting with simple leaf patterns, they progressed, as they were able, to more complicated stitches, and some with deft hands became experts very quickly. Delighted to be able to earn some money for themselves, before long the women of Borris could be seen sitting outside the doors of their cottages stitching for hours, since the interiors were too dark and the delicate fabric needed to be protected from the smells of turf fires and boiled pigs' trotters. Sometimes huddles of two and three women could be seen on the street, poring over a difficult stitch and figuring out how to tackle it. Week by week Frances copied and distributed new patterns, some created by Lady Harriet herself, as she walked along the main street offering encouragement and helping the women overcome any problems.

Soon, through the influence of the Kavanagh family, Borris Lace became a sought after accessory in high-class establishments in Dublin, London and the United States. Ladies at fashionable events in

London were seen wearing decorative collars and cuffs that had passed through the hands of the ordinary women of Borris. They were paid a fair price for their work by the Kavanaghs, depending on its size and difficulty, and the family managed the rest. Harriet ensured that those who needed glasses were assisted in getting them so they could learn the new skill, and prosperity slowly returned to the village streets with a contentment that had been absent for a long time. But Arthur's restless mind was always looking to the future. He constantly wondered what else could he do to make Borris viable and at night he prayed that he would make his late father and ancestors proud.

In January 1857, as baby Walter took his first steps, Arthur set about securing a development to put Borris on the map and secure its financial future. The first railway on the island of Ireland, from Dublin to Kingstown, was designed by a fellow Carlow man, William Dargan, and since then the race to provide a network to serve the rest of the country was ongoing and competitive. The Irish South-Eastern railway proposed a route from Bagenalstown to Wexford and an Act by this name was passed in Parliament in 1854. Arthur's mother, Lady Harriet, had tacitly agreed in 1855 that, if necessary, it could pass through the Kavanagh land. Now Arthur, by granting fourteen miles of land for this purpose, endeavoured to make it a reality. He knew that the easy transport of goods and services would mean that local businesses, particularly the sawmill, could thrive, and he personally supervised the laying of tracks across his estate. The project had some financial backing by an English businessman, Mr George Mott, and the railway looked set to open within a few months.

Excitement was in the air as the great iron tracks snaked their way through the countryside nearing the newly built limestone station house off the main street. The line that would serve the village started in the town of Bagenalstown and, when completed, would open a direct route to the ports of Wexford. For now, only the section as far as Borris was being worked on. Children waved and jumped with excitement as the first steam engine arrived on 11th October, 1858. It was a goods train, pulling ten trucks of iron track and sleepers for the siding in the station. How the railway was going to cross the deep valley on the next leg of its journey to Wexford, and who would fund this next phase, nobody dared to imagine. All were focused on the imminent opening of the Bagenalstown to Borris line and how it might alter their lives.

The day of the opening dawned cold, but dry. It was December and the hoarfrost was slowly melting from the station house windows when the whistle of the steam engine could be heard in the distance, followed by the clicks and rattles of the traction wheels. The passenger railway had finally come to Borris! Bunting was stretched across the railway buildings and newly built sheds, and villagers crowded the platform waving and cheering. A piper played Irish tunes as the Kavanaghs and other gentry stepped into the First Class carriage, which was adorned with red velvet seats and neatly tied back curtains.

On more than one occasion the guard had to urge people to stand back from peering in the windows as the train attempted to leave the station.

The train returned to Borris on two occasions that day and was greeted with the same excitement each time. The villages fell into a hushed silence as the Kavanaghs returned with Colonel Bagenal-Newton of Bagenalstown and his family in tow, having been invited to tea at Borris House. With their top hats and tails, and ladies in fine dresses, they strode down the platform and the locals parted like the Red Sea. Following behind were Arthur and Frances, with Arthur tipping his hat and calling to locals by name.

'Great day for Borris, John! Isn't it wonderful, Paddy?'

'It certainly is, m'Lord. It certainly is.'

For weeks people stood in the fields to watch the goods train and passenger train as they passed by, waving and trying to guess who or what might be on board. Sometimes a newspaper wrapped in twine would be thrown to a farmer as the train slowed down towards the station and from the First Class windows people threw boiled sweets to the children on the platform. Gradually the train became another part of everyday life in Borris. Although beyond the means of many villagers, it meant that parcels and post from relatives abroad arrived in a timelier fashion. Every week, wood from the sawmill was loaded onto flat carriages and at Bagenalstown it was transferred to a train bound for the port of Dublin. Soon, Arthur hoped, the wood could travel directly to Wexford and across the Irish Sea from there.

A meeting between Mr Mott and Arthur was planned for July 1859. Keen to get the next phase of the line up and running, Arthur prepared meticulously for the meeting. His enquiries with the Railway Board, chaired by local MP, John Redmond, were that a viaduct would have to be built to span the gorge which was just outside Borris village. While he knew this would be expensive, there was no other way the railway could proceed towards Wexford. When Mr Mott arrived, his head was low as he was shown to the library where Arthur had maps and drawings laid out on a large table.

'Delighted to see you,' Arthur declared as he walked in. 'Have a seat. Can I tempt you to a cigar?' he said, indicating the silver cigar case left to him by his father.

'No, no. Not at all, thank you. I'm afraid, Mr Kavanagh, I have some bad news.'

'Bad news? What kind of bad news?'

'I'm afraid it's financial bad news. The railway is losing money.'

'Oh dear, well, I'm sorry to hear that, but it's early days. Surely we should give it a bit longer before we judge its success, don't you think?'

'Mr Kavanagh, I admire your optimism, and perhaps if I owned this marvellous residence I could afford to be optimistic too. But I am a businessman. If I don't make money, I have nothing to fall back on.'

With that, a servant arrived with tea and coffee. Lavishly ornate tea and coffee pots embossed with gold, which Harriet had brought back from her travels, were laid on the table with freshly baked madeira cake. Both men fell silent until the servant left and, as Mr Mott put the cup to his lips, Arthur said:

'Let me get this straight. Are you telling me you're broke?'

'Not yet, Mr Kavanagh, but a few more months backing the Bagenalstown to Borris railway may well see me completely bankrupt. I'm going to have to pull the plug. I'm afraid Borris Station will close.'

'Stop right there, Mr Mott. Let's not be so dramatic. I'm very sorry to hear you are in financial difficulty and, believe me, I know what that is like.'

Mr Mott raised an eyebrow and looked around at the mahogany and glass bookcases and gilt-edged portraits, smiling ruefully.

'I very much doubt that you do, Mr Kavanagh.'

'This is my inheritance, Mr Mott. There is nothing here that can be sold, and I have tenants who need supporting or they will starve. That railway is a lifeline. Could I propose a deal?'

'I'm listening.' Mr Mott stroked his beard.

'I will manage the railway and subsidise it for a period of time to the tune of £5000. During this time the viaduct will be underway and confidence in the railway will be restored. You, Mr Mott, will disappear quietly with what you have left of your fortune intact. In return I will give you a letter of recommendation for the bank to allow you to pursue another venture. Nobody will be any the wiser. Are we agreed on that?'

Pausing for a moment, Mr Mott replied: 'So you mean to buy me out?'

'Precisely.'

'Well then, yes, Mr Kavanagh. I can agree to that, but for what my opinion is worth, I think you may as well dig a hole and bury your money in it. The railway will fail. The whole Irish system is chaotic. A line is planned from Dublin right through to Waterford and another through the county of Wicklow. This line is a red herring.'

'We shall see about that, Mr Mott.'

And, having exchanged a few more pleasantries over tea and cake, Arthur rang the bell for the butler to show the businessman to the door.

*

At the Railway Board meeting Arthur mentioned nothing of this conversation except to say that Mr Mott had agreed that he would manage the railway as Mr Mott had other business interests needing his attention. The remainder of the meeting was taken up with plans as to how the gorge would be navigated in order that the next phase of the line could be completed. The engineer who had been engaged was a Mr William Le Fanu from Dublin, who addressed the meeting. In his opinion the only solution was to construct a sixteen-arch viaduct made from limestone with the spans each being eleven yards wide. Drawings were produced and all agreed it would be a magnificent structure.

'Through the chair, may I ask where the money will come from?' The spell was broken by Colonel Bagenal-Newton. 'Personally, I cannot invest further. I am already deeply indebted to this project.'

'Where do we stand with the government grant?' Mr Redmond asked.

The treasurer, with one glance at the accounts, said: 'Almost gone, I'm afraid. The line is losing money all the time.'

'And that's why we need to continue it,' Arthur interjected. 'It was never meant to just link Bagenalstown to Borris. We must carry on to Wexford, then we will see how profitable this railway can be.'

'But what about the funding, Mr Kavanagh. Are *you* prepared to fund it?'

'I will fund the building of the viaduct. Can anyone match that?' Arthur added, with a tight feeling in his stomach, knowing he had no idea how he could come up with the funds.

'A generous offer, Mr Kavanagh,' the Colonel replied. 'I will fund the line as far as Kilcoltrim. Beyond that, I'm afraid, a new sponsor will have to be found.'

And so, the future of the railway was secured for the moment, but Arthur went home in troubled mood.

During dinner he said very little and when the children had gone to bed and Harriet had withdrawn to the drawing room, Frances stayed at the table.

'Whatever is the matter with you, Arthur? You seem so down in the mouth these days.'

'It's nothing, Fan. Nothing you should worry yourself about.'

'Arthur, if something is the matter with you, of course I will worry. Please tell me.'

'Oh alright, but please don't try to change my mind.'

'I can't promise that, but do tell me, please.'

'I'm going to have to sell my yacht. I don't see any other option. The railway is in trouble.'

'But Arthur, *The Corsair* is your only means of relaxation. You can't sell it. I've never seen you as happy as when you're sailing and each trip sustains you for weeks afterwards.'

'I have no choice, Fan. Perhaps when times are better, I'll buy another one. But for now, I've made a commitment and I have to honour it.'

'Is there nobody else who can sponsor the railway? There simply must be.'

'No, there isn't. There's talk of closure if it doesn't start making money soon. I can't think of anybody else.'

'Have you spoken to your mother about this?' Frances asked.

'Frances, I am approaching thirty years old. I am not going to run to my mother to solve my problems. I've decided what to do and nothing will change my mind.'

What Frances didn't know was that Arthur had already borrowed quite a large sum of money from his mother as well as smaller amounts from some friends. The only disposable asset he had that was fully his own, rather than part of the estate, was his beloved yacht and the next day he sent word to New Ross to have it sold.

He wrote: *Just remove my possessions from it and have them sent to Borris. Wrap and label everything carefully. I hope to have use for them again.*

And so, the viaduct was funded in part by Arthur and Colonel Bagenal-Newton as well as by monies raised through grants from government. Mr Redmond, as the sitting MP, was able to raise some funds, but investment in Ireland was not a priority for the Crown, whose growing concern was the wave of nationalism sweeping the country.

'Have you ever thought of running for office yourself?' Arthur was asked on more than one occasion, since his father had been a long-serving MP, but his answer was always the same.

'I'm not cut out for that kind of life. I'll do what I can here in my own locality. This is where my duty lies.'

By now Doyne had retired, and Arthur was no longer hiring an agent for the estate, instead managing it all himself. He had helped many of his tenants to improve their dwellings, but with 1200 holdings in all, it was impossible to improve each one. At night he lay awake, wondering where the money would come from to finish the railway and how he could make Borris profitable into the future. At home he became quiet and broody, only cheered up by the children who always brought a smile to his face. Every day he did his duties, sometimes hunting or cutting down trees, until one day he returned to Frances and announced:

'I know what I'll have to do. I'll sell the hounds. They're excellent hunting dogs and I'll get a good price for them.'

At this Frances stood up from the table and in a rare display of emotion, she threw the napkin down, saying:

'You will do no such thing, Arthur Kavanagh. If your precious railway means that, piece by piece, our lives are going to be dismantled, I will not have it. Those dogs are as much a part of you as this house itself. You have always told me that the Kavanaghs hunt and fish. Those two little boys will do just that, and you will not take that away from them for the sake of a loss-making railway. I've had quite enough of it, Arthur!'

The baby, sensing the change of tone, wailed in his high-chair and Frances lifted him and stormed out of the room.

Arthur, with raised eyebrows, looked at the butler who was fiddling with his buttons nervously, as Walter said: 'Mamma cross, Papa?'

'Yes, indeed she is, Walter. Yes, she is. Well observed, young man!'

Chapter 19

Changes

On the morning of May 15th, 1859, preparations for a party were underway at Borris House. A large marquee with bunting was erected on the lawn, held up by wooden poles with guide wires securing it to the ground. An eight-piece brass band was tuning up in the front porch with discordant sounds echoing around the estate. Servants were scurrying around, laying napkins and cutlery on long trestle tables. Hoddy, along with her husband and two children, had arrived from Corfu the previous day, as had two of Frances' cousins with their families. Guests from the Bruen and Butler gentry families were expected, as well as fifty local landowners. In a second marquee, all the locals were invited to food and ale with a separate area for dancing so they could enjoy the festivities.

Lady Harriet was hosting and funding the party for three reasons. Firstly, a baby girl had been born to Arthur and Frances three weeks before and Harriet wanted to mark the birth of their first daughter in style. Secondly, it had been two years since Hoddy and her family had been home. Her husband's army career dictated that he rarely got leave long enough to travel to Ireland. The third reason was a secret, which Harriet planned to divulge in the after-dinner speeches. She felt a peculiar mixture of excitement and nostalgia as she stood looking out through the main front door. Borris had been her home for over thirty-five years. She had seen so many happy days, but also rather a lot of sad ones. Days when there was a marquee on the lawn were invariably the better ones. But the future hung like a heavy cloud and Harriet found it hard to be optimistic.

Going back upstairs, she looked into the nursery, which was riotous with children running and crawling and laughing. The new baby, Eva, was sleeping quietly in a basket as her two brothers played with cousins they had never met before. For a moment Harriet recalled when her own four children filled these walls with noise and laughter and how two of them hadn't lived to reach their twenty-fifth birthdays. If only Thomas' and Charles' children could be here too.

'Are you alright, Lady Harriet?' One of the nannies approached her. 'You look quite faint.'

'I'm perfectly fine, thank you.' Harriet checked herself. 'I was just looking in on the children. They all look very content indeed.'

And she went to her room to choose her clothes for the evening.

In the afternoon, Harriet asked to meet Arthur and Frances privately in the drawing room.

Arriving a few minutes late, Arthur hopped onto the chaise longue looking irritated and checked his watch.

'We'll have to make this quick, Mother. I'm really very busy getting the horses and hounds ready for the visitors. I'll be taking a party out early in the morning. Is there something important you need me for?'

'I need both you and Frances, Arthur, and thankfully your wife had the common decency to arrive punctually! Now will you sit still and give me a few minutes of your valuable time?'

'Alright. I'm sorry, Mamma. Is there something wrong?'

'I wouldn't say "wrong" exactly, but I do have something important to say.'

Both Frances and Arthur stared expectantly at her.

'We're all ears, Mamma.' Arthur raised his eyebrows.

'Firstly, I have some good news for you, Arthur. I heard that you gave instructions to sell *The Corsair*. And before you look to Frances, it was *not* she who told me. The good news is that the payment you received for it actually came from me. Your yacht is not sold and is ready for you to use when you see fit.'

Frances gasped. 'Oh, that's wonderful, Mother, isn't it Arthur? That's so generous of you.'

Harriet and Frances looked to Arthur for a response but for a few moments he remained silent.

'I really don't know what to say, Mamma. Of course, it *is* very good of you and I'm delighted to be able to sail again, but I feel I have failed once more and you have had to rescue me.'

'I thought you might look at it like that and that is why I didn't tell you, Arthur. And on the matter of failure, could I just say that I believe you are doing a fine job of managing the estate – more than I would have given you credit for.'

At this Arthur looked indignant, but Harriet raised a hand to silence him.

'I'm not finished! You simply must decide which matters *most* to you; the railway or the estate. There is little point in having a magnificent viaduct as a monument to your foolishness while you can't afford to maintain your inheritance and look after your tenants. This is the last time I will come to your rescue, and I know how much sailing means to you or I wouldn't have done it.'

'I'm very grateful to you, Mamma. Thank you,' he said as he moved to get up and leave.

'I will let you know when I have concluded, Arthur.' She gave him a withering stare and he sat back down. 'The second reason I brought you here is to tell you that I am moving to Ballyragget in the next few weeks and will no longer be living here at Borris.'

It was Arthur who reacted first this time. 'What? When did you decide this?'

Before she could answer, Frances gushed: 'Oh no, Mother. But this is your home. It wouldn't be the same without you.'

'I've made up my mind,' Harriet said firmly. 'Both of you and the children are the future of Borris House now. I've served my time and I have decided to retire from public life to paint and travel as much as I can. I've decided and it is final.'

Arthur and Frances exchanged a glance before Arthur said, 'Very well, Mother. I'm sad to hear it but I hope you will be very happy there. When are you planning to move?'

'I have already instructed Bookey in how I want the house in Ballyragget prepared. His work as agent in Kilkenny has kept him very busy lately but he said he will oversee the renovations for me. I've told him he has a maximum of three months, so I'll be in situ before September. I'm planning a trip to India with Hoddy in November. That's all for the moment. You may leave now, Arthur, since you have business to attend to. That's all I have to say.'

Turning at the door, Arthur looked back at Harriet and, with what looked like tears in his eyes said: 'We will miss you, Mamma. Borris will not be the same without you. I'll do everything I can to make you and my late father proud.' And he left the two ladies to discuss the colour schemes for the drawing room in Ballyragget and how the lace-making might continue without Harriet's input.

*

The last guests left the banquet at 4am, having danced and sung their way through the balmy, summer night. There was an audible gasp when Lady Harriet announced her imminent move to Kilkenny, and some of the ladies dabbed their eyes as she voiced her appreciation of the tenants' loyalty to the Kavanagh family. Even those who had originally found her abrasive all those years ago and railed against her, had developed an admiration for this woman who had endured loss and heartache in their midst, and whose tenacity had never wavered.

Kitty Ryan was sitting between Molly Doyle and Mary Quigley when Lady Harriet talked about her admiration for the women of Borris. For once, Molly was quiet as Harriet recounted the enthusiasm with which the local women and girls had taken to lace-making, the standard of their work and their commitment to the industry which had put their little village on the map.

'I have seen them sitting at their doorways until the light fades and I have marvelled at the beautiful creations they have made. Collars and cuffs which are being worn in royal circles as we speak, beautiful tablecloths which now adorn the finest establishments in the land, and vestments worn by clergymen of every persuasion, in veneration of the one true God. Women of Borris, I am proud of you.'

'Will you stop your blubbering,' Molly eventually said. 'Sure isn't it only the truth.'

'I know, but it's so sad that she won't be here no more,' Kitty whispered through her tears.

'She's not dying, for God's sake. She's only moving to Ballyragget.' Molly laughed drily.

'I think it's very sad,' Mary Quigley pitched in. 'I can hardly remember a day when she wasn't in the big house. It's the end of an era.'

'It's the end of nothing,' Molly guffawed. 'The fun is only starting around here, and I don't know if that new woman or her crippled husband know what they're in for.'

'Will you whisht, Molly! Someone'll hear you.'

'I was never one to worry about that.' Molly smiled. 'Oh, will you look. Here's Mr Kavanagh himself to address the peasantry!' And she gave Kitty a nudge.

Positioning himself on a table to be seen by everyone, Arthur cleared his throat. He wore a long black cloak, designed to cover his leg stumps. It had heavily decorated shoulders and hung regally around him with only a hint of metal revealing the hooks in the place where his hands should be.

'Distinguished guests, and people of Borris,' his booming voice addressed the crowd. 'I want to thank you for your attendance at our banquet this evening which marks the birth of my beautiful daughter, Eva. I am blessed more than words can express to have, in addition to my wonderful wife and two fine sons, a little girl to brighten my days. Please raise your glasses to Eva.'

And all present echoed his toast shouting 'To Eva' and holding up their drinks.

'The news that my mother is to leave Borris House is difficult for me. As you well know, my family has been here in Borris House for hundreds of years, and in each generation it was not just the MacMurrough Kavanagh men, but their strong loyal wives who made this estate the wonderful place it is. My mother, in her time at Borris, has been dealt a difficult hand. She has suffered much loss, but she never lost her faith in God and in the MacMurrough Kavanagh destiny. Without reservation I can say she has made me the man I am.' His voice broke slightly as he said this last sentence and, coughing briefly, he continued.

'Borris House will be very different without my mother, but my wife and I will endeavour to continue with the traditions and values my mother and my late father held dear. I would like to wish my mother a long and happy retirement in Ballyragget and hope she will be a frequent visitor to Borris. Please raise your glasses to my mother, Lady Harriet.'

'To Lady Harriet,' the crowd echoed.

'For now,' Molly added, and she shook her head knowingly. 'But not for long.'

*

Through his hard work and kindness, Arthur was earning the respect of many in the locality, not only the tenantry, but also among his peers who were witnessing firsthand his intelligence and determination. Elected firstly to the Grand Jury, he was then nominated as High Sheriff for Kilkenny. As a Conservative, he supported the candidacy of Mr John Alexander of Milford in the election of 1857 to represent the borough of Carlow. Believing that by being a good landlord he could pacify his tenants and dissuade them from joining the more militant factions that were growing throughout the country, he reduced rents, rebuilt and reroofed cottages and actively campaigned for reforms in his role on the Board of Guardians of New Ross Poorhouse.

If people stared at him, and most people did, he merely smiled and carried on. At public meetings when there was a document to be signed, he held the pen in his mouth and steadying it with one or both of his stumps, added his legible signature with flair. On one occasion, when there was a hunting party at Borris House, a visiting child screamed and pointed when she saw a "half-man" sitting on the sideboard with a beard and long cloak. Admonished by her parents, the child was led away pointing and crying. Arthur found this amusing and sometimes revealed a shiny hook just to enjoy the reaction. But, in his official duties at court or at Board meetings, a servant would carry him on their back to a seat and from that moment on, his charisma and personality took over.

In early 1860 Arthur began to suffer from chest problems and couldn't take part in the hunt. While the doctors couldn't find anything specifically wrong with his heart, it was thought that the stress of having so much responsibility so young might have a played a part. His mood was also particularly low – a condition only known to Frances as he hid it from everybody else.

One morning in early spring, Frances visited him in his room and asked:

'Are you well enough to get up today, Arthur? The children are asking about you.'

'I'm so sorry, Fan. I'll come down for luncheon.'

'What is it, Arthur? It's so unlike you. Is there anything I can do to help?'

'There's nothing anyone can do to help, Fan. For the first time in my life, I feel that I might not be equal to the task. I mean I've grown up with such privilege and I'm not sure I've used it to best advantage. I can't stop thinking about my two brothers and the lives they should be leading and perhaps I'm letting them down and all the Kavanaghs before them. And I want so much to create a legacy for Walter and Arthur and Eva and you, Fan. Am I letting you down?'

He was crying now, large tears trickling into his beard.

'No, you are not letting me down. Why would you even contemplate that?' And she put her arms around him as he cried like a baby.

'What if my chest pains don't go away and if the railway doesn't work out? And if the tenants revolt and turn against me?'

'Stop it now, Arthur. You need to calm yourself. I'm going to get Doctor Boxwell and perhaps he can give you something to help. You're just exhausted. It's unlikely that any of those things are going to happen and if they do, I know when you're feeling better, you'll be able to deal with them. Try to rest now, and I'll send for him.'

Frances was shaking as she walked downstairs and asked the butler to send for the doctor at once. This was not the Arthur she knew and the thought of him losing his spirit was even more terrifying than losing him to illness. She could think of only one thing that might help, and that was a complete break from Borris. A sailing trip for a period of time, long enough to rebuild his morale, if only Doctor Boxwell would deem him physically fit to travel.

With the help of Doctor Boxwell, Arthur slowly recovered his health and confidence, attending to his duties outside the house where his ebullience masked the melancholia exhibited at home. With the doctor's blessing, and the assistance of Frances, a cruise was quietly organised. A new bigger yacht, which could accommodate more people, was sourced and named *The Eva* after their daughter. After a few weeks, Frances and the two boys would join him and enjoy a family holiday together far away from duty and responsibility. Perhaps the energy of the open sea could rejuvenate Arthur, as it had done many times before.

Chapter 20

Troubled Waters

The next few weeks were spent on board *The Eva*, sailing towards the Mediterranean. Arthur assembled a small crew, consisting of his valet and one of his Connolly cousins. Equipped with a chart, compass and binoculars, he planned and continually revised their journey. When it came to tacking and jibing, he shouted commands while manning the tiller between his stumps and when it came to tying knots, his hooks were as dexterous as any skilled hands.

Frances and the boys came aboard at Malta and Arthur showed off to his sons by speeding through the water while they squealed with excitement. It was clear to Frances that Arthur's mood and general health were much better and, as they sailed around the heel of Italy in the Ionian Sea, she tried to put his mind at ease by telling him that everything was going well in Borris, although that wasn't exactly true.

Arriving in Albania, a country Arthur loved, lifted his spirits even further. There he could indulge his love for hunting, a sport his burgeoning duties had been drawing him away from of late. A party consisting of the small group of sailors and a local guide was organised to leave on horseback the next day in pursuit of wild pigs. Arthur's chair-saddle was unloaded with the rest of his hunting gear. Frances was stricken with worry when she saw that the terrain was steep and treacherous and the horses skinny and unkempt, used to leaping and springing like goats on mountain tracks. These were not like the sturdy mounts to which Arthur was accustomed.

Setting out on a narrow path with the sea hundreds of feet below to the left, Arthur's horse suddenly sprang from one rock to another, missed its footing and both he and Arthur tumbled over the edge. Frances, who was on foot behind them, screamed and covered her eyes, but miraculously a giant cactus plant about ten feet down had broken their fall. Arthur was hanging precariously sideways, still attached to his chair-saddle and the flailing animal, while the guide scrambled down to try to rescue him.

Calmly, Arthur instructed them on how to free the saddle from the horse to disentangle him. His cousin, John Connolly, held him steady while his valet undid the straps and the guide tried to subdue the frightened animal. Frances cried quietly into her handkerchief, comforted by Connolly's wife, thinking of her two boys back on the boat who might be about to lose their father. After twenty minutes of delicate manoeuvring, Arthur was free and they hoisted him back to the pathway, while the unfortunate horse fell to his death. Kneeling beside him, Frances laid her head on his chest:

'I thought I'd lost you for sure this time.'

'I'm fine, Frances. You know I have nine lives, and I think I've only used six so far.' He tried to make light of what had just befallen him.

'Must you do such dangerous things? Think of the children. They would be heartbroken.'

'I'll be fine, Frances. We have all had a fright. Now let's have lunch and rest until tomorrow.'

To Frances' dismay, Arthur insisted on going hunting again the next day, although by a different route, and she was more than relieved when they landed a few days later in Corfu where they could stay in comparative luxury and safety with Hoddy and her children.

When Arthur arrived back in Borris there were the usual celebrations of welcome with bonfires along the street and cheering crowds. Usually this was something he took for granted, but something had changed within him, and he immediately felt a pang of guilt at the sight.

Looking to Frances he said, 'What have I really done to deserve this adulation? The unfortunate people don't know any better. In other parts of the country, landlords are not being treated so well, and their tenants have all turned against them. I hope I can be worthy of their trust, but please don't ever let me take it for granted again.'

They both waved from the carriage and Frances assured him that he was more than worthy, but, in her heart, she feared that all their certainties were coming to an end and the future was a perilous place.

All around the countryside violent and extreme nationalism was rife. Secret military manoeuvres were taking place and the Fenian campaign was a threat to landlords everywhere. Tenants were demanding rights which they considered reasonable but most of the gentry found totally unacceptable. It seemed to Arthur and the aristocracy that tenants wanted to live rent free as well as being supported by their landlords. In reality, the Irish Republican Brotherhood wanted much more. Their goal was to remove British influence from Ireland altogether and there was increasing willingness to use violence to achieve this aim.

In 1862, Arthur was invited to stand in the parliamentary election to represent the County of Carlow in Westminster. Encouraged by his peers, who had witnessed his eloquence and steely determination on many occasions, Arthur was now keen to put himself forward, believing he might be able to make a genuine difference in the land debates and assert some influence there. His late father, as a respected politician, would have wanted his son to follow in his footsteps, and Arthur always aspired to do him proud. But Frances was adamant this should not happen.

'I won't hear of it,' she said when he brought it up at the dinner table.

'But I view it as an honour, dear. Representing the county in Westminster would be the pinnacle of my career, although I'm not sure if a man with no feet can actually follow in his father's footsteps!' The joke was an attempt to lighten the mood.

'I don't find that amusing and I am absolutely against the idea.'

'Pray tell why, Fan?'

'Firstly, you have just recovered from a very trying period in your life and your health must come first. Secondly, your commitments here are great – the railway, the mill, the Poor House, not to mention the estate. Thirdly, I believe you would hate it. And finally, you have three children who dearly love their father and want nothing more than to have you here to show them how to ride and fish in a way your own father didn't. Please say no, Arthur.'

And so, Arthur respectfully declined the offer, if a little ruefully, quoting business commitments as his reason, but not ruling himself out of contention in the future. Instead, he supported the candidacy of Captain Denis Beresford of Fenagh House.

Sailing in *The Eva* was Arthur's main source of relaxation, although he went for shorter trips than heretofore to ensure he could still manage the estate. On one such trip, he arrived back to Borris House from Albania, much to Frances' dismay, accompanied by a very large ape which he named Jack. Arthur emerged from the carriage with his manservant leading the creature by a long chain and the three children danced around with excitement.

'Where did you get him, Pappa?'

'Stand back, stand well back, children.'

'What's his name?'

'Can he sleep in my room?'

Frances stood stock still with an exasperated look, then shaking her head said:

'What now, Arthur?'

'This is Jack, my dear. He's very friendly, although you have to speak very softly to him, and he will live in one of the stables. Isn't he lovely?'

Frances just turned and walked inside, shaking her head.

217

Jet black with a wide, serious face and a tuft of brown hair on his head, Jack turned out to be very gentle with Arthur, but quite vicious with everyone else and had to be kept tied up at all times. Sitting beside Arthur as he held his weekly sessions with tenants under the Oak Tree, he was a curiosity in the neighbourhood and gradually the horses and dogs got used to him. Sadly, Jack met an unfortunate end. As a shooting party was gathering in the stable-yard to venture out for the day, a visiting Italian accidentally released his gun and blew Jack's head off. Arthur flew into a rage and the merriment of the day was ruined. Eventually, once he had calmed down, the expedition went ahead and Arthur instructed the staff to have Jack buried under the Oak Tree, where he had so often kept him company. A small cross was erected to mark the spot and the Italian was never invited again.

In 1864 another son was born to Arthur and Frances, who was subsequently named Charles after Arthur's brother who died tragically in the fire at Borris House. By now, Walter was eight years old, young Arthur was seven and Eva five. The boys had their own ponies and Eva was promised one for her sixth birthday. An attentive father, Arthur spent more time with his children than most of the aristocracy, riding out with them and teaching them to fish in the shallow stream. When on his sailing trips, he wrote to each of them individually, making sure to let them all know he was proud of them and how he looked forward to seeing them when he got home.

Then, in 1866, the opportunity he had been secretly waiting for came up in the form of a vacancy in the county of Wexford for a

Conservative candidate, when the sitting candidate was appointed to the Queen's Bench. Afraid Frances would again object, he wondered how to broach the subject and decided the direct approach would be best.

'I've been asked to stand for Wexford, but I assume you haven't changed your position,' he blurted after dinner one evening.

Frances was silent for a few moments and then, to his surprise, said:

'It's always best not to assume, I find, Arthur,' and smiled.

'So you're more amenable to the idea then, Fan?'

'Yes, I think so. In fact, I feel regretful for having stopped you the last time. Your health is much better now. Perhaps it would be good for you and good for the country.'

'That's wonderful. You know I wouldn't do it if you were really against it,' which wasn't quite true.

'Thank you, Arthur. I think you should stand and if you're successful, I'll be behind you.'

A broad smile lit up Arthur's face and within months he topped the poll, defeating the Liberal, John Pope-Hennessy, by a convincing majority. Now all he had to do was figure out how he could physically execute the logistics of presenting himself on a regular basis at Westminster.

Having seen how influential her husband had become in local politics and the happiness it brought him, Frances had become satisfied that being politically involved might be good for him, with the added bonus of stopping him from undertaking increasingly dangerous sea voyages. Although only 35 and less prone to melancholy, he wasn't as fit to go hunting and riding as before due to increasing chest problems. She hoped a spell in Parliament would be just what he needed.

*

Realising that his political career meant he would be absent from Borris for long periods of time, Arthur began to worry about the possibility of another siege at Borris, similar to the 1798 rebellion his father had often told him about. Violence was widespread throughout the country and he heard rumours that local agitation was being planned. In case a siege might occur, he bought in vast supplies of food. Ammunition was stored and loyal workmen were assigned to guard the cattle and crops against Fenian attack. Although known as a fair landlord, his new status as an MP marked him out even more as part of the establishment and an enemy of Nationalism. He and his agents were now targets to be made examples of, and while Arthur looked forward to his days at Westminster, the protection of his family and property was a constant worry for him.

At night he sometimes rode out looking for secret gatherings in the woods as he had done in his youth. With his cloak flying in the darkness, he was easily recognisable and the rebels had an early-warning system, sending word to each other that Kavanagh was on the prowl. While they agreed not to harm him, they wanted to make an example of him and break the bond of loyalty he and his tenants shared.

'Pay your rent to Kavanagh at your peril,' they warned.

And Arthur found that tenants were coming to him to apologise for non-payment, saying that it was more than their lives were worth to go against the Fenians. One man even came to him under the Oak Tree, saying:

'Please, Mr Kavanagh. I want to pay you the money and I have it here in my pocket. But will you please give me a letter demanding payment that says I haven't paid?'

'You want me to say you haven't paid when you have?'

'Exactly, Mr Kavanagh. You don't know what it's like out there. If they knew I paid you, they'd kill me and maybe my family too. But you've been so good to me over the years.'

'I'll write the letter, Tommy, but where is this all going to end?'

'I don't know, Mr Kavanagh. But, God help us all, it doesn't look good.'

*

On February 6th, 1867, Arthur MacMurrough Kavanagh was formally sworn in as a Member of Parliament in the Palace of Westminster. Arriving by sea and train, he was wheeled into the building and arrived into the chamber to the astonishment of all those present, astride the broad back of William, his valet, who lowered him deftly into his seat and waited at the back of the chamber. Sensing all eyes were on him, Arthur stared straight ahead at the Speaker and breathed deeply.

Lord, grant that I may serve my people as my father before me did, with honour and dignity, he prayed silently and, closing his eyes, he felt the stinging of tears. Even he, who had always believed anything was possible for him from the earliest age, hadn't dared to imagine this day and yet here he was. He wished his mother could see him and feel a modicum of the pride that was swelling in his chest right now. He thought of how he had let her down in the past and of his two brothers, one of whom would probably have been here instead of him.

I will be the best MP the County of Wexford ever had, he vowed silently, before taking his oath to Queen and Country.

Before long Arthur was no longer a curiosity, entering discreetly through a private door beside the Speaker's chair. Only those who rarely attended Parliament stared at his unusual arrival, and once in situ, Arthur didn't attract attention with his cloak covering his metal hooks and the place where his legs should be. Sporting heavy side whiskers and broad shoulders, he looked like any other handsome parliamentarian and rather than rush into speaking, he watched silently and carefully until he was confident he understood the procedures of the house. While other parliamentarians waved their papers or their hats to get attention when they wanted to speak, Arthur couldn't interject, but he had an arrangement with the Speaker that he could let him know in advance if he wanted to speak on a subject.

During his free time in London, Arthur was to be found studying the historical records and privileges associated with British politics. Discovering he was the only limbless member in the House of Commons' history wasn't a surprise and yet it gave him a shiver of pride and responsibility. It was up to him to show that he was as good, if not better, than any other. But it was the discovery of a particular parliamentary privilege that made him break into a broad smile.

'Perfect! Just perfect!' he announced aloud to himself in the silent library.

'Shhh,' the librarian admonished him.

'Is everything alright, Mr Kavanagh?' William, who had been reading the newspaper, came quickly to his side.

'Couldn't be better!' Arthur whispered. 'Now bring me out of here.'

Outside, Arthur explained what had made him exclaim loudly.

'You won't believe it, my good man. I've just discovered that there is an ancient privilege. I'm not sure if anyone has ever used it before but, by golly, I'm going to.'

'What is it, sir?'

'Members of Parliament have the right to sail their vessels up the Thames and moor them within sight of Westminster. I can bring *The Eva* to work!' And he threw his head back with laughter.

'Do you mean it, Mr Kavanagh? That would be very convenient.'

'Convenient? It will be more than convenient. It will stop them all in their tracks! I'll give them something worth looking at and I won't have to endure that dastardly train anymore.'

Within weeks, people on Westminster Bridge stopped and stared over the balustrade, not only to look at the fine yacht moored alongside the embankment, but at the curious spectacle of a cloaked man being carried down a ladder to a rowboat which made its way to Speaker's

Steps. They then witnessed Arthur being placed in his chair and wheeled into the Parliament building.

'Who can that be?' they asked each other.

'It's an MP from Ireland.'

'Has he no legs? What happened to him?'

'He has no arms *or* legs! Born that way.'

'How did he get to be an MP?'

'I don't know. I suppose he can speak!'

'Are you allowed to sail such a huge yacht up the Thames?'

'Looks like you can if you're an MP!'

'Privileged fops!'

Although Arthur couldn't hear these actual conversations, he saw the gawkers leaning over the bridge so, as he entered the house, he usually turned and tipped his hat with his hook to acknowledge that he knew he was the centre of attention. And, although fundamentally a shy man, he enjoyed the idea that he was making a little bit of history.

Chapter 21

The MP

While Arthur served as an MP for County Wexford until 1868, he never actually made a speech during that time. Watching and listening, he learned the peculiarities and traditions of speaking in the House of Commons, determined that when he did speak, he would appear competent. He participated in votes by communicating to the tellers whether it was an "aye" or a "no", while the other members went to the lobby to cast their votes. When Parliament was prorogued in July that year, an election was called, and this time Arthur was returned for County Carlow, where a vacancy had occurred, along with his friend, Henry Bruen. It was in April 1869 that he made his maiden speech to a hushed house who were beginning to wonder would they ever hear the limbless MP's voice.

When the Speaker called 'Mr Kavanagh' it was as if he had called on the chandelier to speak. A hushed silence fell over the busy chamber and all eyes turned to the place, just under the gallery, where Arthur sat, with his speech placed on his silk hat.

'Honourable gentlemen,' he began, and in an oration lasting twelve minutes, he addressed the issue of Mr Mahon's Poor Law (Ireland) Bill to which he was opposed. He argued that there was no comparison between Ireland and England regarding the land question. He insisted that imposing Union Law in Ireland was effectively a method of taxation, which would mean that a good and benevolent landlord would be treated equal to an absentee neglectful one. He said he believed the poor were leaving the land because of starvation and not because of landlords. Quoting an impressive number of facts and figures, he purported that if taxation ceased to be local, politics and favour would influence the fair distribution of charity. 'What's everybody's business, is nobody's business,' he concluded.

While it was uncustomary to heckle a member during their maiden speech, the silence followed by thunderous applause spoke more of Arthur's eloquence and the admiration in which he was held. He even received a short note from the Speaker, J.E. Denison, which said:

I offer you my compliments on the excellent manner and tone of your speech which, as you will see, has made a very favourable impression on the House.

When in London, Arthur lived and entertained on his yacht. Many fashionable parties were held there. His sister, Hoddy, and her husband were regular attendees, having moved to London from Corfu. The Bruens and his cousins, the Connollys, visited as did other members of the Irish aristocracy who were in the city from time to time. Partial to fine wine, Arthur treated his guests to the finest meat and poultry, served by his manservant and a chef who travelled with him. Good-natured late-night revelry was commonplace on *The Eva* while Londoners gazed from the bridge in surprise and envy.

At home in Borris in 1869, another healthy baby boy was born to Arthur and Frances, their fifth child, who was named Osborne. Walter, now twelve years old and at Eton, was allowed to travel on *The Eva* with Arthur at the start of term. The thrill of manning the yacht with his father took away the sense of homesickness he felt as he said goodbye to his mother and siblings in Borris and Arthur promised that he could sometimes come to visit him when the House was in session. Young Arthur was almost eleven and looking forward to joining Walter at Eton the following year, while Eva was ten and Charles five.

During subsequent speeches on Poor Law in Ireland, Arthur was not treated so kindly by his peers in the Commons. On several occasions he was shouted down and accused of looking after his own interests, rather than seeking justice for tenants. Stung by this criticism, he was nonetheless adamant that the bill was detrimental to the situation that prevailed in Ireland. Cautiously, he supported the Land Bill introduced by Gladstone in 1870 which put forward the idea of dual ownership and ensured tenants were compensated for improvements to their properties, although most of his Conservative colleagues were against it. However, Arthur was staunchly opposed to the notion of sub-letting.

'Sub-letting only facilitates middle-men, and we've all seen what they do. They charge ridiculous rent for hovels with mud floors and roofs that can barely hold out the elements. It should not be allowed under any circumstances.'

There were a few guffaws when he explained how he cared for his tenants and that he believed happy tenants would be loyal and an asset to any landlord.

'Happy tenants! What are they?' one MP near him shouted.

'Never met one!' another said.

227

Gladstone's Act made little impact in Ireland, as Arthur had predicted, the only advantage to some tenants being that they were compensated for improvements they had made to a property if they decided to leave it. Although he had opposed Gladstone's 1869 Act to disestablish the church in Ireland, separating the Church of Ireland from the Church of England, Arthur willingly implemented it. Under the terms of the Act, the Church of Ireland was no longer allowed to collect tithes from the people and some churches were confiscated to compensate clergymen and schoolmasters who had lost their positions. Arthur's solution was to allow the private chapel at Borris House to become the parish church, with the clergyman being given £100 a year to act as chaplain to the family.

'My world is crumbling,' he confided to colleagues in the smoking room at the Commons, 'and I don't know where it's going to end.'

'It's not all that bad, my good fellow,' an English MP chimed in. 'These are small changes in the grand scheme of things.'

'With respect, things are very different in Ireland. The Fenians will not stop when they see a chink in the armour. Systems that have worked for centuries are being thrown out and there's nothing to replace them, except disorder and violence. I fear for my future and those of my class.'

'Have a little faith in humanity, my good fellow. The recent concessions may well appease the lower orders. I think your fears are misplaced!'

'With respect, you don't know the Irish like I do. There are political murders every day. Innocent people are being terrorised and killed for the cause and this is being encouraged by the Catholic clergy. They say they don't support violence, but they are riling the people up. The world of my ancestors is falling apart and having "faith in humanity" is not going to save it.'

*

In Borris, a meeting organised by the local clergy was taking place expressing outrage at the "Borris Evictions." The tenants who had been thrown out of their homes were not tenants of Arthur's, but another local landlord. However, the anti-landlord mood was intense and uncomfortably close to home for Arthur.

'We can't allow this to continue,' Father Carey shouted to the mob in the churchyard. 'Innocent people being put out of their houses with nowhere to go. The latest eviction of an elderly blind man is just the last straw. Poor Byrne gave his life to his landlord, Mr Little of Castlecomer, and what did he get in return?'

'Eviction!' they shouted back.

'In Christian justice, I don't know how any man can defend it. Listen here, now. Every one of you needs to support the Land League. Tenants have rights and we need to demand them.'

Another huge cheer.

'As our advocate, John Mitchel, who was so cruelly deported for speaking the truth said, "The life of one peasant is as precious as the life of one nobleman or gentleman." Stand up for yourselves and believe that fairness will prevail!'

Another roar from the crowd.

'Sadly,' he continued, 'all landlords are not like our good friend, Mr Kavanagh.' He pointed up the hill to the Big House. 'Remember, this meeting is nothing to do with him. He's been fair and generous to the people of Borris.'

Mutters rippled thought the crowd.

'Enough of that! I won't have a bad word said about Mr Kavanagh. If every landlord was as fair as he, we wouldn't be in this mess. Stand up for what's right. Stick together. We are stronger than you think if we stick together!'

Several speakers addressed the assembly and the mood turned so angry that Father Carey walked back into his house shaking his head. One quoted John Mitchel again:

'John Mitchel said another thing, Father. He said: "If the landlord evicts you, shoot him like a mad dog, and if the landlord hides in London, shoot the agent!" '

'No violence!' Father Carey shouted from his front door and then closed it firmly behind him.

In the crowd there were several of Arthur's tenants, and they talked about what they had heard as they walked back up the long main street.

'No landlord is going to be safe, you know. Not even Mr Kavanagh.'

'I know. I wonder should we warn him? He was very good to my family.'

'It's not our business to be warning him, and it's more than your life is worth. Remember that and keep your mouth shut.'

Sitting on a stool outside her front door, Molly Doyle and her friends watched the crowd walking away from the chapel.

'Oh God, I'm sort of scared the way they're all shouting,' Mary Quigley said.

'Nothing to be scared about, you amadán! For the first time in our lives we're going to have the power. Those behind that big wall are going to get the shock of their lives.'

'What do you think is going to happen?' Kitty asked.

'I'll tell you what's going to happen. People like us are not going to be fools for the like of them anymore. We're going to get paid for what we do, and live our lives out in our own houses when our service is over. It's the least they can do for us.'

'But they're talking about violence and burning. Do you think it'll come to that?'

'Whatever it takes.' Molly cackled. 'It might take a year and it might take fifty years, but when the tide turns, there's no holding it back. And I'm not one bit sorry for them.'

*

News of violence and agitation in Borris did not pass Arthur by. Becoming increasingly angry, he regularly spoke in Parliament about the need for protection for landlords and that "peace preservation" measures should include harsh punishments for those who threatened or imposed violence. In the smoking room, he vented his frustration to his peers:

'When is law and order going to be asserted in Ireland? The Fenians are literally getting away with murder and destruction. I'm no Orange supporter, but how is it fair or just that Orange protests are banned and perpetrators punished and yet Irish thugs and rebels get off Scot-free?'

'My good man, don't you think they may have a point?' a Welsh MP ventured. 'It is *their* country after all and they have watched their neighbours starve and emigrate while the aristocracy feasted.'

'I certainly do not think they have a point! I am offended by your insinuation! Firstly, I am not of the aristocracy. I come from a family which can trace its roots back to the High Kings of Ireland. Secondly, as landlords, the Kavanaghs have always sought to be fair to their tenants and I personally have improved many holdings since taking up my role as landlord.'

'Yes, my good man. But benevolence is not equality, is it? And furthermore, you are not representative of the majority of landlords in Ireland, who are indeed of the aristocracy, and who stand by while tenants starve and evict them mercilessly.'

'I accept that, and I believe they should be compelled to look after those whose families have served them over the years. But giving the Irish peasantry more and more rights and entertaining talk of an Irish government is communistic. It upsets the natural order of things and it simply won't work. They'll fight among themselves like cats and dogs.'

'Harsh words, old fellow. I'm surprised you have such a poor view of your fellow countrymen. Don't you see any sense of moral justice in what the Irish are seeking – to have a say in their own affairs?'

'No, I don't and I'll thank you not to lecture me on morality. I'll take my leave of you now. I don't believe we'll have a meeting of minds today.' And he summoned his manservant to take him back to his yacht.

*

In May 1876, just before the Whitsun parliamentary recess, Arthur was summoned from the chamber to receive some shocking news. Hoddy, who had been ill for a short period of time, had died suddenly at her London residence. In tears Arthur was carried to the street where a hackney was hailed to bring him to pay his respects to his sister and sympathise with her husband and children.

Requesting to be seated beside her on the bed, Arthur asked to be left alone with Hoddy. Pale and thin, the dark circles under her eyes made her look older than her years and the stark whiteness of the pillow stole any remnants of colour from her face. Arthur asked his manservant to remove one of his hooks before he left the room, so he could touch her face.

When everyone had gone he released a series of loud sobs. 'Dearest Hoddy, you have been such a wonderful sister to me. I'm going to miss you so much.' And he rested his head beside her on the pillow, crying quietly.

'Has anyone told Mother?' Arthur asked when Hoddy's husband, William, came back into the room.

'Yes, a telegram was sent early this morning.'

This news caused Arthur to burst into tears again.

'Poor Mother. She has suffered enough already. She doesn't deserve to lose another of her children. And she loved Hoddy so dearly.'

'I know that.' Her husband's eyes were full of tears. 'And Hoddy thought so much of her.'

'Now I'm the only one left and I've always been a…' his voice broke, 'disappointment to her.' Arthur sobbed again.

Sitting on the other side of the bed, William took Hoddy's hand and waited for Arthur to gather himself.

'Oh, I'm sorry, William. I'm being really selfish. You're the one who has suffered the greatest loss here. I have no right to self-pity.'

'That's quite alright, Arthur.' His voice was husky. 'I don't know how I'm going to live without Hoddy.'

Back at Borris, arrangements were already being made to receive Hoddy's remains. Frances, knowing how much Arthur confided in Hoddy and how close they had become again over the last few years in London, had a heavy heart. Arthur would be broken by this, on top of all the other things that were going against him lately. Now the mother of seven children, the latest two, Agnes and May having been born in 1870 and 1872, her life was busy with domestic affairs. But on his visits home lately, Arthur spent a lot of time in his bedroom and seemed very low in spirits. This would surely be the last straw....

Walter and young Arthur accompanied the funeral party from London on *The Eva*. Three sombre black carriages arrived in Borris just as darkness fell and people lined the street, bowing their heads and making the sign of the cross in respect. Looking out the window, Arthur felt a mixture of gratitude and contempt. *Do they really hold us in high esteem or is this just a front? Is it something they do for grace and favour? Is anyone out there really sorry that Hoddy is dead?*

At the front door of Borris House, Lady Harriet stood stoically, holding a lace handkerchief in one hand. Dressed from head to toe in black, she looked every day of her seventy-seven years, with her silver hair scraped back in a bun and her pale, pinched face. Behind her stood Frances with Eva, Charles and Osborne by her side. Six servants stood solemnly, waiting to help the party as they arrived.

Hoddy's two teenage daughters stepped from the carriage first and went to embrace their grandmother, sobbing quietly, followed by Arthur who, without waiting for his chair, made his way over to his mother. Tears streamed down his face as he approached her.

'I'm so sorry, Mamma.'

With no sign of affection, Harriet dabbed her eye saying, 'Enough, Arthur! We must be strong.'

Stepping forward, Frances and the children enveloped him in a hug, before the undertaker indicated that the coffin was about to be removed, and the entire party stood to attention as Hoddy's husband, William, Arthur's sons Walter and young Arthur and his cousin, John Connolly, carried the coffin slowly and sedately through the front door and laid it on the round table in the hallway. Lady Harriet watched as the lid was removed and couldn't suppress a gasp as she saw her only daughter, lifeless at only forty-six years old. Holding onto the mahogany table for support, she kissed her finger and touched Hoddy's cheek with it, and without speaking, walked silently to the music room.

That evening, when the children had left the table and the guests were being shown to their rooms, Frances asked Arthur how he was. For a full minute he gave no reply, then indicating the portraits on the wall he said:

'Frances, it's all falling apart. Look at my ancestors. They thought our precious world would go on forever. I know you don't believe in the idea of a curse, but it's hard to imagine that this family is not cursed at the moment. And now Hoddy, the one who united Mother and I and made me feel like I belonged, even *she* is gone.' He started to cry again.

'But you have me, and you have the children.'

'I know that, and I love you all dearly, but I feel like I'm the cause of all the trouble in this family. I *am* the curse.'

'That's quite enough, Arthur. You have brought this family and this village back from the doldrums. You have been true to your calling and been the fairest, kindest landlord you could be. If your mother is not impressed, then she should be ashamed of herself. I am proud of you. The children are proud of you, and I know for sure that Hoddy was proud of you. If anything, you have defied the curse.'

Walking behind his wheelchair, she put her hands on his shoulders and kissing the side of his face, waited till the crying had stopped.

'Now, Arthur Kavanagh, we must do your sister proud by burying her with dignity, and then together we'll face whatever the future holds for us.'

Chapter 22

Ghosts of the Past

Throughout the next day, old friends and relations called to pay their respects to Hoddy and to sympathise with the family. In the morning, the coffin was moved to the small family chapel adjacent to the house and was flanked by Hoddy's children and husband throughout the day. Arthur and Lady Harriet spent most of the day in the drawing room, having tea with visitors whom they hadn't seen for years and listening to stories of times past in Borris House. Frances and the younger children rode out with the Connollys until late afternoon when prayers were recited.

The Bruens of Oak Park called, as did Lady Harriet's Le Poer Trench relations. There were representatives of the Butler family in Kilkenny and the Wandesfordes from Castlecomer. Some of Hoddy's friends from boarding school arrived as did landowners from Wexford and Ballyragget. Doctor Boxwell and his wife came in the afternoon and stayed for prayers in the evening and plans were finalised with the clergyman for a funeral in the morning.

After prayers and just before the evening meal, a carriage pulled up at the front door and a middle-aged lady emerged with a stylish black hat tied underneath with a chiffon bow and a long black flared coat. The butler asked her name as he showed her into the music room.

'Mrs Maud Butterly,' she answered.

When he announced the lady's arrival to Lady Harriet, she said she didn't know anyone by that name and since she was dressing for dinner, perhaps Arthur would deal with her.

Tutting at being disturbed, Arthur stepped into the hall and stopped dead.

'Maud?' he found himself whispering.

'Yes, Arthur. I'm so sorry for your loss.'

Arthur found himself dumbstruck for a few moments, before indicating the drawing room.

'Come in, come in, please.'

'I was so sad to hear about poor Hoddy. Such a shock. How have you been?' Maud sat beside the large marble fireplace, putting her handbag beside her on the brocade seat and removing her hat.

'This is a surprise.' Arthur was just catching his breath, as he settled his wheelchair in front of the window. 'It's been so long.'

'Yes, indeed. And terrible to meet again under such circumstances. Hoddy was such a lady and a very good friend.' Maud exuded confidence and a composure that was absent in her youth.

'Yes. It's been a terrible shock. You said your name is Butterly. You're married then?'

'Oh yes. A long time ago. Ancient history now,' and she laughed nervously.

'Lucky fellow.' Arthur smiled, and they both looked at the floor.

'Well, you did abandon me, Arthur, if I remember correctly.'

'And you didn't reply to my letters, if I remember correctly,' Arthur retorted.

'What letters? If I had received a letter I would certainly have replied. Where did you send them?'

'I sent them to Hoddy to give to you. Did she not pass them on?'

'And I gave her some to send to you!' She covered her mouth as the realisation set in.

At that moment, Lady Harriet came through the door from the hallway dressed for dinner.

'Good evening, Lady Harriet.' Maud stood to greet her. 'I'm so sorry for your loss.'

Lady Harriet looked from Maud to Arthur and he realised she didn't recognise the lady whose hand she was shaking.

'You remember Maud, Mother... Maud Considine.'

Lady Harriet visibly froze and then recovered herself. 'Of course I do. I didn't recognise your *married* name when I heard it. It's very good of you to come.'

The cold emphasis on the word *married* reminded Maud of the day she had left the house in tears so many years before, having been told by Harriet that Arthur was gone away indefinitely.

'Yes, Lady Harriet, happily *married* for many years now.' And she smiled stiffly.

'I believe dinner is served so I'll take my leave of you.' Harriet backed towards the door. 'Thank you again for calling. You won't be long Arthur, will you?'

'I won't be dining this evening, Mother.'

Harriet stopped at the door and stared at Arthur, but he didn't meet her gaze, and she left, closing the door firmly behind her.

Arthur looked at Maud and she could see that he was vexed.

'Am I to understand that you never received any of my letters, Maud?'

'Not one. I presumed you had... well... abandoned me.'

Wheeling his chair over and back with his hooks in an agitated manner, he said, 'I'm so sorry, Maud. I know it's a very long time ago, but somebody did this to us and it pains me greatly to think that it may have been my dear sister, Hoddy. Failing that, it was my mother, and both of those possibilities are devastating to me.'

'Yes, I'm beginning to think I shouldn't have called. The last thing I want to do is cause trouble in the family at a time like this. But, you know Arthur, I suffered greatly.'

'What do you mean?'

'They sent me away to my aunt in Switzerland and she arranged for the baby to be adopted in England. I have no idea where and I think about that child every single day.'

'A baby? There was a baby?' His face looked stricken.

'Yes. I told you that in one... but of course you didn't receive them.'

'Oh Maud. I am so sorry and angry and... so confused. Please tell me you've had more children.'

'I have. Three sons and a daughter. But nothing will ever make me forget my first. Not ever.'

'You know I have seven children,' Arthur said. 'All perfect and each one has brought such joy to me. I've been lucky enough to have a very good wife and family. But, if only I'd known. Things could have been so different.'

At that, one of Arthur's daughters opened the door.

'Mamma asked if you might come to the table, Papa. She says you really must eat.'

'Thank you, dear. Tell her I'll be there in a moment.'

As the door closed, he said: 'Could you wait here for a moment, Maud? I want to get something.' He wheeled himself over to the door, opened it with his hook and disappeared down the hall.

A few minutes later Arthur arrived back with a small box.

'This is something I bought for you when I was in India. Look at your initials engraved on the front.' Grasped in one of his hooks, he held out a silver cigarette case with M.C. in cursive writing on the lid. 'I never lost hope that we might be together again until they told me you were engaged to someone else. Please take it now. It was always for you.'

'I can't take it, Arthur. It wouldn't be right.'

'Please. It's the only small gesture I can make and it will bring me happiness to know you have it at last.' He wheeled closer, still holding out the box.

'Well, thank you then, and I will take it.' There were tears in her eyes as she placed it in her bag. 'And I never forgot you, Arthur… I really must go now.' Standing, she began to rearrange her hat.

'I'll ask the butler to see you out.' He rang the bell by the fireplace. 'And Maud, before you go. Was it a boy or girl?'

'It was a perfect baby girl. Absolutely perfect. And she'd be twenty-six now, wherever she is.'

'Have you any idea where?'

'None. My aunt organised the adoption privately through a contact in London and she died some years ago. There are no records.'

Slowly the door opened and Arthur, clearing his throat, asked the butler to show Mrs Butterly to the door.

'Goodbye, Arthur. I wish you nothing but happiness.'

'And I you, Maud. Safe journey home.'

As the door closed behind her, he realised he hadn't thought to ask her where "home" was.

*

Hoddy's funeral was sombre and solemn. As was customary for funerals of members of the Kavanagh family, the village people lined the street as the cortege left Borris House and wound its way downhill, past the Catholic Church where a crowd was gathered with heads bowed, the men holding their caps to their chests. The black carriages then made their way through open countryside with the Blackstairs mountains looming in the distance, until they reached the ancient burial ground at St Mullins where so many of the MacMurrough Kavanaghs had been lain to rest before.

Arthur barely spoke at all on the journey, which didn't trouble the silent Harriet much, but Frances was very concerned.

'Are you alright, Arthur? You're very quiet.'

Lady Harriet tutted and looked out the window, her clasped mouth a straight line.

Arthur nodded but didn't speak.

'Hoddy wouldn't want this,' Frances whispered. 'You know she always wanted you to be happy.'

'Did she, indeed?'

Frances and Harriet both stared at him wide-eyed at this remark.

'Whatever do you mean, Arthur?' Harriet snapped.

'Oh nothing, Mother, nothing. There's no point in discussing it.'

Frances studied Arthur's face closely, making a mental note to ask him about it later, but now the old abbey was in view and it was time to bury Hoddy.

*

In the evening, after all the relatives had dined, Lady Harriet went to her room, while the other visitors took a walk on the estate.

'Let's go to the drawing room, Arthur,' Frances said, instructing the children they shouldn't disturb them for at least an hour. 'Eva, please look after Agnes and May.'

Eva groaned, but did as she was asked and the boys went to play billiards.

244

In the drawing room, Frances sat in the same chair that had recently held Maud, while Arthur wheeled his chair close to the fireplace.

'What is it, Arthur? Why are you so melancholy.'

'Must you really ask me that when my only sister is dead, Frances? Really?'

'I sense there's more to it than that. What did you mean when you said to your mother "there's no point discussing it"? What is the "it" to which you referred?'

'Oh Frances, there have been so many complications with my mother over the years, they really are too tiresome to go into now.'

'There's something you're not prepared to tell me then?'

'It's of no interest and no consequence to you. I may discuss it some day with my mother, but probably not. Meanwhile I'd like you to trust that there is nothing you need to worry about.'

Frances scowled and lifted up a piece of lace she was working on. After a few minutes, Arthur said:

'If you're going to ignore me, I may as well leave.' Dropping the sewing onto her lap, Frances stared hard at Arthur.

'Arthur Kavanagh, I have managed your household, humoured your mother and put up with your absences for twenty years. I've done my best to be cheerful and positive when the future has looked very bleak indeed. Now the least you can do is return the favour and put whatever is bothering you behind you or else allow me to help you to deal with it.'

'There is nothing to deal with,' Arthur said slowly.

'Very well, Arthur. Then put it behind you and focus on your family and your estate. But may I ask you one question and will you answer truthfully?'

'I will.'

'Who was the lady with the black hat?'

Arthur swallowed hard. 'The lady with the black hat was Maud Considine. She was someone I spent time with when I was young. She was a good friend of Hoddy's and she came to pay her respects.'

'Then why did your mother seem so agitated by her presence and why have you barely uttered a word since?'

'That would be two further questions, Frances. I only promised to answer one. But I'll indulge you. Mother didn't like her, and I liked her very much.'

'And do you still *like* her very much?'

'A fourth question!'

'Oh, do stop being so tiresome, Arthur. Do you like her or not?'

'Frances, I love you and have loved you for many, many years. I cannot imagine life without you. You and the children are everything to me. And if that isn't enough for you, I'm afraid I don't know what is.'

'Which doesn't answer my question.' Frances shook her head.

'I think it does. Now can we talk about something else, please? What did you think of how the vicar handled the ceremony?'

And as far as Arthur was concerned, the matter was closed.

*

Back in the House of Commons, 1876, Arthur was increasingly disillusioned. He was frustrated by talk of Home Rule for Ireland and spoke against it at every opportunity. Parnell's obstructionism was viewed as an embarrassment by him, and his peers began to view him as intransigent in his views on the Irish situation. When summer recess came, he was relieved to escape to the serenity of *The Eva*, which on this occasion he sailed through the Caledonian Canal to Orkney and Shetland. The tranquillity of the still waters of the Scottish lochs soothed him and gave him time to think and the questions clouding his mind were relentless.

Should I tell Frances about the baby? Would that be the moral thing to do? But would it change things? Would it ruin the near perfection of our lives together? Why tell her about something she can't do anything about? And what about Mother? Should I tackle her about the letters? Is there anything to be gained from it? Would it just be revenge or is it the least I can do to acknowledge the daughter I didn't know I had?

Writing to Frances, he told her about the scenery and the stark beauty of the mountains reminding him of Borris:

The dark, broody mountains in the distance are reminiscent of Mount Leinster and make me feel quite at home. Speaking of broody, I'm sorry my mood has been so low of late. I promise things will be better when I return in a few weeks.

Enquiring about the children, he mentioned each by name and sent a short message to them. He told her how much she meant to him and that he was looking forward to returning to see her.

I don't deserve you, Frances, but I'm very glad you have put up with me for so long and I look forward to many more happy days in your company. I'm so sorry I vexed you, and I know now that what you said is true. You have done so much for me over the years and humouring my mother can't have been easy! Please know that you are the centre of my life now and always. With all my love, Arthur.

Chapter 23

Cometh the Hour

In January 1877 Walter Kavanagh came of age. Since Arthur was attending Parliament in London, the celebrations were postponed until the October recess. Preparations being made for weeks in advance with a temporary roof being built over the courtyard, illuminated by large gas chandeliers. Garlands and decorations were strewn along the walls and diagonally across the interior and new glasses arrived which had been specially ordered from Venice.

Arthur was looking forward to presenting his son to the public as his successor and heir. Walter, a tall steady young man with an earnest demeanour, lacked his father's adventurous spirit, but shared his work ethic and conservative values. He would be worthy of the title "The MacMurrough" when Arthur died and, in the meantime, there was so much Arthur wanted to show and teach to him in a way his own father had not been able to do for him. In truth, he was probably more like Frances with his calm personality, but the Kavanagh blood ran through his veins, and it felt good to be passing the baton on to the next generation.

Gentry families with long associations with the Kavanaghs were invited to share in the occasion. The Bruens, Ormondes, Connollys, Butlers, Alexanders, Beresfords and many more, along with tenants from the three counties in which the Kavanaghs held estates – Carlow, Kilkenny and Wexford. One notable absence was Lady Harriet, who had become suddenly ill days before and was recuperating at her home in Ballyragget. Candles and flowers adorned the long trestle tables, and a fine meal of beef, roast potatoes and local vegetables was served, with ale and wine flowing freely. When the meal ended, Arthur, speaking from his wheelchair, addressed the crowd:

'Esteemed friends, clergymen, neighbours, it brings me great pleasure this evening to present my son, Walter, to you on the occasion of his reaching the age of majority.'

Loud applause interrupted him.

'Hold your applause, friends, or we will be here until morning.'

A burst of laughter.

'I'll begin again. I have great pleasure in presenting my son, Walter, to you. Many of you know him already from various walks of life and know that every word I say about him here this evening is true. Nobody knows a son like his father, and I can assure you that the future of this family is in safe hands with this fine young man.'

More applause.

'In presenting Walter to you, I have to compliment my good wife, Frances. It is twenty years since I first presented her here to you and since then you have grown to know and respect her. She has not only been a model parent to our seven children, but also has involved herself in the rebuilding of this wonderful community in ways I know you all appreciate.'

More applause.

'I know that, having reached the age of majority with Kavanagh blood in his veins, and the guidance of such an exemplary mother, Walter Kavanagh will be a man of duty and integrity, someone you can rely on to look after your interests above all else and to uphold the traditions and values of our noble family.'

Another burst of applause.

'So, without further ado, may I present to you, Mr Walter Kavanagh.'

Dressed in a formal dinner suit, Walter's response was brief and lacked the eloquence of his father, but the tone was sincere. Thanking the assembled crowd for their presence and good wishes, he acknowledged his allegiance to them and to his noble family traditions.

'I pledge to follow my father's excellent example and I look forward to living among you and working with you for the good of our estate, our village and our country.'

Polite applause and a few calls of 'Long life to the Kavanaghs,' followed, before Father Carey, the local Parish Priest got up to speak.

Arthur, knowing that this very clergyman had been responsible for rabble rousing, watched nervously, but he needn't have worried. Clearing his throat, Father Carey set out his stall immediately by saying that this was an evening where politics should be left aside. Praising not only Arthur, but specifically Frances for their service to the community, he acknowledged how both had cared for the poor in the area – Frances, by her generosity and commitment to the lace-making industry while Arthur was a landlord among landlords, who was known for fairness and a lack of bigotry.

'Indeed, if Mister Kavanagh was prone to bigotry, I would not be here among you tonight.'

He finished by wishing Walter well as he took his place as an adult in society and with a gentle allusion to the challenges that lay ahead, assured him that Catholics wanted equality but not to harm or subsume the place of this fine and noble family.

'Long life and happiness to Walter and God's blessing on the entire Kavanagh family.'

After the speeches, the invited guests made their way to the great hall where a brass band was waiting to entertain them with dance music for the evening while the tenants, having eaten and drunk their fill, made their way home.

Molly Doyle, now in her mid-seventies, walked slowly alongside her friend Kitty.

'Do you remember all that talk about the curse?' Kitty asked.

'Of course I do. And wasn't it true! Sure that family had nothing but bad luck until the cripple took over.'

'Do you think the bad luck is over now, then, Molly?'

'Don't be ridiculous, girl. Sure, bad luck is never over, but didn't he have seven fine strong children.'

'At least!' Kitty answered and the two of them cackled.

'But, mark my words, the same bad luck is coming to them that's coming to all people of their sort. They can dance tonight in their finery, but not for long more.'

'I suppose you're right, Molly. Aren't we the lucky ones if the truth be told!'

*

Two days later, when all the visitors had left, Arthur set off early for Ballyragget with a manservant to see for himself what his mother's state of health was. The maid showed the two men into the drawing room where Harriet was reclining on a chaise longue.

'That will be all for the moment.' Arthur dismissed the servant once he had carried him into the room and deposited him in an armchair. 'Come back for me in one hour.'

'Do I get an entire hour of your time?' Lady Harriet said sarcastically.

'Well, I was about to enquire after your health, but judging by that remark, I think you're not too bad.'

'How did Walter's celebrations go?'

'They went very well indeed, Mother, although you were missed.'

'Yes, I deeply regret being unable to attend, although these occasions bring back unhappy memories for me.'

'So how *is* your health, Mother?'

'I'm seventy-eight years old, Arthur, and feeling every minute of it. Frank Boxwell was here, although you may have heard he's retired from his practice now.'

'Yes, I heard that.'

'He assures me he'll continue to look after me, which relieves me greatly.'

'Indeed!'

'He's given me something for my cough, but it's keeping me awake at night and I really don't feel up to travelling.'

'There's something I want to talk to you about, Mother. I've been waiting to see you alone for some time.'

'Arthur, Arthur, it's not a good time. I'm not well.'

'Something tells me, Mother, that there will never be a good time. So, I'm going to pose a question to you. Should you choose not to answer today, that's fine, but I will expect an answer soon. Why did you not pass on Maud Considine's letters to me or mine to her?'

Lady Harriet sat up.

'Did that woman come around to cause trouble in our family after all these years and in the guise of sympathising on the death of my only daughter?'

'Why she came around is irrelevant. I want to know the answer.'

'I'm sorry, Arthur.' She coughed.' I have no idea what you're talking about.'

'Really, Mother? I must have sent fifteen letters and she informed me she sent quite a few, but you didn't see any of them?'

'Were they addressed to me?'

'No, Mother. They were addressed to Hoddy, but she is not here so I can't ask her.'

'As I said, I have no idea what you're talking about.'

Harriet started to cough dramatically and rang the bell beside her. 'I really must get my medication now,' she spluttered.

'Of course you must,' Arthur said drily.

As the maid came in, Harriet coughed loudly again.

'Nellie, could you fetch my cough bottle and the tablets Doctor Boxwell left for me please?'

'Certainly, my Lady.'

'And will you tell my man that I'm ready to go now,' Arthur interjected.

'You're leaving already?' Harriet raised an eyebrow.

'Yes, Mother. Goodbye. Think about what I've said and perhaps you might recall what seems to have slipped to the recesses of your mind. I wish you a speedy recovery.'

And hopping onto his manservant's back, he left for Borris, wondering had it all been Hoddy's idea, although that thought made his stomach churn.

*

Walter Kavanagh, having completed his secondary education at Eton, and attending Christchurch College in London, spent the next couple of years learning the intricacies of estate management while his father attended Parliament. His younger brother, Charles, was at Harrow while young Arthur was at boarding school in Dartmouth. Arthur was keen that all his sons would take their place in society, but he feared for Walter, knowing the weight of responsibility that would fall on him. On a daily basis, Commons discussed the Irish question and while Arthur's political career was highly successful, he could see that ultimately landlordism in Ireland was becoming impossible and his objections were falling on deaf ears.

In 1880, Arthur was elected Lord Lieutenant of Carlow, arguably the highest rank one could possibly hold in the county, making him the Monarch's personal representative, with the right to call able-bodied local men to arms if necessary. While his father would have been honoured that this title was bestowed on him, and indeed Arthur was quietly proud, he knew that, to the local militia, it aligned him firmly with the Queen and the establishment and might not bode well for him in the upcoming election.

The election campaign of 1880 was marked by violence and a growing movement to end the era of landlordism. The Home Rule candidates were Donald McFarlane and E. Dwyer Gray, the Lord Mayor of Dublin. Both addressed a meeting in Borris and while they didn't condemn Arthur directly, they were vociferous in their condemnation of the Feudal system which had "had its day" and would now make way for a new dawn. A booklet, designed by a local curate, was distributed entitled *The Political Services of Kavanagh and Bruen and what they have done for Carlow* which, when opened, revealed only blank pages. Arthur was being made a laughing stock in his own backyard.

On the day of the ballot, Arthur travelled to Kilkenny to cast his vote for Lord Butler. He felt trepidation about his own situation, knowing that if he regained his seat, it would be close as the Home Rule candidates had gained momentum. On the return journey, in the darkness of the evening, he could see bonfires in the distant hills as he had on many of his victorious occasions before. Relieved, he turned to Frances who was sitting beside him in the carriage, and said:

'By golly, I must have done it! I can't wait to see the margin. I feel sure it was very tight.'

But, on reaching the village, he saw that the faces of the villagers who lined the streets with torches, were actually jeering and booing and outside the church, a limbless effigy was being burned. Frances tried to distract him from seeing the glee on the faces lit up by the bonfire, but he sat open-mouthed, staring until the gates of Borris House were before them and the square mansion loomed like a monument to the past.

In the hallway, Walter waited for them.

'I'm so sorry, Father. I don't know what to say.'

'I know, Walter. We can talk about it another day, but right now I'm going to my room.' Turning at the bottom of the stairs he asked: 'Walter, was it close?' But Walter just shook his head. It had been a landslide for the Home Rulers.

The feeling of betrayal was far worse than the reality of losing his seat. During the election campaign, many locals had come to him secretly, assuring him that they would vote for him. People who had so recently been hosted by him and cheered for his son at his coming of age, and who had lamented the loss of Hoddy, were Judas figures, now dancing in the streets on his downfall. The portraits on the stairs seemed to jeer at him as the one Kavanagh who had let the family down, stabbed in the back by his own people.

Having asked the kitchen staff to prepare a tray, Frances brought it to Arthur, but he refused to eat.

'Frances, I really need to be alone. I'm sorry, but this is a sharp blow. I know it's not completely unexpected, but I'm not ready to talk about it yet.'

'Very well, Arthur, but remember that in defeat or victory your family stands with you and we will overcome this setback.'

'I know that, but it doesn't comfort me right now. I'm sorry.'

It was three days before Arthur came downstairs and joined the family again and when he did, he was solemn and crestfallen. In the afternoon, Frances asked him if she might push his chair out to the garden so they could talk. Outside, she sat on a garden bench and asked Arthur how he was feeling.

'It's time to talk, Arthur. You can't keep it all to yourself. This is affecting all of us.'

'I know and I'm sorry for being selfish. I've had a good run in the Commons and I look forward to spending more time on *The Eva*. But you know what I find so difficult to come to terms with?'

'What's that?'

'It's the betrayal. They looked me in the eye and told me they would vote for me as they always did. My own people! The ones I've sat under the tree for hours listening to and trying to solve their problems.

The idea of having to look at them and live among them for the rest of my days makes me ill.'

'I know. I feel the same. But you know, Arthur, it's not personal. The same thing is happening all over the country. Landlords are targets now. It's not because of anything you've done.'

'But that's precisely it. I haven't been like the other landlords. I've worked so hard to be different and caring and look where it got me!'

'I wish there were something I could do to help. But I must say, I do look forward to spending more time with you. You have been away a lot and I haven't had much chance to visit London because you were always so busy. Perhaps we could spend more time in the townhouse there and you could show me around. We could go to shows and attend some of the parties you never have time for.'

'My dear positive Frances. Always coming up with happy outcomes.' He smiled for the first time in days.

'There is life after politics, Arthur.' And she embraced him.

'You can help me with one thing, Frances. I really don't want to poison Walter's mind against the people he will, hopefully, serve and that's one of the reasons I have stayed out of the way for the last few days. Can you help me to give him hope, Frances? You're naturally inclined to see the future in a more positive way than I. Help me not to ruin it for him.'

'Of course, I will. Walter will find his own way forward and what will be will be, but he still has so much to learn from you. This hour will pass, and the Lord has looked after us this far. He won't let us down now.'

Slowly Arthur emerged from under the cloud of bitter disappointment. While courteous to his tenants, his enthusiasm for dealing with their concerns was replaced by minimal and strictly necessary exchanges. He spent time riding out with Walter and sharing his ideas with him of how the estate might be developed and where the best places to hunt were, while avoiding the subject of his election defeat.

When a letter arrived from Lady Harriet, whose health had improved slightly, Arthur looked at it for a long time before opening it. The two hadn't spoken since he asked the question about Maud Considine and no answer was forthcoming. He knew that, yet again, he was a disappointment to his mother now, as she was to him. It was unlikely any words could ever repair the damage. Finally, when he opened the envelope, it revealed a short note:

Dearest Arthur, I was sorry to hear of the election result. It is a hard blow, I'm sure. Perhaps Walter might stand at a future date and resume the Kavanagh tradition at Westminster. Love to Frances and the family. Yours truly, HK.

*

In July, Arthur was appointed by Gladstone to the Bessborough Commission, along with Messrs O'Connor, Dowse and Shaw. A welcome distraction for Arthur, their duty was to travel throughout Ireland, taking account of the plight of landlords, tenants and members of the Land League, and reporting back on their findings. The next few months were an eye-opener for Arthur who learned that, in many ways, he was one of the luckier landlords, as well as one of the kinder ones. In the west, some landlords were being blackmailed by their tenants who refused to cut their corn or dig their potatoes. They listened to tenants whose rents had been increased overnight to an amount they couldn't pay and were subsequently evicted. Land leaguers explained their demands and the lengths they were prepared to go to achieve them. They heard about tenants living in unbearably overcrowded conditions with parcels of land that couldn't possibly sustain them. Violence and destruction were being instigated far and wide.

So struck by the intensity and peril of what he was hearing, Arthur wrote to the Chief Secretary for Ireland, Mr Forster, and urged that no more land legislation should be introduced until the people of Ireland agreed to abide by the law. He expressed the opinion that the upcoming Queen's Speech should include words to that effect. His letter added that while a suspension of habeas corpus would be regrettable, it may be necessary and would help restore order.

Although Arthur Kavanagh was not present for the first day of Parliament and many of his colleagues were astonished he hadn't been re-elected, his influence was great, as on that day Forster introduced the Protection of Persons (Ireland) Bill which allowed for internment without trial of anyone suspected of involvement in the Land War. When the Bessborough Commission Report was issued, Arthur refused to add his signature as there were aspects he didn't fully agree with. Instead, he separately submitted his own report. Staunchly against the idea that tenants should be allowed to sell their holdings, he believed this compromised the landowner's right to decide what became of his own property. He simply wasn't prepared to compromise on this.

In Parliament, as Gladstone introduced his land legislation, he not only acknowledged Arthur, but paid tribute to him as one of the most able gentlemen he had ever encountered among the Conservative party in Ireland, an independent thinker and a man of great scruples and honour. These words meant a great deal to Arthur, helping to soften the blow of defeat and giving him reason to believe that his voice was still being heard and valued.

Chapter 24

For Better or Worse

If Arthur wanted his sons to be proud traditionalists, bringing honour and distinction to the family name, what he wanted for his daughters was what every member of his class hoped for – a good match. To marry into a suitable family with similar values and to find a kind caring man with whom to rear a noble family was the ultimate goal. In this regard, Arthur and Frances sat proudly at the front of St Saviour's Church, Hans Place, London on July 27th, 1882, for the wedding ceremony of their eldest daughter, Eva, to Cecil John Alexander, son of the Bishop of Derry. The Alexanders were a respected religious family – something which particularly pleased Frances. She was doubly delighted to know that Eva's new mother-in-law had written the famous hymn "All Things Bright and Beautiful" and other well-known hymns for children.

The groom's father presided at the ceremony, with his mother and siblings sitting to the right of Arthur's family. Lady Harriet, who was well enough to attend, sat beside Frances, dabbing her eyes as Eva made her way down the aisle in a rich white brocade dress trimmed with Borris lace, her face covered with a fine hand-worked veil. Carrying a bouquet of orange blossoms, she reminded Harriet so much of Hoddy on her wedding day, that she gasped as she tried to compose herself. Eva's two younger sisters, Agnes and May, were bridesmaids, wearing coffee-coloured dresses with feather caps and satin sashes.

Arthur had delegated the role of giving his daughter away to Walter, as he didn't want to accompany her in his wheelchair, but when she reached the top of the aisle, she bent down and kissed him on the cheek before taking the arm of her husband-to-be.

The wedding reception was held in the home of Mr and Mrs Henry Stoche of Lowndes Square in fashionable Belgravia, where the small wedding party was treated to a catered feast and after-dinner entertainment in the form of a string quartet. At the going away party the next day, Frances took Eva aside:

'I do hope you will still visit Borris as much as possible, dear. It won't be the same without you and you know your sisters will miss you very much. As will I, and your father,' she added.

'I know that, Mother, and I will visit as much as I can. My heart will always be in Borris and when we get settled in our new home here in London, I hope you and Father will often come to stay.'

At the same time, Arthur called Cecil to him.

'Be good to my daughter, young man, or the wrath of the Kavanaghs will come down upon you.' They both laughed, but then Arthur said: 'I'm serious, Cecil. That young lady means the world to us. Treat her as the precious jewel that she is, and I hope your marriage is as long and successful as mine.'

'I will, old boy. You needn't worry. Eva will be treated like a queen. I guarantee it.'

Staying on in London for a few more days, Arthur and Frances visited the Houses of Parliament where a big fuss was made of Arthur by his former colleagues. They also visited Madame Tussaud's wax museum – a first for both of them – and marvelled at the likenesses of royalty, politicians and statesmen.

Pushing Arthur's wheelchair through Regent Park, Frances suddenly said:

'It's going to be hard to let them go, isn't it?'

'Let who go?'

'The children. One by one we'll be attending their weddings and then they'll be gone. It's truly hard to believe they're all grown up already.'

'They're not all grown up yet, Frances. Osborne and the girls are still quite young.'

'Yes, but with young Arthur away in the navy now and Charles in Eton, Borris is getting very quiet.'

'That's true. I know, as a father, I shouldn't have favourites and in truth I don't, but I have to say I am so proud of Arthur. If I could have realised one ambition for myself, it would have been to serve in the navy and it cheers me up each time I think of him, serving his country on the ocean waves.'

'I'm proud of him too, Arthur, but I'm proud of all our children. They've turned into fine young adults.'

'They have. We've been blessed, and I've been blessed with you, Frances. I'm sorry if sometimes I don't show it.'

'Arthur, there's something I want to tell you.'

'Oh dear. This sounds serious.'

'I've received a few letters from Arthur and I don't think he's very happy in the navy. He didn't want to tell you because he knows how much his service means to you, but he's talking about perhaps leaving and going into commerce.'

'You can't be serious, Frances! Commerce! What kind of commerce? What would a Kavanagh know about commerce? That's ridiculous, Frances.'

Frances took the opportunity to sit on a park bench facing the lake and Arthur rotated his chair to face her.

'I knew you wouldn't like the idea, but if he's not happy – and you know his health is not good.'

'I'll write to him as soon as we get home. He mustn't leave. My brother Charles could never face his comrades when he deserted. It would be a terrible mistake. Service to one's country is the most noble of professions where he can fraternise with his own class. Commerce is for every Tom, Dick and Harry. His talents would be completely wasted.'

'Don't upset yourself, Arthur. Write to him, but please remember he is twenty-five years old now and he must make his own decisions.'

'We'll see about that.'

Arthur began his letter that very night, sitting up by lamplight and determinedly moving the pen that was lodged between his stumps.

Dearest Arthur, it troubles me greatly to hear that you would consider leaving the Royal Navy. In my opinion, that would be a decision you would regret for the rest of your life. Not only that, but there is something I haven't shared with you before, probably because I was too reticent. You see, the truth is that the realisation of my ambition and the seat of my hopes for our noble family lie with you, and not so much with Walter. I know he will do a fine job, but your chosen profession is one that for me holds the highest of honour and gives me most pride. In moments of melancholia, one of the things that cheers me is to think of you as a Royal Navy Officer, bearing our family name and bestowing greatness upon us. I implore you, dear son, to stick with your fine profession and to continue to do your utmost to serve Queen and country. Your loving father.

The letter served its purpose and Lieutenant Arthur knuckled down and continued his service, although recurrent bronchitis made life very difficult for him. By October he was too ill to continue and was sent back to London to recuperate. When he was brought to visit Arthur and Frances at their London townhouse, they were shocked to see him arrive in a wheelchair. Thin and gaunt, his breathing was laboured and he was only barely able to propel himself. Within a few weeks, he was bedbound, and his doctor's advice was to go on a cruise to Madeira to restore his health. Recollections of his brother Tom's death at sea haunted Arthur and they decided that Frances and Walter would go with him, while Arthur stayed in London. Seeing them off at the pier, Arthur sensed in his heart that he would never see his son again.

Writing to his mother to fill her in on young Arthur's poor health, Arthur told Harriet that his son's suffering was immense and that, if he couldn't be cured, he wished for God to take him. *I fear the worst and I'm afraid that another Kavanagh will be buried at sea.*

267

A few days later, a telegram arrived to tell Arthur the news he had been dreading. Two days into the voyage, the young man had breathed his last. In a dignified ceremony, a clergyman onboard had said prayers for his repose with Frances and Walter present. The Captain agreed to store the body until they returned to England, so a proper funeral could be organised. Having heard the news, Arthur cried for a full day, only stopping for long enough to instruct his manservant to contact the other members of the family by whatever means possible.

In silent prayers he asked God if his own pride had brought this about. *If only I had allowed him to leave the navy, would he be alive now? How long did he endure pain and ill health so as not to disappoint me? I am cursed. I am a curse and now I have condemned my son to be cursed too.*

The only thing that soothed Arthur's distress was a letter from Frances, now on her way back to London, telling him of the peace with which young Arthur had faced death:

He told me he was ready to go and that he wasn't afraid, Arthur. And if you saw the serene smile on his face when he died, he looked just like he did in his basket in the nursery all those years ago. Don't blame yourself, Arthur. I know you are inclined to, but this is God's will and I have accepted it. Please accept it as such and we will remember our son as a loyal servant of his country and the Lord. We will be together soon. Your loving wife, Frances.

When Frances and Walter returned, Arthur told them that he had decided that young Arthur would not be buried in Borris, but rather in

Woking Cemetery, a place he often passed when travelling by train to London.

'But Father, Kavanaghs are always buried in St Mullins. Shouldn't we take him home?' Walter was tearful and deeply upset by the loss of his closest brother.

'Absolutely not. Those hypocrites who promised me their votes would line the street and pretend to mourn my son when they would as soon stab me in the back. I couldn't stomach it.'

Walter looked alarmed at this, the first time his father had vented his anger at the people of Borris in front of him.

'I... I don't think that's entirely true, Father, but if you feel so strongly about it. What do you think, Mother?'

'I think if that's what your father wants, I'm happy to go along with it. Sadly, young Arthur is gone and as long as his body rests in hallowed ground, I'll be content.'

Over the next few weeks, letters of condolence from Arthur's shipmates and superiors confirmed that he was a very hard working and popular crewman. They heard how he had insisted on doing his duty even when very unwell and eventually had to be ordered to leave for London to get medical attention. Arthur and Frances read and reread these accounts on their return to Borris until the pain of losing their loyal son began to ease.

*

Having been warned to keep his movements secret because of threats from the Fenian militia, when Arthur was in Ireland he remained on his own estate most of the time. In order to collect any rent, subterfuge had to be employed, as those who were found to have paid their landlords were in grave danger. Arthur had clandestine meetings with some loyal tenants who made him promise never to reveal that they had paid and not to issue any receipts. Some even arrived in disguise or posted their rent from distant post offices, but many availed of the opportunity to evade payment and aligned themselves firmly with the rebels.

While some landlords went bankrupt quite quickly, and Arthur's estate suffered heavy losses, Arthur's anger spurred him to action to try to reverse the trend. In response to the Land League, he was instrumental in establishing the Land Corporation of Ireland as well as the Irish Patriotic Union. Their purpose was to form a company to take over farms from which tenants were evicted, having refused to pay their rents. He knew that unless landlords worked together, they would suffer and be defeated by the might of the Parnellites. However, not enough landlords bought into the scheme to make it successful and both organisations struggled to gain any traction.

Since young Arthur's death, Lady Harriet rarely visited Borris. Her health was very poor and she was now in her eighties and increasingly frail. She made it clear in letters to Arthur that she disapproved of the decision to bury her grandson in England.

Kavanaghs are buried in St Mullins. I hope to join them there soon and it is a travesty to me to think that my grandson will not rest close to me and all his noble ancestors. It was a selfish decision you made, although not your first.

In the summer of 1885, Arthur was summoned to Lady Harriet's bedside, having been told by Doctor Boxwell that she had only days, if not hours to live. Arriving on horseback, he was helped inside by his manservant and carried upstairs to her bedroom.

'So, you came,' she said. 'I must be dying after all.' Harriet's voice was quiet and hoarse.

'Of course I did, Mother. How are you feeling?'

'Let us not pretend this is a head cold, Arthur. I'm feeling wretched, but I know it won't be for long.'

'I'm sincerely sorry to hear that, Mother.'

'I believe that, Arthur, and there's something I want to say to you.'

It was difficult to hear Harriet's voice and Arthur leaned forward to catch the words.

'Yes, Mother, what is it?'

'You and I have had our differences,' she croaked slowly, 'but I am proud of you and your fine family.'

'Thank you, Mother.'

'And I also want to say…' She breathed heavily.

'Yes, Mother?'

'I'm sorry.'

'Sorry for what, Mother?'

'Oh Arthur,' she closed her eyes and took another breath. 'Will you take the apology when it's given. Now, I need to sleep. I can't speak any more.'

The drapes around the four-poster bed were dark and heavy and the candles beside the bed threw eerie shadows all over the walls. Arthur sat by the bedside for two hours in a wing-backed chair, finally falling asleep himself, and when he awoke in the middle of the night, Harriet's maid was sitting on the opposite side of the bed, crying quietly.

'She's gone,' she whispered to Arthur. 'An hour ago.'

Arthur hung his head, but no tears came. Just a heavy weight in his chest to add to the heaviness already there. Feeling completely alone, he wished Frances had come with him. She would know what he should do. As the morning broke, Doctor Boxwell arrived and Arthur felt a pang of guilt that the doctor was far more upset than he was. But now, yet another funeral had to be arranged and there was no one to do it but him. Lady Harriet's wishes were clear – she was to be buried in St Mullins and, whether he liked it or not, the people of Borris would line out to pay their respects to a woman they had grown to admire and look up to.

On the day of the funeral, prayers were said in both churches in Borris. Father Carey in the Catholic Church paid tribute to a woman ahead of her time, a woman who had travelled the world and brought back skills which had enhanced the village of Borris and provided an industry which would live on long after her death. He told the villagers that Borris lace was a lasting tribute to Lady Harriet and that her generosity to the poor of the village would never be forgotten.

'Now let us leave politics aside and go to pay our respects in a dignified peaceful way,' he urged. 'Lady Harriet deserves nothing less.'

Filing out onto the street, the Catholic brethren lined the main street as their Protestant neighbours followed the large black hearse through the arched gateway and down the centre of the village. Never before had so many black carriages been seen, one after another, all containing family members and dignitaries, dressed in fine dresses, suits and top hats. Arthur was in the first carriage along with Frances, Walter, Agnes and Mary. The rest of the family were in the other carriages, including Eva and her husband, who had travelled from London. Arthur looked firmly forward, not making eye contact with anyone on the street and after the burial, he asked to be helped back to the carriage immediately.

This time, Eva climbed in beside him.

'Are you alright, Father? Are you very upset about Grandma?'

'I'm very upset about everything, Eva. But I don't want to trouble you with my morose thoughts.'

'I'm happy to listen, Papa.'

'No, Eva. This will pass and you don't need to be listening to the ruminations of an old man.'

'Father, firstly you are not old. And secondly, I have some exciting news that may cheer you.'

'What is it?'

'I'm expecting a baby. Very soon in fact. This black coat hides it very well.'

'That's wonderful news, Eva.' He kissed her cheek. 'I needed some good news today.'

'If it's a boy, I'm going to call him Arthur, after you and, of course, my brother.'

Arthur swallowed and broke into a smile, which suddenly turned to a sob.

'I'm sorry, Papa. I didn't mean to upset you.'

'No, no, it's wonderful.' Arthur tried to regain his composure. 'Forgive my tears. I really am delighted.'

Chapter 25

In Sickness and in Health

Although only fifty-four years old and in relatively good health, the disappointment of political failure followed by the loss of his son and mother left Arthur's mood very low. Frances encouraged him to spend more and more time in London, often accompanying him there, since she noticed how much happier he was when spending time with Eva and his grandchild. He enjoyed the political discourse he could have at the Carlton Club, where he was a life member, and spent many evenings dining and smoking cigars with his peers. Being in its civilised opulence made him feel like there was a future for members of his class, a feeling that deserted him every time he stepped on Irish soil.

At home, Walter was managing the estate with only the occasional need to consult his father, although when Arthur visited Borris they had long conversations where father and son aired their opinions and Walter was quick to bow to his father's intellect and experience. He was now engaged to Helen Louisa Howard, daughter of Colonel John Stanley Howard of Ballina Park, Wicklow. A quiet, pretty girl, she was well liked by Arthur and Frances, reminding them both of the shy Frances who had first arrived in Borris many years ago. They both felt confident that she would uphold the Kavanagh traditions and be a support to Walter in his challenging role.

In 1886, another honour was bestowed on Arthur when he was appointed Privy Councillor of Ireland, making him an advisor to the ruling sovereign on the exercise of royal prerogative. It was a very welcome recognition for his service to his country and Arthur didn't waste any time in taking up the role. As soon as he heard that Gladstone, having supported Home Rule for Ireland, was rejected in the House of Commons, Arthur strove to bring about a Coalition Government that would tackle the Irish question as a priority. He would use what influence he had to bring this about.

*

When Arthur and Frances returned to Borris in time for the Christmas celebrations, Walter immediately commented on how gaunt his father had become.

'Are you not eating, Father? You seem to have lost quite a bit of weight.'

'I'm eating like a horse, Walter. I suppose it's just the decrepitude of old age.'

But Walter wasn't happy with this explanation and later, when Arthur was at his desk in the library, he spoke to his mother about it.

'Don't you think Father has got very thin, Mother? He doesn't look at all well.'

'I have begged him to visit a doctor, but he refuses. He believes it's just the turmoil of the last few years taking its toll. But what worries me is that he is actually eating more than ever. He's constantly hungry and thirsty and yet he's losing weight.'

'When Doctor Boxwell makes his Christmas visit, he will surely notice and advise him, although I've heard the doctor is in failing health himself,' Walter said.

'He must be almost eighty now. Perhaps he won't visit this year.' Frances looked worried.

'He's already accepted the invitation to the party on Christmas Eve.'

'Oh, I'm relieved. He always listened to Doctor Boxwell.'

In the kitchen, the staff all whispered their observations of how Mr Kavanagh looked so poorly, how the joy was gone from him and how he struggled on the stairs now like never before.

On Christmas Eve the huge tree was in the hallway, as usual, and the local children sang carols and were treated to gifts and sweets. Eva and her family were home from London, and Walter's fiancée was there, with Arthur's other children all arriving during the day from their schools and universities. When Doctor Boxwell arrived, it was hard to tell who was more shocked, he or Arthur. Shuffling into the house with a walking stick and head bent low, the doctor was clearly in decline. When he lifted his head to greet Arthur, he couldn't disguise his shock.

'What's the matter, Arthur? You didn't tell me you were ill.'

'Because I'm not ill,' Arthur retorted. 'Happy Christmas to you too, Frank!'

Walter and Frances both hurriedly intervened, making a fuss of Mrs Boxwell, taking their hats and coats and showing her to the drawing room where tea was served. Arthur, although clearly annoyed by what Doctor Boxwell had said, put it to the back of his mind and brought his friend and mentor to the library. Both of them struggled on the stairs, but neither complained and soon they were having a cigar in the library, discussing the hunt and the state of Irish politics. It was after dinner when Doctor Boxwell broached the subject again.

'Would you mind if I examined you, Arthur? You really don't look well.'

'Oh Frank, you're retired now. You don't need to be worrying about me.'

'Well let me ask you a few questions at least. How is your eyesight?'

'It's funny you should say that, because it's a little blurry actually, but I suppose that's to be expected in one's fifties.'

'And do you find that you're very thirsty at all?'

Arthur stared at the doctor.

'Extremely. And hungry too.'

'And do you have to use the chamber pot during the night?'

'That's a very personal question, Frank, but yes.'

'I'm almost certain you have diabetes, Arthur, but it will have to be confirmed by a blood test. Will you give me your word that directly after Christmas you will go to the new physician in the village and tell him what I have said?'

'I will. What will it mean for me if I do have it?'

'Well, you'll feel much better with medication if that's the case and your eyesight might be saved. The outlook if you don't deal with it is very bleak indeed. So will you promise?'

'I will. I'll do it once the festivities are over. And how are you, Frank?'

'I don't have long, Arthur. But that's to be expected at my age and I'm resigned to it. I don't have much pain and I'm well looked after.'

'I'm very sorry to hear that.'

'Don't be sorry, Arthur. I've had a long and interesting life and I'm ready to meet my maker. I have no regrets and I really appreciate my long association with this fine family.'

With tears in his eyes, Arthur said, 'You know you've been like a father to me.'

'I do and I'm very proud of you.' He reached forward and placed a hand on Arthur's shoulder. 'Don't let the world disillusion you, Arthur. Look after your health, dust yourself off and embrace the changes that are coming. You've done your best to influence matters for the better. Now you need to look after yourself.'

From downstairs they could hear singing and Walter came to the door to urge them to join the company.

'We'll be down in a moment,' Arthur said, sliding off the low chair he was sitting on.

Doctor Boxwell winked at Walter to let him know the matter had been dealt with and the two men made their way slowly down the stairs.

*

In early 1887 the diagnosis was official. Arthur was suffering from advanced diabetes and needed daily medication. Furthermore, the doctor was uneasy about his persistent cough and prescribed antibiotics, urging him to return for another check-up in a couple of weeks. In defiance of his failing health, he continued to attend meetings in Carlow, Kilkenny and Dublin with short boating expeditions in between. He was anxious that the Land Corporation would be successful, so much so that it became known colloquially as "Kavanagh's Scheme." The Corporation was now providing armed protection to the poorer tenants, while damages for non-payment of rent on instruction from the Land League were taken from local taxes to which tenant farmers contributed.

Arthur's movement found an unlikely ally in Pope Leo XIII, who condemned the Land League's activities on the grounds that tenants were unable to enter into lawful contracts and also on the grounds that boycotting was unchristian. The mostly Protestant landlords were surprised by this turn of events but willing to take support from anyone whose influence might help.

Arthur's illness somewhat overshadowed the wedding of Walter to Helen in February, although he did his utmost to present as well as possible. The marriage took place in Holy Trinity Church, Marylebone, with the reception at the Howard family townhouse in Kensington. Arthur made a fine speech, praising his eldest son's loyalty to family traditions and admiring the way he had assimilated into his role as landlord and more recently as High Sheriff and Magistrate. He welcomed Helen into the family and toasted the beautiful bridesmaids who were sisters of the bride, wishing the happy couple long life and happiness. Colonel Howard spoke of his delight at the choice of husband his eldest daughter had made and welcomed Walter into the Howard fold. As soon as they could reasonably do so, Arthur and Frances slipped away to their townhouse at Cadogan Place so Arthur could take his medication and rest.

By now *The Eva* had been sold since it was too big for Arthur to manage and been replaced by a smaller craft which he named *The Water Lily*. In the summer of 1887, he and Frances, along with Agnes and May, who were now aged eighteen and sixteen, took a cruise to Holland. With a crew of three, including a cook, Arthur's mood visibly lifted at his daughters' delight at being on the open sea and seeing their father's sailing skills. His younger children had missed out on the sailing trips taken by the older Kavanaghs and due to ill health and being so busy, he had reneged on promises to bring them over the years.

On reaching Flushing, or Vlissingen as the Dutch called it, the young ladies and Frances marvelled as they saw the tall ships, yachts and pleasure boats in the vast harbour. Going ashore on that first evening, Agnes and May walked ahead while Frances wheeled Arthur on the long promenade with the vast beach below, stopping to watch the side-shows and to taste ice-cream from a local stall. The girls were slightly embarrassed by the way people stared at Arthur eating the ice-cream with his hook, but Frances waved her hand dismissively.

'This is one of the happiest days I have had in so long,' she said.

'I was just thinking the same thing,' Arthur said, and they smiled at each other.

'I never realised why you liked travelling so much, Papa, but I think I do now,' May said.

'Except for the seasickness.' Agnes laughed.

'It will get easier from here on,' Arthur reassured her. 'For the next few days, we'll be cruising around the coast and upriver to Leyden. You won't encounter rough seas there.'

'Well, thank heavens for that.' Agnes sounded relieved.

'But we still have to sail home!' May teased.

'Oh, do be quiet, Sister. I'm not thinking that far ahead, thank you very much.'

In Amsterdam they took a boat trip on the canals before having a brief meeting with Prince William III at the majestic Paleis Amsterdam. While the Prince didn't speak much English, he said he had heard of Arthur. If this was true, Arthur knew it meant he had heard of his disability but, since this was something he never discussed, he smiled in appreciation and offered the Prince best wishes from the people of Ireland. Touring the building, the baroque architecture took their breaths away as did the opulent decoration of the interior. The Citizens Hall, with its marble floor covered in detailed maps which showed Amsterdam as the centre of the universe, was the highlight of the visit. Arthur, with his navigational skills, was fascinated by the detail on the floor-maps and eventually the girls had to plead with him to move on.

Outside they bought tulips from a flower seller which the ladies put in their hair and in Arthur's buttonhole. Then, taking a carriage back to the harbour, they dined on the deck and sang songs late into the evening, with Arthur reciting pieces from Scott's novels and from Shakespeare.

Going to bed that evening, Frances said:

'This is turning out to be a truly wonderful trip. I wish we never had to go home. It's as if the years have been rolled back and it makes me so happy to see you enjoy yourself.'

'You know you mean the world to me, Frances. And to have the girls with us on this trip is truly special. If we never take another cruise, I'm deeply satisfied that we've had this marvellous time together.'

Before returning home, they visited Leyden where the country's oldest university was situated. In the Botanical Gardens they learned that this was the place where the tulip was first introduced to Europe and were surprised to find that the orangery there was very similar to the one in the Botanical Gardens in Dublin. In the Museum de Lakenhal they viewed Rembrandt's paintings and, for the first time, Arthur felt a pang of sadness that his mother, who would have loved to see them, was no longer alive.

By the time they returned to Ireland, Arthur was in much better spirits and his cough seemed to have eased. Saddened to hear that

Doctor Boxwell had died while they were away, he immediately sat down to write a letter of condolence to his family. There was also some good news: after dinner, Walter and Helen announced that they were expecting their first baby, and they all raised a glass to the continuation of the Kavanagh clan.

'Another generation of Kavanaghs at Borris House,' Arthur declared. 'A happy day indeed.'

Frances fussed over Helen, urging her not to exert herself, while Agnes and May were thrilled to hear that a baby would be coming to the nursery. For the next few months, the household settled into a mood of calm expectation, with Arthur occasionally riding out and hunting, although he very rarely went alone anymore. Huge amounts of correspondence came for him daily, mostly to do with the Land Corporation. Arthur dealt with them meticulously, sometimes writing up to thirty letters a day, although when Frances thought he was too tired, she instructed his manservant to say "there was no post today."

Chapter 26

Until Death Do Us Part

The year 1888 began with great celebrations at the birth of baby Arthur Thomas, the new heir to the Kavanagh Estate. The church bells in Borris rang out and the granite walls bordering the main street were festooned with flowers and bunting. But Arthur was saddened to see that there were very few houses on the main street decorated, and although there were lots of congratulations forthcoming as he rode through the village, people looked furtively over their shoulders before addressing him and very few were willing to declare it publicly.

Seeing a baby in the nursery again gave Frances great joy. May and Agnes made a huge fuss of the baby until they returned to Finishing School, nursing him in their arms and singing to him. Walter was now managing the estate completely independently of Arthur and was serving on most of the committees on which his father and grandfather had also served. He had developed a good relationship with most of the tenants, and expressed the opinion to his father that he thought the only way forward was to allow tenants to own their own land. This led to heated discussions between them, which usually ended in Arthur going into a coughing fit so intense that the conversation had to be postponed.

In early summer, Arthur was feeling well enough to take a boat trip on the Barrow to St Mullins, accompanied by his cousins the Steeles, his son-in-law Cecil Alexander and three maids. On the Kavanagh land there, they picnicked outside a small cottage, which had often been frequented by Lady Harriet. The sun shone as the family group sat on the lawn, reminiscing on their childhood adventures, with Cecil listening in amazement at some of the dangerous things Arthur used to do. In mid-afternoon, Cecil and the Steeles went for a walk upriver while Arthur took a rest, returning to Borris in time for dinner.

He attended meetings in Dublin on a few occasions between September and Christmas, although Frances urged him to keep them to a minimum and usually accompanied him on the journey. All the committee members who met him were shocked at the deterioration in his appearance. His shoulders, once broad, seemed shrunken and his face was pale and barely recognisable. His handwriting had also deteriorated, since the firm grip he once had on the pen within his stumps was now affected by his weight loss. But Arthur was still well able to assert his opinion, insisting that the future of Ireland depended on the reinforcement of law and order and that union with the crown was the only way forward.

After Christmas, and just after baby Arthur's first birthday, Frances made an announcement over dinner one evening.

'Your father and I are going to spend the foreseeable future in London.'

'Why is that, Mamma?' Walter asked. 'Do you have business to attend to there?'

'Your father and I have discussed it,' she looked to Arthur for confirmation, 'and we believe it's time you and Helen had this place to yourself, now that you have started your family. We'll visit regularly, of course.'

'Is that what you want, Father?'

'Yes, yes. Your mother wants me to see a physician in Harley Street about this cough of mine and we do enjoy being in London, so it seems like a good idea.'

'I suppose it would be good to get an expert opinion. You do seem very troubled by that cough.'

'I dread physicians!' Arthur said. 'How I miss Doctor Boxwell.'

'Dear Doctor Boxwell,' Frances added. 'He looked after us all so well, God be good to him.'

And so, in February large trunks were stacked in the hallway and there was an air of finality to this trip to London.

'You'll be back in the summer?' Walter ventured.

'Of course, of course,' Arthur said as he climbed into the carriage. 'And you might come to see us, if you have the time?'

Frances kissed baby Arthur on the head, saying, 'You'll be a big boy by then.' And, hugging Walter and Helen, she turned her head quickly and they were quite sure there were tears in her eyes.

In Harley Street, Arthur underwent a series of blood tests, and doctors listened to his heart and lungs. His pallor, along with the intensity of his cough and chest pain, led to the diagnosis of consumption, complicated by his diabetes.

'Is there a cure, Doctor?'

'Not a very reliable one sadly, Mr Kavanagh, and your disease is at such an advanced stage, I'm afraid even that might not work. The prognosis, I hate to tell you, is grim.'

Arthur sighed. 'What might I try?'

'Fresh air at high altitude is the only thing that has been proven to work, but that would be mostly when the disease is at an early stage. I'm not sure that you are fit to travel.'

Arthur shook his head. 'Thank you for your help,' Arthur said. 'Kindly keep this from my wife. I will explain it to her in my own way.'

'As you wish, Mr Kavanagh.'

When the doctor walked out of the examination room, pushing Arthur in his wheelchair, Frances looked anxiously from one to the other. Knowing Arthur would not like her to question the doctor directly, she just said, 'Thank you for your help, Doctor. Is a hospital stay necessary or can Arthur come home?'

'I'm coming home,' Arthur interjected, 'And I'm going to the Cowes regatta in July.'

Both Frances and the doctor looked startled at this announcement, but neither said what was in their minds, which was that the frail figure in the chair didn't look like he would last till then.

But last he did, and although unable to sail *The Water Lily* himself, he hired a small crew to bring him there, accompanied by Frances. His face, when he saw the flotilla of boats coming into view, made the trip worthwhile for all aboard. So thin now that his teeth looked too big for his mouth and his eyes bulged slightly, many nights were spent sweating and coughing while Frances held cold compresses to his head and gave him liquorice to settle his stomach. When his boat was moored, word went around that Arthur Kavanagh had arrived and old friends began to queue up to see him.

Hugh Grosvenor, the Duke of Westminster, asked to come aboard first. Shocked at the deterioration in his previously robust friend, he spoke about boats and sailing with Arthur as if nothing had changed, but he shook Frances' hand solemnly as he left, and her sad eyes confirmed what he suspected. Lord Dufferin, Viceroy of India and a noted travel writer, came afterwards and he and Arthur talked about their voyages over the years. From a distance Frances watched Arthur's animated face as he relived the foreign adventures he took with his mother and brother and couldn't help thinking that he would be reunited with them soon.

Looking out to sea they saw the Kaiser Wilhelm II arriving, escorted by twelve German warships. A grandson of Queen Victoria's, it was one of the first times this Kaiser had been seen in public since it was the Year of the Three Emperors – Wilhelm's grandfather died earlier in the year and then his father died of cancer, having only been in office for ninety-nine days. Arthur looked through binoculars to catch a glimpse of the new Kaiser and noted that he looked 'very young indeed.' The German warships were vast with high sails and huge crews and Arthur spent hours studying them and comparing them to other warships he had seen on his travels.

The highlight of the trip was on 5th August when the Royal Yacht arrived with Queen Victoria on board. In full view of the other sailing vessels, she commissioned her grandson as Admiral of the Fleet, a five-star naval officer rank. Ship sirens were sounded amidst loud clapping and cheering, and champagne glasses were raised in toasts onboard the vessels and on the quayside. That evening, Arthur's lifelong friend and former government colleague, Admiral Charles Beresford, came on board and the two men discussed the navy and politics until Arthur's cough became troublesome and Charles bid him farewell.

At the end of the regatta, Arthur insisted that they sail on for Holland, remembering the lovely time they had spent there the previous year. But the weather this time was incessantly wet, and Frances, knowing that these conditions were the worst possible for her husband's cough, prevailed upon him to return home. Waiting for them at the pier in Dover was Eva, who had a carriage and driver ready to bring them back to London. When she saw her father, she looked at her mother panic-stricken, but Frances shook her head silently, indicating that she shouldn't say anything, and fussed about the luggage, hailing the driver to come and help with Arthur's chair.

By November, Arthur was completely bedridden. In the evenings Frances read to him, sometimes from the newspapers, but more often he requested the poems of Byron.

'Read me "When We Two Parted" again,' he said one evening.

'But that's a sad one, Arthur. Wouldn't you prefer me to read something uplifting?'

'No, that's the one I want to hear.'

Frances began:

'When we two parted

In silence and tears,

Half broken-hearted

To sever for years,

Pale grew thy cheek and cold,

Colder thy kiss;

Truly that hour foretold

Sorrow to this.'

Her voice was breaking and Arthur asked her to stop.

'I know I'm dying, Frances. I've known for some time, but I wanted to keep living as long as I could.'

Tears were running down Frances' face now and she couldn't speak.

'Lie beside me, Frances?'

Arthur was so tiny now and Frances didn't want to hurt him by placing her head on his chest so she pressed her lips to his cheek, finally finding her voice.

'We've had a good life, Arthur, and I'm glad we spent it together.'

'As am I, Frances. I know at times I was unbearable and for that I am truly sorry.'

'You were never unbearable, just difficult,' she whispered through her tears, and they both smiled.

'I have one request,' Arthur said. 'I don't want to be buried in St Mullins with the tenants who didn't vote for me as chief mourners. I want to be buried on our own estate in Borris, beside the old Ballycopigan church, where I spent so many happy days when I was young.'

'Will that be permitted, Arthur? Is it consecrated ground?'

'I don't see why not.'

'I'll ask Walter to arrange it with the clergyman. And Arthur, if you're going to be buried there, so am I.'

'As you wish, dear.'

It was another month before Arthur died on Christmas morning 1889. Eva, Frances, Agnes and May were with him as his breathing became very laboured. At 2am it became clear that he was trying to say something, and Eva put her ear to his mouth so as to hear him better.

'He wants us to sing Christmas carols,' she said, looking alarmed.

'Then we shall,' Frances said, and began with "Once in Royal David's City". Soon afterwards, to the strains of "Away in a Manger", Arthur slipped from this world peacefully at fifty-eight years old.

*

Back in Borris, in a two-column tribute in the local newspaper, *The Nationalist and Leinster Times,* Arthur's death was lamented:

"By the death of Arthur MacMurrough Kavanagh, a striking personality is removed from Irish political life and the failing cause of Irish landlordism has lost an able and devoted champion."

In St Canice's Cathedral, in Kilkenny, the Bishop of Ossory described him as 'a great and good man, and a tower of strength whose unique position by ancestry and birth linked him to the history of Ireland. A formidable and fair opponent, a loving husband and tender father.' The *Leinster Express* described him as "one possessing more than the usual amount of wisdom granted to one man," and listed the vast number of dignitaries who attended, including Bruens, Ormondes, Lecky Pikes, Alexanders as well as members of the Privy Council and many men of high office who served with Arthur in his various official roles.

If Arthur turned his back on the village in death by being buried privately on his own land, they didn't turn their backs on him. The coffin was carried from his own private chapel and placed in the hearse, then instead of turning left for the main street, as the other Kavanagh funerals had, it wound its way down to the river and the woods where Arthur spent his youth. Borris House looked cold and desolate as the horses bore its master farther and farther away.

Directly behind the hearse was a single carriage containing Frances and her daughters, followed on foot by Walter, Osborne and Charles as well as close friends and dignitaries. Then, at a respectful distance, a huge crowd of tenants and local people streamed behind, while others watched from the fields and terraces. Reaching the small disused church at Ballycopigan, the coffin was placed in the moss-lined grave, in the ground which Arthur had secretly had consecrated two years previously. Under a weak January sun, in the shadow of Mount Leinster, Arthur MacMurrough Kavanagh was laid to rest, surrounded by his family in the place that he loved, home at last.

Acknowledgements and Bibliography

Research included reference to local and national publications including *The Nationalist and Leinster Times, The Leinster Leader, Carloviana* and *The Irish Times,* as well as *The Kavanagh Papers.* Valuable information was also gleaned from the following publications:

The Incredible Mr. Kavanagh by Donald McCormick (1960), *Born Without Limbs* by Kenneth Kavanagh (1989); *The Right Honourable Arthur MacMurrough Kavanagh* by Sarah Steele (2017), *The Cruise of the R.Y.S. Eva* by Arthur MacMurrough Kavanagh (1865); and *Burke's Irish Family Records.*

I am grateful for the support of Carlow County Council, and Carlow Library for their support and financial assistance. Also, for those who have supported my writing over the years including Tim Sheehan, Gerard Quinn, Joseph O'Connor, Donal Ryan, Sarah Moore-Fitzgerald, Martin Dyar, Barry McKinley, John MacKenna and Angela Keogh. Gratitude also to Helena Mulkerns for editing and Mark Turner of Marble City Publishing for his help in getting this book to print.